IF YOU CAN'T STAND THE HEAT . . .

"You are Mark," hissed the fire phantasm.

"Nope, I'm Max," said the boy. "Close, but no cigar—guess you got the wrong furnace. What's this Mark's last name? Maybe I can—"

"Silence!" cried the apparition, its grating voice cracking.

"Not a conversationalist, then," muttered Max, eyes flitting about for a way out of his fix. Once again, his messenger bag was out of reach, on the floor across the basement, smoke curling from the canvas. "Can we start again? Hi, I'm Max. You must be Flaming-Hellspawn-Ghostly-Guy. Pleased to meet ya!"

"You must die, Mark!"

"Max, actually, but whatever," he said with a shrug. "Seriously, though, what is *happening* today? Is it open season on me or what?"

"*Marked!* You are Marked!" cried the flaming phantom, staggering ever closer. Max could smell his hair burning now, the stink assailing his nose and throat. It was now or never. "You must die! The fire take you!"

MAX HELSING
AND THE THIRTEENTH CURSE

CURTIS JOBLING

PUFFIN BOOKS

PUFFIN BOOKS
An imprint of Penguin Random House LLC
375 Hudson Street
New York, New York 10014

First published in the United States of America by Viking,
an imprint of Penguin Random House LLC, 2015
Published by Puffin Books, an imprint of Penguin Random House LLC, 2016

Text and illustrations copyright © 2015 by Curtis Jobling

THE LIBRARY OF CONGRESS HAS CATALOGED THE VIKING EDITION AS FOLLOWS:
Jobling, Curtis.
Max Helsing and the thirteenth curse / by Curtis Jobling.
pages. cm.—(Max Helsing: Monster Hunter ; 1)
Summary: "Max van Helsing and a group of friends try to save the world
after he discovers he has been cursed by an evil warlock who intends to
reclaim the earth for monsters"—Provided by publisher.
ISBN 9780451474797 (hardback)
[1. Magic—Fiction. 2. Monsters—Fiction. 3. Blessing and cursing—Fiction.]
I. Title. II. Title: Thirteenth curse.
PZ7.J5785Max 2015 [Fic]—dc23 2015006094

Puffin Books ISBN 9780147516114

Printed in the United States of America

3 5 7 9 10 8 6 4 2

Designed by Kate Renner

For Emma . . .

Woof! Woof!

PROLOGUE

xxx

THE WALDEN WOODS HORROR

The twigs snapped underfoot like skeletal fingers crushed before they could snatch and seize hold. The teenager's steps were hurried, kicking up wind-tossed leaves and weather-beaten branches as she swiftly climbed the slope. She glanced back occasionally, spying through the trees the neighborhood lights, twinkling into life at dusk. Her dorm backed up to the woodland's edge, her bedroom window overlooking the forest, this wild, wonderful world, right at her doorstep. His world.

Her eyes darted, searching the shadows on either side of the trail, checking to see that she was alone. He was a recluse for good reason; the folks who lived in this quiet corner of Lincoln, Massachusetts, were suspicious of strangers. Where better for him to hide away than up here, in the woods? She knew how he felt. She'd never fitted in, always the outsider, even in her own family. It wasn't easy being a Goth when one's younger sisters were preppy, pony-loving princesses. She'd imagined life might get easier once she got to college, but she remained a square peg in a round hole. Yet those misfit days were behind her now. That the two of them had found one another was a miracle. It filled her heart with hope that there was somebody out there for everybody, even the loneliest soul.

Stepping through the forest, the young woman emerged at her destination. She stopped for a moment, taking one last cautious peek back the way she'd come; nobody on her trail, nobody in pursuit. She turned about, toward her lover's home. The old mill loomed out of the darkness, its windows boarded, the stream rushing through its broken waterwheel. It looked sinister at twilight, but that didn't bother her.

It gave her a thrill, truth be told. Spooky things got the pulse racing, the blood pumping; they made her feel alive. A nighttime rendezvous in an abandoned timber mill? This was their secret place. She reached for the long black scarf about her neck, fingers twining through the material to brush her flesh. She would be in his arms again soon enough. She'd waited too long for his kiss.

"Lovely evening for a stroll!"

She looked up, startled to see a figure standing in the tree line at the top of the slope.

"Who . . . who's there?" she asked, squinting through the dim, dusky light. "Come out where I can see you. I'm not scared, you know."

He stepped out of the shadows. He was just a kid, a middle-schooler. His face was hidden within the hoodie cowl that poked out of his bomber jacket's collar. The scuffed leather had seen better days, as had the drain-pipe jeans and battered Chuck Taylors. In his right hand, a yo-yo spun lazily up and down; he made it rise and fall with the deft skill of a seasoned slacker. Over his shoulder he carried a khaki satchel, the bag resting against his hip. Finally, the boy tugged the hood back, his grin emerging in the gloom.

"You should be."

MAX HELSING HAD HOPED HIS SMILE MIGHT PROVE disarming to the young woman in black. Unfortunately, accompanied by those words, it just came across as creepy. She gave him a sideways look, reaching a hand into her pocket. Perhaps a can of pepper spray in there? Or something worse? Not that Max was too bothered. Nothing could be as bad as last summer's Colorado job and the Case of the Cold Canyon Killer. The petrifying spitting venom of a dust dragon had turned his baseball cap into a bonnet of stone. That was his favorite hat, he recalled with a pang.

"Sorry," said Max, pocketing his yo-yo and raising his hands peaceably while stepping closer. "I didn't mean to freak you out. I promise, I'm totally harmless."

"That's close enough," she said, backing away in the direction of the ruined mill. "What are you doing here?"

Max made an embarrassed face. "Well, I was kind of hoping I could dissuade you from going in there."

He pointed at the dark building. She stole a glance, as if it might have transformed since the last time she looked.

"Why's that?" Her hand emerged from her pocket, clenching something solid and rectangular. It looked ominously like a gun. Max cringed; okay, so that could possibly rival the dust dragon.

"Haven't you heard? Legend says the old mill's haunted. Well, at least the locals do. They say it's cursed. That terrible things happen to anyone who enters. Some big bad juju went on here in the past."

"So?"

That wasn't the reply Max had hoped for. Usually the "big bad juju" line would put even the most numbskulled norm off. The fact that it hadn't only confirmed what he feared.

"So you're not scared easily? Cool. Maybe we can go in together?"

The woman eyed him suspiciously. "You shouldn't be here."

Max strolled toward the building, its double doors slightly ajar. He peered through the gap, the dark void impenetrable. A host of smells assailed his nostrils, none of which was pleasant. He was getting the musty aroma of mold and damp, a hint of rotten timber, and the sweet scent of decaying flesh; a heady bouquet indeed. This was the place, all right.

"I said you shouldn't be here," repeated the young woman.

Max looked back at her. She was in her late teens, no doubt a student from the university in nearby Waltham. A Goth, too, judging by her dark attire. He might have known; they were so often Goths. He spied the scarf bound around her throat. Hiding something? Before he proceeded any further, he needed to discover just how deeply she'd been glamoured.

"There's no harm in taking a look inside, is there?" he said finally, fishing a flashlight from his bag. "It's abandoned, isn't it?"

"It's not abandoned. Somebody lives here."

"Don't be silly. Nobody would *choose* to live in a wreck like this."

"My boyfriend does."

Max arched an eyebrow as he seized a door and tested it. It groaned, resisting his pull. "Boyfriend? Is he a hermit?"

"He just doesn't get along with people," said the student, her words both cautionary and concerned as she stepped suddenly toward him. "You really should leave."

"It doesn't look like he's in," said Max, before ducking between the doors into the gloom beyond.

While she called after him, he flicked his flashlight switch. A bright beam lanced through the pitch black, the atmosphere alive with a swirling sea of dust particles. Max gagged now, the woodland aromas no longer providing adequate cover for the stench. This was the lair, undoubtedly.

Behind him, the Goth girl struggled through the entrance, cursing the intruding twelve-year-old. Max ignored her objections, instead searching the chamber for signs of life. Or worse . . .

Exposed rafters were vaguely visible in the darkness overhead, the rest of the ceiling shrouded in shadows. A rusted saw was suspended from a wall bracket up high, while log chains hung like iron curtains against the boards. The odd hand tool remained pegged in place, covered in cobwebs after decades of neglect. Long-forgotten offcuts littered the dirty floor, wedges of rotten timber that crawled with spiders and slugs.

"When you say he doesn't get along with people, what do you mean exactly?"

"He doesn't like crowds. Can't say I blame him." She seized Max by the shoulder and spun him around. "I said you shouldn't be here, and I meant it."

Max now recognized the item in her hand, and was shocked to see it leveled at him. "Um . . . you appear to have a Taser pointed at me. What gives?"

"You shouldn't have come here," said the woman, snatching the flashlight from his hand. She glowered, gesturing for him to move deeper into the mill. "I gave you fair warning, but you didn't listen, stupid little jerk."

Max smiled sheepishly. "Seems we might've got off on the wrong foot," he said, attempting to step within reach of her. If he could get in close, there was a chance he could disarm her. Slim, but better than nothing. He'd hate to be at Taser-point when the master of the house finally woke up. The teenager shone the flashlight beam directly into his eyes.

"Back up, and don't try anything stupid. You're going nowhere."

Max quit trying to get close to her, his dazzled eyes now searching the earthen floor of the building. *Where are you?* he wondered, seeking a sign that would reveal the occupant's resting place. His present predicament confirmed the girl's mental state; she was in the monster's thrall, completely under its spell.

"The man-purse," she said. "Throw it over here, now."

Reluctantly, Max unhitched his messenger bag, regretting the fact that he hadn't tooled up before arriving at the mill. There was an old, homemade catapult in the bag, his earliest childhood weapon, which might have come in handy if he'd had the foresight to pack it in his pocket. The canvas satchel that now sailed through the air to land on the floor between them was his box of tricks.

"So this boyfriend of yours," said Max as he backed up into a wall, the tools that adorned it rattling overhead. "He doesn't sound like a people person. Is he a bit of a shut-in? Only comes out at night?"

"He only comes out for *me*. We have something wonderful. Special. Our love's timeless. You wouldn't understand."

"I think I would," Max muttered, eyes still flitting across the floor. Maggots squirmed blindly in the soil, trying to avoid the student's booted feet. Unless Max was very much mistaken, the earth there was stained dark. Dried blood, perhaps? Was she standing over the beast? Maybe it would burst from the ground at any moment, just like in the movies. He shuddered. It was rarely like in the movies.

He looked back to the young woman. A goofy, lovey-dovey expression had appeared on her pale face.

"You got indigestion, or has something tickled you?"

"You'll meet him soon. Then you'll understand the nature of our love. Maybe, right at the end, you'll realize what a fool you were."

"The end? Sounds a bit final."

"My love will be hungry when he wakes. He'll need to be sated." She placed the fist that held the flashlight against her chest, caught up in the Gothic drama, the beam illuminating her face from below as in a Halloween prank. Her scarf hung loose, revealing the punctured skin of her throat.

"He sounds like a real catch. I take it he's the silent type? Broody and moody? I bet he even sparkles . . ."

"He's intense," she said dreamily, before frowning as she caught Max smiling. "Ours is a unique love. He and I shall live forever. He'll make me his bride."

"They all promise that," muttered Max, searching in vain for a way out of the fix, still mindful of the Taser. He glanced up. The one weapon that might prove useful was the saw, and that was a good ten feet above his head, balanced against the wall at his back. How to reach it . . .

There, by his right foot; one of the chopped hunks of

wood. Max slowly began to crouch, extending his hand down his leg, straining his fingers to reach the block.

"Hands where I can see them!" the young woman hissed, causing Max to snap to attention, arms in the air like those of a puppet on a string. She glanced toward the boarded-up windows, Taser still trained on the boy. The light between the planks was pale blue, the sun's warm rays replaced by those of a chill moon. Her voice was a whisper.

"He rises."

Max's eyes were fixed upon the earth, expecting it to crumble and part as the creature rose from its pit. Instead, a shower of descending dust caused him to sneeze. The student raised the flashlight skyward, settling its focus upon the building's resident.

The figure hung upside down from one of the loftiest beams in the mill. Its hairless head was opalescent, pulsating as the flashlight's beam caressed it. Even from a distance, Max spied the twitching blue veins that carried corrupted blood through the monster's foul flesh. Its arms, originally folded about its torso in a frigid embrace, slowly extended from either side of its body, fingers flexing to reveal long yellow nails. Translucent wings connected its arms to its bony hips. Its gnarled feet trembled, crooked knuckles cracking as it prepared to disengage from the beam. It tipped its head, neck craning to look down upon Max and the teenage girl. Coal-black eyes blinked. Its nose was withered away to nothing, dark, slitted nostrils twitching as it sniffed at the air. A puckered mouth yawned open, revealing a maw of jagged teeth dominated by enlarged central incisors, each fully an inch in length.

The girl returned her gaze to Max at the precise moment his sneaker connected with the block at his feet. Those Saturday morning soccer games in elementary school hadn't been a waste of time after all. He went for a controlled pass with the inside of his shoe, surrendering the power of a penalty kick in favor of accuracy. His foot struck the piece of timber sweetly, propelling it at the student's head. There was a resounding *thunk* as the rotten wood hit her temple before she crashed to the floor in a crumpled heap, Taser and flashlight tumbling from her hands. He dived forward, snatching up the stun gun as the monster hit the ground.

Max jumped and turned in time to see the creature advancing on spindly legs. The flashlight rolled back and forth across the earth, its flickering beam flashing wildly around the mill. The creature's pale skin was stretched taut over every bone, granting it the appearance of a staggering cadaver. Its dead, hungry eyes bulged in their sockets, fixed upon the young adventurer, a dark tongue fluttering across those familiar, hideous teeth. Max checked the Taser in his hands.

"Fool," groaned the girl from where she lay slumped at the monster's feet. The abomination came to a halt, chuckling as it ran a grotesque hand affectionately through her dark hair. "You really think that can harm my love?"

"No," said Max, aiming the weapon overhead and firing it up the wall.

The two Taser probes whistled through the air, wires trailing, catching themselves on the old saw blade. In a fluid motion, the young monster hunter yanked the stun gun back like a fish on a line. The rusted tool tore free from its bracket, spinning dangerously through the air toward him. Max made a silent prayer as his hand shot out to catch it, hoping to maintain a full complement of fingers. He snatched it by the handle and brought it around in a scything arc toward the creature.

"But this should do the trick!"

The monster's black eyes went wide as the rusty saw blade tore a jagged path through its neck. The decapitated head tumbled, landing neatly in the girl's lap as she let loose a startled shriek. It was as if a switch had flipped in her head—with the glamour lifted, the effect of the spell ceased instantly. No longer the beast's consort, she was just a confused young woman cradling a hideous, stinking, slack-jawed skull.

"Vampires," said Max Helsing, with a shake of his head. He tossed the bloodied saw aside as the monster's corpse collapsed into the dirt. "Terrible boyfriend material."

VAMPIRE (ADOLESCENT)

OTHER ALIASES: lamia, vampir, vampyras, wampir

ORIGIN: Transylvania, Europe

STRENGTHS: Great speed, high intelligence, immunity to many conventional weapons.

WEAKNESS: Daylight, Holy Water (blessed), and Holy Symbols. Particular fear of the crucifix. Aversion to garlic and silver. Wooden stake to the heart = instant dispatch.

HABITAT: Anywhere dark and removed from daylight. Grave, tombs, and crypts all popular, but also known to roost in caves, disused buildings, and tunnels.

Despite the fearsome visage, the Adolescent (also referred to as a "Stage II") is less dangerous than its Mature brethren. Post-pupation, this is the second stage of the vampire life cycle, in which it has discarded many human features since its Infancy (Stage I). Regardless, NEVER underestimate a vampire, whatever its age.

—Erik Van Helsing, January 12th, 1853

PHYSICAL TRAITS

1. Enlarged canines—Used for puncturing flesh before feeding.

2. Night vision—It hunts only at night.

3. Wings—Akin to those of a bat. Unlike those of Mature & Elder vampires, Adolescent wings afford limited gliding ability as opposed to actual flight.

4. Opposable toes—Able to grip as easily as hands.

—Esme Van Helsing, March 22nd, 1862

5. TELEPATHY!!!
Watch out for MIND CONTROL!!
Telepathy NOT limited to MATURE or ELDER suckers!

MAX HELSING Feb 14th, 2014

ONE

xxx

BREAKFAST-A-GO-GO

The fried eggs quivered, threatening to leap from the pan at any moment. With deft flicks of the spatula, Jed sent droplets of hot oil across their surfaces, the yellow yolks clouding over like cataracts. He only partly paid attention to the frying pan, his eyes drifting over the *New England Examiner* that lay open before him. Beneath the kitchenette counter, a battle of wills was under way.

"He's a hellhound?" asked Max incredulously.

The ugliest dog in the world sat on the linoleum floor opposite, locked in a staring contest with Max. He was a small black pudgy thing, unblinking bug eyes regarding the young monster hunter vacantly. With a face like he'd been chasing parked cars, he wasn't going to win any puppy pageants any day soon, not unless some terrible accident took out every other dog in the western world. He'd probably still lose out to a strategically shaved warthog. A bright

HELLHOUND (JUVENILE)

OTHER ALIASES: barghest, "Black Shuck," gytrash

ORIGIN: Northern Europe, especially British Isles

STRENGTHS: Infravision, heightened sense of smell, fiercely loyal.

WEAKNESS: Hot-headed—suffer from tendency to rush into battle. Loyalty can be their downfall.

HABITAT: Deserted highways, woodlands, scenes of great horror.

Featuring widely in European folklore, these "hounds of hell" are considered Bearers of Death, their arrival often portentous and heralding a person's demise. On occasion they are used by vampir to protect them as they slumber. This "guard dog" variety of hellhound can always be found close to its master's nest . . .

—Erik Van Helsing, October 10th, 1858

PHYSICAL TRAITS

1. Lightning speed—Deceptively quick, even in its ungainly juvenile form.

2. Jaws—Bite is as powerful as that of an adult crocodile—BEWARE!

3. Fire Breath—Adult hellhounds can belch bolts of fire at their enemies. No reported instances of pups having this ability.

4. Growth—They get BIG . . .

—Esme Van Helsing, May 11th, 1862

EIGHTBALL!!
Got one of these for my BIRTHDAY!
NOT convinced—all he does is fart
and slobber! He's worse than Jed!

MAX HELSING

Nov 16th, 2015

pink tongue poked out of his panting mouth, a glob of pendulous drool suspended from his lip like ectoplasm.

"Eightball's pedigree," said Jed, reading glasses focused on the newspaper. "You shouldn't be so quick to judge a book by its cover."

Never a truer word spoken, thought Max. Jed was old as the hills, with a bum leg, but you underestimated him at your peril. A boxer in his youth, the man had fought alongside Max's grandfather and trained his father. Jed's own monster hunting exploits had been cut short when he went toe-to-toe with a minotaur in a Minneapolis junkyard. He'd killed the monster, but not before it gored him good and proper, leaving his left leg busted and locked at the kneecap. It had taken him out of the field, but there was still plenty of fight left in the old warrior. Max hadn't been awake long, but Jed had been up for hours, hitting the punching bag before sunrise. His white vest left his arms exposed, the honed muscles belying his seventy-odd years, brown skin still glistening with beads of workout sweat.

"Where did you get this mutt?" asked Max with a blink, now wondering if the dog even had eyelids.

"Odious Crumb. He passed on his best wishes. I thought you'd be more grateful; you've always said you wanted a pet."

"I wanted something cute."

"Like a Pomeranian?"

"What's that?"

"Fluffy dog, looks like a teddy bear."

"I *wanted* a puppy," said Max, rising from the floor and

taking a seat at the counter. Eightball smacked his lips, sniffing expectantly at the air. "I don't know *what* this is."

"Stick with him. He's a remarkable wee beast. He might surprise you."

"You know, most people get regular-looking dogs."

"We ain't most people," said Jed, sliding the eggs from the pan to a plate. He shoved it across the counter just as the toaster popped. Max caught the two slices and juggled the hot bread. He didn't stop to butter them; he was already running late for school. Eightball watched hungrily.

Jed raised a steaming mug of coffee to his lips. He took a slurp, pondering the newspaper as Max tore apart a slice of toast and dunked it into an egg. "You sleep okay?"

"Yeah. I was wiped out after that Walden Woods job."

"Vampires will do that to you."

"Actually, I think it was the fresh air."

Jed arched a gray eyebrow over the rim of his half-moon spectacles. "Sorry it turned out to be a sucker, son."

Max shrugged. When possible, he tried to rehabilitate the creatures he encountered, or at the very least relocate them. Sadly, some beasties were beyond his help. Vampires fell firmly within that category. There was nothing grand or romantic about those particular demons. They were parasites that gorged on the blood of the living. Once drained and dead, their thralls would rise from the grave as newly made vampires. Thankfully, few of these monsters survived. The world had the Van Helsing family to thank for this, not that it would ever know.

Max's family had dropped the Van prefix before their surname during the war years, on account of it sounding too German. That it was actually a Dutch name was neither here nor there. The family's unique line of work required them to remain inconspicuous, so the last three generations had all been plain Helsings. Max tossed a crust to Eightball, the pup's lips smacking as he snatched it from the air.

"Don't feel badly about how it went down," said Jed.

"I don't. I was just out of options. Only hope the girl can come back from that. Being enthralled by a sucker ain't nice at all."

"Let's count ourselves lucky that the few vamps that linger are a weaker, late-generation variety. Nowhere near as dangerous as the Elders your forefathers faced."

Max chased the yolk around his plate with the toast, nodding toward the newspaper. "So what's happening in the world today?"

"Which world do you want to know about?" Jed sighed, returning to the *Examiner*. "Politician popularity polls or baseball batting averages?"

"That's news?"

"My sentiments exactly," said Jed, rifling through the paper to the culture section. A long finger trailed across the articles. "You gotta look below the surface to find the real stories. Here we go. A showing of rare Native American art at the Waterfront Gallery; the opening of an early settlers exhibition at the Museum of Anthropology; an archaeological dig out in Rockport that's turned up some strange finds. This is where the real stories are, hiding in plain sight behind the slick senators and snarling sportsmen. This is *our* world."

Max nodded. "I'd better get going."

Dabbing up the last bits of egg with his toast crust, he snatched up his messenger bag. He paused beside the stove, where something bubbled in a covered pot. Taking a wooden spoon, Max removed the lid and gave the contents a stir. Lumps of indiscernible meat bobbed to the simmering surface of the soup, the unmistakable stench of shellfish rising on the steam.

"It's your favorite," said Jed. "Homemade clam chowder."

Max blanched at the old man's bad joke, and his signature dish. Besides eggs, it was Jed's *only* dish. He regularly made a great batch of the soup, which would feed them for a week. Max couldn't bear the stuff, but a boy had to eat. Sometimes.

"I'm not hungry."

"It's for tonight, numbnuts."

"Still, doubt I'll be hungry," replied Max, popping the lid back onto the pot. "You ever think of expanding your repertoire beyond eggs and soup?"

"Your chores all done?" retorted the old man, eyes still on the paper. "Garbage taken out? Leaves brushed off the steps? Velcazar's Words of Warding memorized?"

"Yep, yep, and yep!"

"Creaky floorboard outside the Liu apartment? That still needs nailing down . . ."

"Remind me again why I have to fix things for everyone in *my* house?"

"Strictly speaking, Helsing House ain't yours any-more. It's owned by the Cole Corporation. We're building superintendents."

"Glorified janitors, more like."

"Be thankful you've a roof over your head, even if it is the attic. Now scram before you're late for school again."

Eightball leaped after him, giving chase as Max scampered through the door.

"And get yourself straight home tonight, y'hear?" the elderly guardian shouted, but the boy was gone.

The staircase shook as Max's sneakers struck one step in six, carrying him down the flights in swift succession. He paused on the second floor outside the Liu apartment, placing his heel on the misbehaving floorboard. The warped wood groaned. He made a mental note of the job for later. He was determined to be punctual today. On too many occasions in the last few months, his unusual life had conspired to make him late for school, resulting in trips to Principal Whedon's office. Turning from the Lius' threshold, he charged straight into the stationary figure of Mr. Holloman.

Max bounced off him with a *clang*, his head ringing as he regathered his senses. He looked up at the statuesque fellow from 2A. Mr. Holloman's broad, slablike face stared down without emotion, his expression as blank now as on the day he was forged. Max hadn't even heard him open his door. For an iron golem, his neighbor was awfully light of foot.

"How you doing today, Mr. Holloman?" said the boy, stepping around the towering figure. "Anything interesting planned? Hijinks ahead? Shenanigans afoot?"

Max always hoped it might be the day that the peaceful giant spoke. Sadly, it wasn't. Mr. Holloman's face only turned with a creaking groan as he watched Max pass by. With his tarnished metal flesh passing for dull, dark skin, the man could be mistaken for a regular human in the street, if it weren't for the empty holes where his eyes should have been. The sunglasses he wore helped conceal these iron sockets and kept him from scaring his neighbors, who were unaware of his remarkable condition.

"Have a good one, Mr. H!"

One more flight of stairs and Max was hurdling the banister, hitting the first floor with a thump. Dust billowed where he landed. Another chore for his list, Max mused. No menial task was too boring for Jed to set him on, no drain too blocked for Max to wrestle with. Jed said these were life lessons. Max suspected they were jobs the old-timer didn't want to do himself.

When Max arrived in the lobby he was surprised to find Eightball waiting, head cocked, drool dribbling, stubby tail thumping the welcome mat.

GOLEM, IRON

ORIGIN: Prague, Kingdom of Bohemia

STRENGTHS: Almost impervious to physical harm, magic resistance.

WEAKNESS: Low intelligence, vulnerability to water attacks, reduced speed. Steamheart in chest—remove this to deactivate.

HABITAT: Golems are predominantly used by minority/oppressed communities as guardians. Often reside in or near houses of worship or shrines. Can easily be mistaken for statues when inactive.

Golems are anthropomorphic beings first recorded in Jewish folklore. While that version is a construct of clay, the animated iron variety is a more powerful, complex creation, often the handiwork of a magus. The clay golem is charged with defending the weak and disadvantaged from prejudice—less is known about the iron golem. The purpose of this metal man's creation is always particular to the individual enchanter.
—Erik Van Helsing, March 18th, 1858

PHYSICAL TRAITS

1. Chest Cavity—Houses steamheart, key to golem's animation.

2. Hammerhands—Mechanical fists strike like morningstars!

3. "Shem"—Word of power, stored within head, either in mouth or hollow eyes. The shem connects the golem to its master.

—Esme Van Helsing, March 21st, 1863

Golems have, on occasion, been known to run amok. This is often on account of either the death of their master or the shem (a holy word of power hidden within its form) being removed. Keep a bucket of water handy when dealing with these iron giants. —Algernon Van Helsing, July 2nd, 1938

MR HOLLOMAN in 2A:

—Are GOLEMS mute? Still waiting for the BIG GUY to say something! No sign of a SHEM either—maybe he keeps it up his butt!

MAX HELSING   Nov 3rd, 2014

"You're pretty speedy, considering you've got cocktail weenies for legs."

Cracking the front door, he slipped out onto the pristine, freshly swept front steps of Helsing House, leaving a whimpering Eightball behind.

Helsing House towered behind Max, a mountain of dark bricks and spires reaching for the heavens. It dated back to the mid-1800s, a fine example of the neo-Gothic architecture of that period, or so Max had been told. The wind whipped around the boy. The town of Gallows Hill was firmly in late fall's bare-knuckled grasp. Skeletal trees swayed, their twisted branches stripped of foliage. Dead leaves had transformed the long driveway into a river of rippling reds, browns, and yellows, the occasional straggler fluttering on the breeze.

A low granite balustrade flanked the entrance, with rampant stone lions roaring silently on either side of the door. Checking for a moment that he wasn't being observed, Max jumped up onto the head of the lion on the left, reaching into his jacket pocket to pull out a blueberry muffin wrapper. A birdhouse stuck out from the brickwork above, its wooden wall and roof dappled with moss. Unlike most birdhouses, this one had a door on it, currently closed.

"Yo, Mrs. Fairweather," he said, lightly rapping a knuckle on the outside of the box.

There was a rustle inside, and then the door swung open to reveal a tiny, smiling humanoid figure. She was perhaps four inches tall, and as she stepped out a pair of thin gossamer wings peeled away from her back. The pixie fluttered into the air, graceful as a hummingbird. The bickering of tiny voices in the nesting box made her warm smile vanish.

"Will you kids keep it down in there," she called back irritably. "I'm trying to talk to Max!"

"Hey, Max!" the children called from inside the birdhouse, raising a smile on the boy's face as Mrs. Fairweather gratefully took the sweet, crumb-coated wrapper.

"It's very good of you, Max. The brood and I appreciate it."

"No problem," he replied. "Now get back indoors before the mailman—or a hawk—spots you!"

The little lady winked, rolling the muffin wrapper under her arm before fluttering back into the box. "Kids! Breakfast!"

Max hopped back down onto the porch, chuckling. Sure, the menial jobs could be a drag sometimes, but life in Helsing House was never dull. He didn't know many people who had a golem and a family of pixies as neighbors. He sprang down the steps and set off toward the rear of the building.

Eightball awaited him.

"Didn't I leave you inside? How'd you get out?"

Max sidestepped the peculiar dog and crossed the drive to the side door of the detached garage. He yanked the clanking collection of keys from his pocket, sifting through for the one that matched the industrial-strength padlock. The key went in, and the brass mechanism popped apart in his hand. Stuffing the bundle back into his pants, key chain looping around his belt, Max opened the door, ducking in briefly to grab his Raleigh Chopper. There was no car in the garage: there wasn't room for one. Workbenches crowded the floor alongside Jed's gym equipment, while all manner of unusual and deadly looking ephemera adorned the walls and ceiling—the Helsing armory.

He backed the bicycle out of the building, oblivious to the figure that crept up behind him. A crunching footfall suddenly alerted Max to approaching danger.

Max's left heel dug into the gravel as his right foot kicked the Chopper's rear wheel into the air. He spun around instantly, his retro ride suddenly a weapon as he propelled it toward his follower by the high-rise handlebars. Almost too late, he spied the innocent—and terrified—face of his ten-year-old neighbor, Wing Liu. Max pulled back on the handlebars just enough for the kid to jump clear and land on his rump in a shower of dead leaves.

"Whoa," gasped Max, booting the Chopper's kickstand. "You were nearly wearing that bike for a moment. You okay?"

Wing took Max's offered hand, and the older boy hauled him to his feet. Wing peeled leaves from his clothes sheepishly, rubbing his butt.

"You bruise your behind there?"

"That and my pride."

"You're in one piece," said Max, straddling the bike. "That's all that matters."

Wing cast his eyes over the Chopper in wonder. "Epic wheels, dude."

Wing cracked Max up. Everything was *epic* to his home-schooled neighbor. Wing was obsessed with myths, monster sightings, and weird goings-on, always reciting facts out of Ripley's or trawling the Internet for the latest cryptozoological gossip and conspiracy theories. *Too bad I can't show him something* really *epic*, Max thought.

"Thanks, man," said Max, trading a quick fist bump with his disciple. "What's up?"

"My violin teacher is coming for my lesson in about a half hour."

"I timed my escape pretty well, then," chuckled Max.

"Hey, have you seen that new Bigfoot footage?" said the boy, suddenly animated. "It's *epic*!"

"You can't believe everything you see on the Internet, Wing."

"Aw, c'mon. The Internet's your friend!"

"Not mine. I put my trust in a good book, every time."

"The clip's about twenty seconds long; you can see it clearly. There's no way it's not real."

The boy was in his element now. Max admired his passion, which made his skepticism act that much tougher to perform.

"Where was it sighted?"

"Oregon. A party of hikers filmed it, and their sighting was corroborated by a delivery man later that day. He nearly hit it with his van, apparently. You should see it, Max. It's epic, I swear!"

Max laughed and shook his head. Truth was, the story was probably right on the money—there was a long history of Sasquatch sightings in the Pacific northwest. But the last thing Max needed to do was feed the flames of Wing's fascination with the fantastic. The Lius wouldn't be happy, and he was pretty sure Jed would skewer him if he shared their secret with the chatty kid.

The two turned as Eightball suddenly emerged from some nearby bushes, dragging a huge branch behind him in his slobbering jaws. He deposited it beside the bike and looked extremely pleased with himself.

"Who's this little guy?" asked Wing.

"Name's Eightball." The puppy answered to his name, scrabbling at Max's leg until he bent to pick him up. Max patted the twigs from his coat, receiving a stinky lick in return. He grimaced. "We think he's a dog."

"He's adorable!"

"Really?" Max handed Eightball over as the puppy transferred the slobberfest to his new victim. "Play nice with Wing, Eightball."

"You're leaving him with me?"

"I've got lessons of my own to get to," said Max, pedaling

away from both boy and dog. "But be careful: if you feed him after midnight he turns into a Pomeranian."

"A pommy what?"

Max's Chopper cut up the gravel as he disappeared down the drive.

"Look it up, Wing! The Internet's your friend!"

TWO

"You're cutting it awfully close," said the girl, lifting her sunglasses as he approached.

She sat astride her BMX as Max cycled up to the gates of Gallows Hill Burying Ground. The girl wore skinny jeans and an oversize black sweater with her trademark white loop scarf, looking every inch the hipster.

"I was worried you were going to be late," she said. "Again."

"Don't worry about me, Syd," said Max, skidding to a dramatic halt beside her. "I could be an hour late, but I'd still make up the time on this beauty."

"Oh, so it's a time-traveling bicycle now? It certainly belongs in the past."

Max grinned as he caught his breath. His Chopper *was* an antique. He and Jed had lovingly restored it to its former glory after rescuing it from a garage sale. Syd's BMX was another story. Matte black carbon fiber frame, welded rims, custom chain tensioners, aluminum heads, stainless steel spokes—Max didn't know what *any* of these words meant, but he knew them nonetheless, thanks to Syd never shutting up about them. "You're just jealous."

"Yeah, that must be it," she said with an amused snort. "Good to go?"

"Ladies first."

"Don't be getting all chivalrous on me."

Max grinned and set off first. Syd might act like a tomboy, but he knew there was a girl beneath the disguise. Her olive skin was flawless, and (although he'd never tell her) her hair always smelled of strawberries.

In the distance, the towers and office blocks of Boston reached for the sky. Gallows Hill was removed from the hustle and bustle of the city, but it wasn't a sleepy town. Far from it. This was where many of Max's people lived, humans and monsters alike trying to get by and get along with each other. The regular folks of Gallows Hill—the "norms," as Max called them—had no idea that another society lived and thrived alongside them.

Max stared through the wrought-iron railings as they cycled beside the graveyard. The world beyond took on a life of its own, graves and headstones flickering by as if viewed through a zoetrope. A crow kept pace with them, flying above the sleeping dead, its beady black eyes fixed upon the two cyclists. The Van Helsing family crypt was there, deep in the cemetery's heart. Max would visit it on occasion, to feel closer to his father and contemplate his crazy life. People said the graveyard was haunted by the ghosts of witches hanged during the trials of old, and the neighborhood kids did their best to keep that legend alive. It was the oldest burying ground in all of New England, and Helsing House's close proximity was no coincidence. *Everything* seemed to be haunted by *something* in Gallows Hill. Rumor had it Max's school had its own ghost, though it had yet to introduce itself to him.

The crow cawed, its harsh call stirring Max from his daydream before it winged off into the graveyard's depths.

"Seriously, though, you promised me on Friday you'd be on time today. 'I'm turning over a new leaf on Monday.' Those were your words. Did your weekend go loco? If you make me late I'll give you such a beatdown."

"I went hiking in Walden Woods last night. It took more out of me than I expected."

"You? A *hike*?"

"Yeah. It was a work thing."

"Oh," said Syd, arching an eyebrow and nodding.

Max felt lucky that there were no secrets between him and Syd. She knew all about what his work entailed. She'd first witnessed it when the two were in their last year of elementary school together. Syd had lost a baby tooth unexpectedly while chomping on an apple, and Max had jumped in swiftly to purchase it from her. It had cost him a week's allowance, but he'd happily parted with the cash. Intrigued,

Syd followed the boy after school to a derelict dentist's office, where she discovered Max feeding her abandoned incisor to a wizened and grateful tooth fairy. Her gasp had given her away to the tiny creature and the Helsing boy. From that point on, Max had welcomed Syd into his world. Now she helped him out on jobs, supplying him with gadgets and gizmos she created.

"Then there were the house chores," Max continued. "Jed never gives me a break. And this morning he gave me a puppy. That was kinda left field."

Syd squealed. "Ooh! A puppy?"

"Why does everyone keep doing that?"

"Because it's a puppy, Max! Puppies are cute!"

"When I say *puppy*, I mean it in the loosest possible sense of the word."

"You can be so mean, Max Helsing. I'm sure he's precious. What's his name?"

"Eightball. You can meet him tomorrow, if you're still coming for dinner. You clear it with your folks?"

"I cleared it with my *mom*," she snapped. "Perry's not my dad. They're going off on some date. And besides, I wouldn't miss your party for the world."

"I wouldn't call it a party. *Party* suggests streamers, paper hats, and a crowd. It's just a gathering of people I care about."

"Aw, you're such a sweetie!" Syd reached across and rabbit-punched him in the arm. The Chopper veered away, threatening to careen into the road before Max righted it again. He sucked his teeth. Syd punched harder than any girl he knew. Harder than most of the boys, too.

"Maybe I'll get you an alarm clock as a gift," she said, picking up the pace as they climbed the hill past the creepy All Saints Church. The last school bus appeared, destined to arrive right at the bell.

"You'd miss this." He grinned, pedaling furiously.

They turned the corner and hit an intersection, only a block away from the school now. The light shone red, halting their progress momentarily, as traffic barred their path. Parents' cars drove south back down the hill, away from the middle school, overprotective moms and dads having safely deposited their little darlings. Hearing shouts across the road to his left, Max caught sight of a panicked sixth grader dashing down the intersecting street, away from the school.

Max sighed, drawing Syd's attention. "Check that out."

Two eighth graders followed the boy into the side street, laughing. Max recognized one of them straightaway: Kenny Boyle.

"Dude," said Syd, tapping his shoulder and pointing up the road toward the school. "We're so close!"

"You're right, we are."

Boyle was a head taller than Max, a great streak of sneer and sinew topped off with a shock of red hair. Max knew where he stood with most monsters, but he was less sure when it came to humans. He knew one thing about Boyle, though: the eighth grader was a stone-cold bully.

"This isn't your fight," Syd reminded him.

Even from this distance, they could spy the stunted figure of Principal Whedon at the gates, ushering children across the threshold. He was staring up at the school's clock tower, watching the hands shifting slowly, inexorably closer to eight o'clock. Then the bell would sound and the gates would close.

"Max, if you miss that bell . . ."

"I know, I know," he said, nodding. He straightened the high handlebars, pointing the Chopper dead ahead, up the hill toward the school. The crossing light counted down, flashing and beeping. "Be on time. Turn over a new leaf. All that good stuff."

The light changed. *Walk.*

Max pushed off, taking a hard left and setting off down the intersecting street, straight after the bullies and their victim.

"It's not your fight!" shouted Syd.

"It never is!" came the reply as he pedaled away. The girl shook her head and continued up the hill, racing toward a glowering Principal Whedon at the school gate.

Max found Boyle down an alley, the sixth-grader in his grasp as he shook him down for lunch money. His henchman was tipping the contents of the poor kid's schoolbag onto the ground and sifting through it.

Max jumped off his Chopper, booted the kickstand, and dashed up to the trio. He slammed Boyle hard in the back, forcing the older boy to release the poor kid. Boyle turned, snarling, unrattled. As the bully's fist connected with Max's face, he thought he could hear bells ringing.

He did. It was the school bell. He was late.

Again.

THREE

xxx

ALL KINDS OF VERMIN

Max stood outside the principal's office, across the hall from Kenny Boyle, and smiled. It took some effort, for a number of reasons. First, Boyle was an intimidating fool who took delight in picking on those smaller than him. Second, the mere sight of the sneer on the eighth grader's milk-pale, freckled face brought on a wave of nausea that made Max want to hurl. And third, and perhaps most importantly, the young monster hunter's fat lip felt like it might tear apart at any moment, thanks to the powerful punch Boyle had landed.

One thing made the painful smile bearable: Boyle's left eye had swollen shut, the bully's features frozen mid–Popeye impression. It was sure to become the mother of all black eyes as the day progressed. In all fairness, it wasn't technically Max's handiwork. He'd ducked during the melee, and Boyle's friend's fist had caught the lanky lout in the face. It seemed Max was being blamed, but he didn't mind taking the credit.

Max's yo-yo descended toward the floor and back up into his palm. He had been here before, preparing to experience the principal's hair dryer impression—a blast of hot air delivered straight to one's face—on numerous occasions. Like his forefathers, who were touched by magic through generations of interaction with monsters, Max had developed certain special powers, but those powers were useless when dealing with Whedon.

Mrs. Perlman, the elderly school secretary, kept watch over both boys as she tapped away on her keyboard. Occasionally she'd stop typing to fiddle with her hearing aid, listening in on the conversation that was under way in the office. Max could see the silhouette of Whedon's visitor through the door's frosted glass panel, and could hear the man's rumbling voice. There was a burst of awkward laughter—Whedon's. Max shifted nervously as the door finally opened.

The two men exited the office and clasped hands in a friendly shake. *Never a good sign,* figured Max. Chief Boyle had clearly come straight from work, his police hat tucked under his arm. The police chief had the same red hair as his son, only his was thinning on top and graying at the sides. Whedon, a good head shorter than Boyle, pumped his hand vigorously.

"Good man, Whedon," said Boyle gruffly, a distinct Bostonian twang to his voice.

"It's my pleasure," said Whedon cheerfully, his face creased by a great, fawning grin. "And please, call me Irwin."

The chief glowered at Max, sending shivers up and down the boy's spine. The yo-yo went slack in his hand, losing its rhythm as Max reeled it in and pocketed it. The police officer popped his hat back on and ran a finger across the visor. Max had encountered all manner of monsters in his short time on earth, but Chief Boyle gave him the heebie-jeebies. The man turned back to the principal and nodded.

"Thanks again, Whedon. Come on, son, let's get you out of here. You're taking the rest of the day off. How about a frappe on the way home?"

It was the bully's turn to smile as he rose and followed his father out of the room. Max winked and mimed the word *ouch*, pointing at his own eye. Boyle's grin slipped as he vanished through the door.

"Come by anytime, Chief!" Whedon called after them. He reminded Max of a lovestruck sixth grader who'd fallen for the eighth-grade quarterback. "And remember, it's Irwin!"

Max stifled a snort of laughter, regretting it instantly. Whedon turned sharply. He straightened his brushy black mustache with a thumb before extending a stubby finger toward his door.

"My office. Now."

Max slumped past Mrs. Perlman into the room. Whedon closed the door behind him, stalking around his desk before settling into his leather chair. The principal lounged back in the seat, bringing steepled fingers to his chin. He was doing his best Bond villain impression, and it wasn't very good. Max had been more intimidated by Chicago-style deep-dish pizzas.

The young monster hunter saw a chair on his side of the table. "Mind if I take a seat, Irwin?"

The bristles of Whedon's mustache twitched, hairs rippling along his lip like an angry caterpillar. "You think you're pretty funny, don't you, Helsing?"

Of *course* Max thought he was funny, at least when it came to dealing with Whedon. But even if the man was the lumpiest, dumpiest, grumpiest fellow he'd ever met (when it came to humans, anyway), Whedon was also the guy who would eventually send Max on to high school. As things stood, Max's report card was going to look like a horror screenplay. If he didn't turn a corner with his behavior soon, there'd be serious long-term repercussions. Monster hunting was his reason for being, but as Jed often reminded him, he still needed an education.

"No, Principal Whedon," he said finally. "I don't think I'm funny. Sorry, sir."

"That's more like it," said the little man, chest puffing out.

"If I could just say one thing, sir. What happened this morning; that was all Boyle. He and Walker were bullying that sixth grader. I was just trying to help—"

"Young Boyle and his friend were assisting that lad after he'd dropped his schoolbag. The younger boy told me so himself."

Great, thought Max. Boyle had clearly gotten to the sixth grader, intimidating him enough to lie on his behalf.

"Helsing, let me give you some advice. Nobody likes a busybody. You need to knuckle down, start cutting out the dumb decisions."

Max was startled. "Dumb decisions?"

"You could actually *make* something of yourself one day, boy. But the way you're going, you'll be cooling your heels on a street corner with the bums. I'm trying to help you out here. You think I enjoy shouting at you?"

Max didn't answer, instead letting the principal rant on.

"Grow up. Take responsibility for your actions. You think life's all fun and games, getting cheap laughs at the expense of hardworking people. Your father was the same. I went to school with him, you know." Max knew this fact, but again remained quiet. "A lazy individual, a show-off and poseur, always swanning off on vacation somewhere or other, shirking his responsibilities."

Max cringed. It was well known that Conrad Helsing had died young, and that Jed had raised the man's son as his own. And those weren't vacations; they were monster missions. But how on earth could Max explain any of this to his principal?

Whedon leaned across his desk and pointed at Max, jabbing his finger in the air repeatedly.

"I'm watching you. Step out of line again and I'll have you out of Gallows Hill Middle School quick as a flash. You might think me cruel now, but you'll thank me for these chats one day. I'm providing you with that one thing that's missing from your life: discipline."

Max nodded, pretending to be suitably admonished. "Is that all, sir?"

Whedon waved his hand as if dispersing a terrible smell. "You're dismissed." Max trudged to the door, relieved to be leaving the tyrant behind.

"One more thing, Helsing," said the principal as Max slowly opened the door.

"Yes, sir?"

Whedon handed Max a pink slip of paper. "Detention, after school." The man's smile poked out from beneath that hideous excuse for a mustache. "Have a nice day."

FOUR

xxx

HUNCHES AND HEADSTONES

Dusk was closing in when Max finally left school. He and a handful of other miscreants had spent an hour in the company of Ms. Kingston, the young librarian keeping her watchful eye on them as they sat and did their homework. That hour had probably dragged on for the other kids, but Max had rather enjoyed it. He found plenty of interest in the history section and even hung around for an additional hour to share a fascinating conversation with Ms. Kingston on Native American folklore. All in all, time well spent. He'd be sure to thank Irwin the next time he saw him.

As Max's Chopper churned up leaves on the sidewalk, Syd's BMX rolled down the street alongside him. She was still wearing overalls from her afternoon spent in Mr. Landis's machine shop, with sunglasses perched atop her head. Unsurprisingly, Whedon was the topic of conversation.

"He may be a jerk, but it sounds like his heart was in the right place," said Syd.

"You're seriously defending him?"

"No, I'm trying to see from his point of view, is all. He's a teacher at the end of the day, and when he looks at you he sees . . . well . . ."

"What?"

"Trouble," she replied with a shrug. "It's never far away, is it? Lurking off your shoulder like some shadowy specter."

"School's a distraction from the serious stuff—from my *real* work. Whedon thinks I'm just a troublemaker."

"Trouble magnet would be closer to the truth," Syd said, laughing. "I did warn you this morning, though, didn't I? You need to start staying out of trouble."

Syd was speaking from the heart, having learned the hard way. Just a year earlier, she'd been caught breaking and entering the school on a dare, using her mechanical know-how and a well-placed lock pick to spring a skylight on the roof. Her so-called friends fled, and she was left for the police—and bailed out by Jed. Since then, she'd ditched that whole crowd and stuck closer to Max.

"It's not like I go *looking* for trouble," said Max as they approached the top corner of Gallows Hill Burying Ground, the familiar black railings coming into view. "But I always seem to land in it. And Boyle got taken out for a milk shake!"

"Don't worry. Bullies always get what's coming to them."

Chief Boyle was a bully and didn't seem to be suffering unduly. "Anyway, enough of my trials and tribulations."

Max sighed. "What are you working on at the moment?"

"Officially, I'm helping Mr. Landis renovate an old VW Beetle. Unofficially, I'm modifying an antique crossbow."

Syd was never happier than when she was in the garage, up to her elbows in grease. Machines were her passion. The rest was just background noise.

Max pulled on his brakes, but Syd didn't notice. He sat up in his saddle, craning his neck as he looked through the railings. The cemetery was cloaked in mist, headstones rising like jagged mountain peaks through a boiling blanket of clouds. Syd went on down the road, oblivious.

"Jed was throwing it out—can you believe it? He can be shortsighted sometimes, the old—"

She suddenly realized Max was no longer beside her. She brought the BMX to a halt and looked back.

"What is it?"

"Not sure," muttered Max. "Something."

"Could you be any more vague?"

"Not really."

"Could be nothing."

"Nope."

"How do you know it isn't?"

"Call it a hunch," replied Max, as he turned off the sidewalk and through the open gates. He hopped off his bike, booting the kickstand and continuing on foot. The gravel crunched as he disappeared into the mist.

Syd begrudgingly parked her bike alongside Max's. "I know all about your hunches."

She quickly caught up to Max as he headed uphill, parallel to the road and railings. His instincts, which Max had once jokingly referred to as his "Helsey sense tingling," were guiding him toward the source of his hunch. The boy occasionally got a gut feeling when something monstrous or magical was approaching. He never knew *what* the danger might be—only that it was impending. He picked a path gingerly between the graves, occasionally stopping to get his bearings. Syd was silent now, watching her friend at work. Max took a turn and headed deeper into the burying ground, smoky tendrils of mist swirling about them. He was slowing now and gradually came to a halt.

It sounded like a big dog feeding in the darkness, a low growl hidden behind a grinding noise. The moon and stars were obscured by clouds, and the two friends were some distance from any of the lamps that lit the graveyard. Max reached into his messenger bag, his eyes remaining fixed on the gloom ahead. The hairs on his neck tingled. He fished a six-inch plastic rod out of his satchel and snapped it. The high-intensity glow stick shone white, illuminating the area with a crackling light.

The grave was old, the headstone weather-beaten and its occupant's identity illegible. Turf was piled high around it, splinters of ancient timber half-buried in the earth. Max took another step forward to throw more light into the crudely excavated pit. He nodded.

"Well, that figures."

A naked creature straddled the broken coffin. It was

an emaciated humanoid, hideously desiccated, leathery skin drawn tight over wasted muscles and joints. The odd wisp of white hair still clung to its blotchy scalp, but it had long ago departed the world of the living. In its skeletal hands it held two halves of a human femur, gnawing on it, the brittle bone already snapped in two like a stick of celery. As the light fell on it, the monster ceased its feeding to look up. Unmistakably undead, its pale white eyes shone back eerily, reflecting the glow stick, black pinprick pupils focused on Max. It ground its teeth together in its lipless mouth.

"Out you come," said Max, clicking his fingers and pointing to the turf beside the grave. "And you can tidy this mess up while you're at it."

Syd inched closer, grabbing her shades to keep them from falling off her head. She peered over Max's shoulder, using the monster hunter as a human shield.

"Zombie?"

"Nope. Ghoul, and a young one, too, I reckon. Still got a bit of hair left, and it's not completely blind yet. Probably rose . . . let's see, fifty years ago?"

The creature clapped its crooked teeth together, gums drawn back and exposed. Max grinned.

"You appear to be hiding behind me," he called over his shoulder, chuckling. "Ghouls are carrion feeders. They're relatively harmless."

"*Relatively* is the key word there. Who knows where that thing's been?" Syd wrinkled her nose and shoved Max

GHOUL, LESSER

ORIGIN: Persia

STRENGTHS: Feels no pain, immune to most physical attacks.

WEAKNESS: Head shots and daylight.

HABITAT: Burial grounds, often nesting in large groups in subterranean tunnel systems.

These relatively harmless monsters are associated with graveyards and the consumption of corpses, their principal diet. Although undead, they provide little danger to the living, only feeding upon decayed flesh. Not to be confused with the infinitely more dangerous zombie.

—Erik Van Helsing, March 16th, 1851

PHYSICAL FIELD ACCOUNT— THE GETTYSBURG GHOULS

The unmistakable stench of the foul fiends reveals their location long before one encounters them. Their tunnel system is ingenious, carrying them beneath each grave so they may feed upon the war dead without fear of discovery by the living. Unable to reason with them, I have reluctantly resorted to the blade. I have labored for two weeks dispatching them, the president and his company oblivious to my presence, and rightly so.

—Esme Van Helsing, November 24th, 1863

The only good ghoul is a dead ghoul. Do not be lulled into a false sense of security by this devil. It is a wicked, soulless demon, no doubt in league with the rest of its undead brethren.

—Algernon Van Helsing, July 15th, 1936

GRANDPA had a serious problem with ghouls. He got it WAY WRONG—they are HARMLESS!!

MAX HELSING

Feb 27th, 2015

forward. "Do your thing and let's get out of here, Helsing. Chop, chop."

Max turned back to the ghoul in the grave. He crouched on his haunches, holding the glow stick overhead. The creature raised a hand through the air and raked at him, rising unsteadily on its filthy, clawed feet. Max leaned back.

"Hey, cut that out. Now we can do this the easy way or the hard way. I've had a pretty lousy day, so I'd rather we go with the former. I need you to put the bones back exactly as you found them—well, the parts you haven't already eaten, anyway—and then haul your skinny butt outta there. Then you've got to fill this earth back in. I know, I know, chores are a drag, so how 'bout Syd and I help you, okay? Teamwork always gets a job done!"

"Speak for yourself, hombre," said Syd. "You and Bones are on your own."

"Ignore Ms. Crankypants back there," said Max, gesturing toward his friend. "She'll help if I make her."

Syd snorted as Max smiled at the undead grave robber. Whether the ghoul understood Max was entirely unclear, but the boy continued regardless, giving the monster every opportunity to do the right thing.

"So whaddaya say? You going to do what I ask?"

The ghoul snarled and turned its back on him, reaching back into the coffin to rip loose a clutch of ribs. Max sighed and rose in resignation.

"Why do they never choose the easy way?" he asked, reaching back into the messenger bag and fishing around for what he needed. Grabbing the crucifix, Max presented it with a flourish and began the ritual. Words of Latin spilled forth, the mantra Max had learned parrot-fashion before he was even wearing big-boy pants. The ghoul was instantly scrambling, gurgling as it went, seizing the headstone to drag itself up. Syd let loose an involuntary squeal, backing up as the monster squirmed out of the pit. Max was on the move, maneuvering around the hole in the earth, maintaining a healthy distance from the creature.

The ghoul landed in the pile of soil, writhing and kicking as Max continued chanting, the crucifix glinting in the dim light where it rose from his knuckles. Crawling now, the beast drew closer to the shadows and the mist. Max switched back to English.

"That's right, run along, and tell your pals I'd better not see them here either. Gallows Hill Burying Ground is off-limits, Bones. I see you here again, I may not play so nice!"

"Well done," said Syd. "For a moment there, you almost sounded like a real Van Helsing."

"And you almost sounded like a real girl. Where did that squeal come from?"

"I'll *never* get used to the monsters," said Syd, readjusting her shades. "I'm the Q to your 007; fieldwork ain't my thing. *Now* can we go?"

"This grave still needs filling," said Max, tossing his jacket onto the headstone. Rolling up his hoodie sleeves, he returned to the pile of earth. He started shoving the dirt back into the ground with his hands. "You *could* help and we'd be done quicker. Many hands make light work, et cetera."

With a grumble, Syd joined her friend, kneeling in the soil and setting to the task.

"You know, back in the bad old days your dad would've just lopped its head off."

"Well," said Max, throwing a great armful of mud onto the splintered coffin below, "I'm not my dad."

"That's something *all* monsters should be grateful for."

FIVE

xxx

UPSTAIRS, DOWNSTAIRS

Max stood beside Jed, peering over the superintendent's shoulder into the bubbling pot of chowder. He shuddered, returning to the kitchenette counter to take a seat. Syd sat cross-legged on the floor, reading Jed's hand-me-down newspaper. Her overalls were covered in fine black hairs—Eightball had spent the last half hour cuddling in her lap and performing all manner of tricks, including fetching toys and treats. That Syd could strike up a rapport with his dog in mere moments annoyed Max no end. The peculiar puppy now whimpered at the apartment door, his little tail thumping as he watched the handle.

"He's really smart," said Syd, reaching across to pat his jet-black coat. "Who taught him to stay, seek, and fetch?"

"He came like that," said Jed. "His breed has a heightened intelligence compared to other dogs. Frightening, really."

Max watched Eightball whirl repeatedly, trying to catch his stubby tail in his slobbering jaws. "Yeah. Frightening intelligence."

"Does he need to go out?" asked Syd, folding the paper and rising to join Max at the counter.

"If he's out, he wants to be in, and vice versa," said Jed. "So, what are we going to do about Whedon?"

"I can handle Irwin," said Max. "I've seen scarier characters on *Scooby-Doo*. But I need to stay on his good side. I'll kill him with kindness—maybe start taking gifts in for him. Any good at baking apple pies, Jed? Or do your culinary skills stop at eggs and clam chowder?"

Jed slopped the soup into bowls and passed them across to Max and Syd. Max winked at his guardian, and the old man's glower cracked into a half smile.

"Whedon, I can deal with," said Max. "But Chief Boyle? He scares me."

Jed grunted as he took a stool across the counter from the kids. He whipped a penknife from his pocket, snapped out the blade, and speared an apple in the fruit bowl. A second later, the knife was a blur as the peel coiled off in a continuous loop.

"You're not having any?" asked Max suspiciously, sniffing at the strong-smelling, steaming soup.

"I had some earlier."

"Sure you did," said the boy as he gulped it down.

"Boyle," sniffed Jed as the kids worked on their meals. "That name's a blast from the past."

"How so?" asked Max.

"He was a beat cop when I was first teaching your father. This was back in the day when the streets *really* weren't safe after dark, for mankind or monsters. Criminal gangs brought their business to the *real* underworld."

"The Undercity," put in Max, his eyes wide.

"That's right," said Jed, his eyes narrowing. He took a crunching bite from the apple, swallowing it down. "Anything you need to tell me, Max?"

"About what?"

"Something I found in your bedroom. Under your mattress . . ." Max blushed as Syd arched an eyebrow. "Scrolls, Max. About the Undercity. Maps. What have I told you about that place?"

"There's no harm in *reading* about it, is there?"

"You *cannot* go there." There was anger in Jed's voice. "It just ain't safe for a Van Helsing. It's dangerous enough for *me* to head downstairs, let alone you."

"Dad went to the Undercity—"

"When he was a full-grown man. You're a boy. You're not ready for that. The Undercity ain't the lion's den—it's the dragon's lair. So forget about going, not on my watch."

Thanks to his reading, Max knew all about criminal connections with the Undercity, or "downstairs," as some called it. Right beneath Gallows Hill, the fabled Undercity was home to all manner of monster. Many of his predecessors had taken their fight to the Undercity, cutting a bloody path through the denizens of the dark places on their occasional crusades.

"What's Boyle's connection with the Undercity?" asked Max.

"Let's just say that Officer Boyle's loyalties were called into question at times, not just by the public but even some colleagues in the department."

"But he's the chief of police," said Max. "He's one of the good guys, right?"

"I love you, Max, but you're naive. Boyle's blood was corrupted long ago. I don't doubt for a moment he's the same backstabbing, bribe-bagging, double-dealing weasel he ever was. Steer clear of him and his boy, you hear me?"

Syd patted Max's back. "Chin up, dude. Stick to where you're safest: hunting monsters."

"Speaking of which," said Jed, "you sure it was a ghoul at Gallows Hill?"

"Positive," said Max confidently. "Feeding on the dead rules out most other kinds of undead. I'd rank it as a Class II, judging by the state of decay, and it wouldn't surprise me if its lair was somewhere close to the burying ground. Probably part of a pack."

"Something for you to investigate."

"No need to be too worried," said Max. "They're no danger to humans."

"Everything's a potential danger, son," grunted the old super. "At the end of the day, monsters are monsters."

"Boyle's not a monster and I'm supposed to be wary of him."

Jed sucked his teeth. "There are all kinds of monsters in this world, Max. Trick is to spot 'em coming."

Max pushed his empty bowl away to spin around on his stool. He patted his lap, enticing Eightball. "C'mere, boy!"

Syd laughed as Eightball's rear left paw scratched behind a stubby ear. The little dog whimpered, ignoring his master, and clawed feverishly at the door.

"It's no good," said Max, exasperated. "My dog's broken."

"You have to earn a dog's trust before it warms to you," said Syd. "Besides, he probably just needs to pee."

Max jumped down from the stool and crossed to the door, grabbing the knob. The door opened inward, Eightball squeezing through the growing gap. As the light from the apartment spilled out, Max was surprised to find Wing Liu on the attic landing, looking slightly taken aback. How long had the kid been there?

"Oh, hey, Wing!" said Max with a big smile, his voice loud enough to alert Jed and Syd that they had an unexpected guest. "Fancy seeing you here, dude. What's going on?"

Wing looked sheepish, his cheeks flushed with color as Eightball scrambled into his arms, tail wagging. He had the look of guilt about him. Just how much had he heard?

"I came to see if I could play with Eightball," said Wing. "You don't mind, do you?"

"Come in, young Master Liu," said Jed. "You're just in time."

"In time?" asked the boy, stepping into the apartment. Max was surprised at Jed's invitation. Jed had always ensured they kept their distance from their neighbors, at least those who were unaware of what their true business was. Their apartment was their sanctuary, yet here he was, inviting Wing in.

"Of course," said Jed, busying himself at the kitchenette counter, opening cupboards and rattling through drawers. "I was going to wait until tomorrow evening, but seeing as all of Max's friends are now here . . ."

Wing was looking around the apartment, face full of wonder, especially when he caught sight of the extensive bookcases. This was Jed's library, home to a wealth of information on the magical, mythological, and monstrous. As Syd stepped up to Wing and began chatting, distracting him, Max sidled up behind Jed and whispered in his ear.

"What are you doing, inviting him in? Have you lost your mind?"

Jed kept his voice nice and low as he replied, Eightball's woofs and Syd's banter cloaking their conversation.

"Better to keep Wing close and discover what he heard than to send him away."

"I hope you know what you're doing. I'd hate to see Wing drawn into anything monstrous. The Helsing world's no place for a kid."

Max saw the old man's cheeks rising, as a rare smile flickered on his face.

"What is it?"

"I may not say it enough, Max, but I'm proud of you. What you've achieved already, in spite of losing your folks at a young age."

"You did a pretty decent job, you lovable old fart."

Max put his arm around Jed's hip briefly, giving him a squeeze.

"Love's the strongest magic there is, Max, the stuff that connects each and every one of us through family. You draw so much strength from your forefathers, young man."

"I draw my strength from you, Jed. Now shut up and show me what you're hiding behind that cabinet door."

The old man retrieved a cake, a thick slab of chocolate icing adorning its top. Thirteen candles flickered, their flames casting an eerie glow beneath Jed's chin as he limped toward Max.

"My commiserations, Max," said his guardian as they all gathered around the counter. Syd paused by the door, extinguishing the apartment lights.

"Commiserations?"

"Indeed, my boy, for tomorrow marks your birthday, and a truly chilling, terrible transformation shall take place." He settled the cake onto the counter as Max leaned in, ready to blow out the candles. Wing looked terrified upon hearing Jed's words.

"Transformation?" whispered the ten-year-old as

Eightball licked his lips and Max gathered his breath. "What kind of transformation?"

"It's awful, Master Liu," said Jed, seizing the boy's wrist in his iron grip. Max blew out the candles, and the room was plunged into darkness.

"He'll turn into . . . a *teenager*!"

SIX

THE NIGHT WATCHMAN

Each of the themed rooms in the Gallows Hill Museum of Anthropology had its own appeal, but one in particular kept drawing Wilbur Cunningham back. The American Room featured artifacts from as far back as the indigenous Massachusett tribe who once inhabited the lands around the bay. The European Room hosted a fascinating exhibition on the British Royal Family and their connections by marriage across Europe. The Australasian Room had all manner of curiosities, the most macabre of which, until recently, had been the tattooed head of a Maori warrior. The museum had recently repatriated it to New Zealand. But it was the Egyptian Room that fascinated Wilbur.

Though the night watchman had never been much of a student, Wilbur had always been intrigued by history. His duplex was decorated with military memorabilia from around the world. He was even a member of the local volunteer infantry, joining up with his comrades in the Irish Brigade to carry out reenactments statewide. Sure, he was out of shape, and his uniform was ill-fitting, but Wilbur didn't care. Once a month, he got to travel back in time, participating in the battles he'd read about. He'd been the happiest soldier in the Union when he got the gig as night watchman at the museum.

Wilbur stood before the sarcophagus, flashlight passing over its surface. Here was a genuine Egyptian coffin from 1,400 years before Christianity existed. There were two of these burial boxes in the room, one much larger than the other, belonging to parent and child. They were surrounded by jewelry and gems, death masks, and daggers of the sacrificial variety. Framed and faded newspaper clippings charted Carter and Carnarvon's ill-fated Tutankhamun dig, supposedly dogged by curses and disaster.

The child's sarcophagus was open, the tiny mummified occupant long gone. The adult's was closed, battered and devoid of decor, likewise missing its resident linen-wrapped body. At one time they had probably been covered in gold leaf and gems, but such prizes had been long since stolen, pillaged by tomb-robbers. The former occupants' identities were unknown. Not for the first time, Wilbur wondered who these people had been in life.

Each coffin was protected behind reinforced glass. It was the adult sarcophagus he stood before now, his double chins jiggling with wonder, his blue eyes shining bright. His friend and fellow security guard Joe Dembinski had mentioned that the museum had received shipment of a third sarcophagus recently, this one complete with its own mummy. Wilbur couldn't wait to see it on show.

The famous bells of Old North Church rang out in the distance, chiming at midnight. Something clattered in one of the adjoining rooms, making Wilbur jump. He rested his hand on the nightstick at his hip and aimed his flashlight beam dead ahead. In that instant he was momentarily transformed from Wilbur, the amateur history buff, to Ace Cunningham, private detective. He'd flunked his police entrance in his midtwenties, thanks to poor fitness and asthma, but he had a vivid imagination.

He stepped carefully through the Egyptian Room, keeping to the carpeted walkway so his footfalls remained silent, and rounded an enormous gold and ebony urn, decorated with scenes of a great and bloody battle. As quietly as he could, he stalked past a long display table, the covered glass lid protecting a variety of grisly looking embalming tools. Wilbur smacked his parched lips, his heart speeding in his broad chest.

A short corridor ran directly into the American Room. Wilbur crept carefully over the threshold, unhitching his nightstick from his belt. He'd been in this job for eighteen months, but the most he'd had to deal with was the alarms going off one stormy night. There had never been any disturbances in the museum itself. No attempted burglaries or break-ins. No thefts or threats. Everything was locked down, everything secure. Wilbur did his rounds hourly, and they were always uneventful. He was the only person in the building. Or at least, he was supposed to be.

"Anyone there?" he called out, instantly cursing himself for being so stupid. *Just us thieves*, he mused angrily.

The flashlight flickered around the room, sending shadows dancing across the walls. A diorama of early Boston dominated the middle of the chamber, the centerpiece of the exhibition. The room was lined with tableaux, featuring mannequins in traditional dress: soldiers, clergymen, fishermen, and farmers, to name just a few. They appeared lifelike under the flashlight beam, and Wilbur jumped as faces loomed, then gave a nervous laugh. He circuited the exhibits, pausing to check that the fire doors were still padlocked. The American Room, like all the others in the building, was empty. Wilbur was the only living soul in the museum.

"There's nobody here, you oaf," he muttered to himself. "Too much coffee. No wonder my blood pressure's through the roof."

He started back in the direction of the security office. The flashlight beam swung like a pendulum before him, left to right, arcing as it lit his path. His left foot caught something, sending it clattering across the floor and under the diorama table. Wilbur hitched his belt to avoid cutting his gut in half and crouched down awkwardly, peering beneath the display. A wooden box sat there, quite innocuous but clearly what his foot had connected with. He grunted and reached forward, chubby fingers latching onto the cube and retrieving it.

Wilbur heaved himself upright, straightening and casting his light over the box. It was perhaps six inches square, and made from a rough, unfinished wood. He turned it in his hand, but couldn't seem to find a lid. He gave it a shake and heard something rattle inside. Where had it come from? The night watchman looked around, retracing his steps back to the point where his foot had connected with it. The flashlight beam illuminated an old iron gibbet hanging bolted from the ceiling, a hokey-looking gallows beside it. Two mannequins were posed side by side, a dour-looking manacled woman and an angry, fire-and-brimstone priest. Etchings and accounts of witch trials had been reproduced and enlarged, displayed on tall boards in all their grim glory.

A tall, empty wooden plinth stood within this sinister collection. Wilbur leaned in close, spying a tiny brass plaque that had been fixed to the top of the polished mahogany pedestal. Two words were engraved into the metal: VENDEMEYER'S BOX. Wilbur shrugged. It meant nothing to him. He looked back at the box he held, then promptly popped it back onto the stand. No sooner had he done this than a clicking sound emanated from the strange device.

"Curiouser and curiouser," said the night watchman, peering in close again.

There was a thin sliver of darkness running along the top side of the cube, clearly revealing that the uppermost plane was removable. The gap between lid and box was perhaps only a couple of millimeters wide, big enough to poke a knife into but little else. Wilbur reached out once more.

As his fingertips brushed the rim of the lid, a hissing sound escaped the box, wisps of strange green smoke emerging from the pitch-black crack. The cloud wafted straight into Wilbur's face, making him choke and splutter. Tendrils of acrid vapor snaked into his nostrils and rolled down his throat, crawling into his lungs and settling there. Wilbur coughed, trying to hack up the awful green mist, but it wouldn't budge.

He staggered back, banging into a fisherman and knocking over lobster pots. Wilbur gasped for air, fingers clawing at his throat. He tore off the clip-on tie, his nails raking his neck as he wheezed and struggled in vain for oxygen. A terrible cold sensation spread through him, from his chest into the pit of his belly, traveling along arteries and veins, finally finding his heart. Death's icy hand squeezed hard and tight.

Wilbur Cunningham collapsed with a thump onto the carpeted floor, flashlight rolling from his lifeless hand and halting beside the plinth's base. The museum was deathly silent once again. The night watchman's body remained as motionless as the mannequins for a few minutes. Then his right hand twitched. Ten seconds passed and it twitched again, quickly followed by the right foot. His left hand curled into a fist as his head flinched. Wilbur Cunningham's eyes slowly flickered open.

They were no longer blue. They shone brilliantly, malevolently, like emeralds in the sun.

SEVEN

RUDE AWAKENINGS

"Hey there, beautiful."

The face in the mirror glowered back gloomily.

It wasn't a pretty picture. A tangled mop of brown hair hung over his eyes, his complexion pasty and sallow. There was a zit by the dimple on his chin, just begging to be popped, and the bags under his eyes would put Gandalf's to shame. If this was what being a teenager meant, Max didn't want any part of it. He'd gone to bed a butterfly and emerged a caterpillar. Stepping into the shower stall, he turned on the faucet. Within moments he was being pummeled by a torrent of scalding water, reviving his weary limbs and spirit.

He didn't *really* look any different, of course. That same face awaited him in the bathroom mirror every morning, rain or shine. He always felt the same first in the morning: rotten. He was still Max Helsing, full-time monster hunter and part-time schoolkid. Suitably reinvigorated, he grabbed his towel from the radiator and exited the bathroom.

"Morning," he called as he strolled through the apartment, securing the towel about his waist. There was no sign of Jed. Books and scrolls littered the coffee table and floor around his La-Z-Boy, the old fellow having clearly burned the midnight oil reading the previous night. As Max walked by, something caught his eye: a familiar red leather photo album, sitting on top of the other books. Max sat down in the recliner, picked it up, and opened the first page. Such a long time had passed since he'd looked through it, and as he did, he was assailed by a wave of emotion.

There was an exceedingly old photograph, clearly pre-1900s. Its sepia coloring was faded by the years, but the figure shown was unmistakable. The man bore the same square jaw and dimple that marked Max as a Van Helsing, in addition to a marvelous handlebar mustache. A snowscape surrounded him, but there was one particular feature that placed him in the Himalayas. Decked out in thick furs, he struck a pose like a big-game hunter, one foot on the slain corpse of a yeti.

Max shook his head. He flicked through the album as the pictures of his ancestors gradually became more recent. Each featured a dimple-chinned, heroic-looking Van Helsing front and center, posing beside another monster hunter or some butchered beastie.

He was into the color photos now, the seventies and the eighties. There was Jed, looking a great deal younger, his hair in a thick Afro. He had two men alongside him, all three wearing desert robes and turbans, and each holding an enormous scimitar. One of the figures he didn't recognize— a barrel-chested fellow, a white guy with arms like a gorilla's. Max thought his guardian was tall, but this other guy had six inches on him, even with the hair. And there, on the other side of Jed, was Max's father, Conrad Helsing.

Whereas Jed and the other man both looked like they could step into the ring and go a few rounds, Conrad cut a more modest figure. Like his son, he was lean, but with a glint in his eye that said he meant business. Max wondered how he would measure up to his dad as a warrior. He was never going to find out.

There were no photos after that one, no happy snapshots of victors post-hunt. Had the world become more dangerous for Conrad and Jed after this last snapshot? Did the moments where they could smile become few and far between? Max closed the album and replaced it on top of the pile. He had one other picture of his old man, of father and baby taken in a photo booth. He kept it in a memory box under his bed, along with other precious curios. Maybe he'd take it out and look at it tonight, when he went to bed.

Max rose from the recliner and straightened his rather wet towel. He looked down, spotting a circular damp patch on the La-Z-Boy where he'd sat. *Good start to the day,* he figured, worrying already about how Jed would react when he discovered what he'd done. Max booked it across the apartment to the kitchenette, spying Eightball asleep in his basket beneath the breakfast bar.

"Yo, Eightball, where's my good morning slobber?" said Max, opening the fridge and grabbing a carton of milk. He popped the lid open and took three huge gulps before returning it to the shelf. He heard a guttural snarl.

"What's up, pup?" asked Max, closing the door and looking about to see what had startled Eightball. He looked past the counter and toward the apartment door, half-expecting to find an intruder. "Nobody there," said Max, turning back to the little black bundle of blubber.

The mutt was looking straight at Max. His teeth were bared, and he clearly was not a happy puppy.

"Eightball?" said Max, trying to keep his voice light. He'd only known the dog for a day, but this was out of character. The puppy hauled himself from his basket, squashing his chew toy in the process, a wheezing squeak escaping as his fat belly rolled over it. His little legs landed on the linoleum floor as he began trotting slowly toward his master. He growled, deep and distinctly menacing. Max began backing away, completely thrown by his pet's behavior. He reached onto the counter, grabbing the box of dog treats and withdrawing a bone-shaped biscuit.

"You want a Scooby Snack?" He tossed it behind the dog, back into the basket. Eightball ignored it, advancing on stubby paws. The glare the little round dog was throwing set alarm bells ringing for Max. He'd encountered monsters that had looked at him the same way, creatures hell-bent on tearing him into tiny, bloody pieces.

If he could get to his bedroom and shut the door, perhaps he could wait in there until Jed got up and sorted out the devil-pooch. He threw the box at Eightball, showering him in biscuits as he dashed around the counter and over the piles of books.

The puppy was waiting for him, blocking the doorway into his bedroom.

"How do you *do* that?" said Max, about to move once more, when Eightball pounced.

For a little guy, he moved like greased lightning, paws barely touching the carpet. His jaws opened—wide—and Max scrambled back, hitting the bookcase. Eightball's teeth clamped down on the wet towel, the puppy worrying his head from side to side. Max experienced his second shower of the day, old books clattering down on him. The towel nearly came free, but Max seized one corner and held tight.

Boy and dog wrestled over the damp towel. One fierce tug from Eightball sent the wet bath sheet flying across the room. Max suddenly felt awfully exposed, in more than one way. The dog snarled once more as Max leaped around the La-Z-Boy. Eightball ran up the length of the recliner and leaped, hitting the wall with a thump just as Max ducked. The naked monster hunter rolled across the floor, trampling books, snatching up his towel as he went. He crashed into the broom closet, the door swinging open and almost hitting him. He spun around just as the puppy righted himself, shaking his head and sending great strings of slobber flying.

Max stood, the towel held before him like a toreador's cloak. Eightball charged. The puppy hit the towel and Max stepped to one side, letting go as Eightball hurtled into the closet, blinded by the terrycloth covering his face. Brooms, brushes, and buckets toppled onto him as Max back-heeled the door shut. He looked up.

Jed stood across from him, staring in disbelief at his nude young charge.

The youth snatched up the first thing that came to hand, an old edition of *Moby-Dick*, which he held in front of himself. Eightball continued to snarl and hammer at the door behind him.

"What in the name of all that's holy happened here?"

"He attacked me, out of the blue," said Max, edging through his bedroom door. "Completely unprovoked, and mad as hell. Either he has distemper or a serious issue with towels."

Jed shook his head in disbelief. "I'll look into it. Get yourself dressed."

"Right you are," said Max, poking his head back around his doorframe as he tossed the book back to Jed. "Oh, and I think I caught him peeing on your La-Z-Boy, too."

The bedroom door slammed, and Jed was left, book in hand, listening to the howls of a hellhound puppy, unhappily regarding the wet patch that stained his favorite seat.

EIGHT

BREAKING STORM

By the time Max departed Helsing House, he was running horribly late. The business with Eightball had thrown his already poor timekeeping off kilter. His homework was done (a rare accomplishment in itself) but had been lost among the books and papers strewn across the apartment. His sneakers had been stored in the broom closet, the puppy managing to savage them with drool once he'd sniffed out that they belonged to Max. Soggy Chucks did not make for a happy Max. He and Jed couldn't believe the transformation that had taken place in the formerly friendly pet. In all the chaos, breakfast didn't even make it onto the agenda—no toast, eggs, or bacon—and this was his birthday!

The sky boiled overhead as Max weaved along the road on his Chopper. Fast-moving black clouds churned over one another, flashes of lightning illuminating them from within as they threatened to burst at any moment. It didn't surprise

Max that Syd was no longer waiting for him at the entrance to Gallows Hill Burying Ground. The Chopper hopped the curb and hit the sidewalk. Max flicked his gearshift as a raindrop fell and landed on his cheek. Just one; perhaps nature was going to go easy on him after all. A heartbeat later, the heavens opened.

The downpour was almost blinding. He heard a roaring noise, surprised to find it was his own voice shouting against the sudden maelstrom. The gloom accompanying the torrential weather transported Max to a twilight world of whirling wind and water. He felt like a deckhand on *Deadliest Catch*, half-expecting a wave to crash over the graveyard fence and wash him away.

But it wasn't a rogue wave that knocked him off his Chopper. Too late, he spied a pale, spindly branch sticking out from the railings. Max had no time to evade it, and it caught him right across the throat. The bicycle skidded into the gutter as Max landed with a wet thump on the leaf-littered sidewalk, breathless.

His head spun and his tailbone hurt like hell. The last time he had been concussed was during weapon training, when Jed had brained him with a bokken. Admittedly, Max should have ducked before the wooden sword knocked him out. It wasn't a pleasant sensation. He squinted through the rain at the white branch that had struck his throat. *Remarkable that the folks at Parks and Rec had allowed a branch to grow through the railings like that*, thought Max. It was a lawsuit waiting to happen. He was toying with the idea of hiring an injury lawyer on a no-win-no-fee basis when the branch reached down and seized him by the hood.

Max was hoisted off the ground, spluttering, blinded by the rain, as the branch dragged him back against the railings. He felt it tight across his throat as a foul stench invaded his nostrils and caused him to heave. Then he was being lifted, his assailant dragging him up the wrought-iron bars at his back. Max recalled the sharp spikes that topped the railings.

He began twisting, bending his body, and hooking his own limbs through the bars. Within moments he was at a ninety-degree angle, parallel to the ground. The white arm around him strained as he torqued it to an impossible angle. The limb could bend no further. Max heard an agonized gurgle from behind that almost matched his own. He was choking, nearly blacking out. He threw his right leg up, the sneaker finding purchase between the spikes, and yanked himself up farther in a quick, savage motion.

The arm snapped, instantly releasing its grip on Max. The teenager prepared himself for the fall to the sidewalk, but he never reached it. He hung there, suspended upside down, a rusty black spike spearing through the right-leg hem of his jeans. His head was perhaps three inches from the paved path. He craned his neck and looked through the rails. It was exactly as he feared.

There stood the ghoul Max had encountered the previous evening. It might have been a gloomy, stormy morning with no soul on the street, but an undead emerging during the daytime, brazen and unafraid of exposure—this was unheard of. The natural instinct for nearly all monsters was to hide from human sight, especially during the daytime. If they had to operate within this period, they would usually do so incognito, disguising themselves so they could fit into human society. The creature now squeezed its face against the bars, black tongue running along its filthy teeth. Max swung his fists at the monster, jabbing at it through the rails, causing it to back away. Its pale white eyes looked up the length of the iron bars. It started to climb.

Max placed his left heel against the crossbar at the top of the iron fence, frantically trying to force his right leg free. He heard the denim ripping as he twisted and turned, only for the stitched hem to resist, holding out against a complete break. The creature crouched on the top of the railings, bones and ribs protruding against its fetid flesh. Max could feel the blood rushing to his head. The undead grave robber was poised, looking down like some ghastly mockery of a mausoleum angel. Its jaws snapped together, and its clawed fingers scratched hungrily at its belly. *What if this ghoul is no longer exclusively a carrion feeder?* Max wondered fearfully. He stamped at the bar for all he was worth.

The denim tore and the boy fell. Max went into a tumble, head, neck, back, and legs tucking into a ball as he safely halted a few yards from the iron fence. The ghoul screeched angrily, seeing its meal escaping, and leaped from its perch on the railings, flying straight down toward the boy. Max was still in the tuck position on his back, looking up as the monster descended. He took its weight on the soles of his sneakers, the wind forced from his lungs as the creature landed on him. It may have been skin and bone, but from that height it still packed some force. Its hands closed in on Max, reaching for his throat, as that long black tongue flickered at him, almost licking his face. Max pushed back. Hard.

His legs straightened, launching the ghoul skyward. Its trajectory didn't carry it over the railings, but that hadn't been Max's intention. The monster came down with a splintering squelch onto the spiked heads of the rails. Four of them found their way through its torso, one through its skull. It hung there, limbs jangling in the gusting rain like some grotesque Halloween wind chime.

Max staggered to his feet woozily. He looked down at the torn leg of his favorite drainpipe jeans. A wave of nausea washed over him. He grabbed hold of the rails to steady himself and let the heavy rain wash over him. It could have been the adrenaline rush of the fight. It could have been the blood rushing, now that he was the right way up again. It could have been the low blood sugar of an empty stomach.

"And this," said Max, panting and wagging a cautionary finger at the slain ghoul, "is why you should never, ever skip breakfast."

NINE

xxx

A WARM WELCOME

There had been no point in heading to homeroom. The best Max could hope for when he finally got to Gallows Hill Middle School was sidestepping the main office altogether. Chaining his bike to a rickety, overflowing drainpipe, a soaking-wet Max had shanked open the boiler room window. With the heavens hammering down around him, he had squeezed through the opening into the basement, followed by a deluge of rainwater.

After draping his damp clothes over an old pommel horse beside the furnace, Max tied his Chucks together by their laces before suspending them from the furance's grilled door. Then he sat down on an overturned bucket in his underwear and stared into the flames. Once first period ended, he'd get dressed again, head up into the school, and simply blend into the mob. If asked, he'd claim to have been in school all along. The boiler room was the ace up his sleeve, just waiting for the right moment to be played.

The Eightball incident seemed a distant memory now, merely an amusing anecdote after the ghoul attack. What kind of rotten luck was he experiencing today? He looked across the room to where his rain-soaked sneakers hung. It was wishful thinking that they might be dry in the next hour. He picked up his messenger bag and began rummaging inside it. Max bypassed his schoolbooks, instead withdrawing a far more interesting tome.

The *Monstrosi Bestiarum* was one of the oldest books in the Van Helsing library, a field guide to all things monstrous. The original author was a Teutonic Knight by the name of Buchner, a papal warrior who specialized in the hunting down and butchering of "unholy entities." A fearsome swordsman, he was also a mean hand with ink and quill, recording the strengths and weaknesses of every monster he encountered. The book had eventually found its way into the Van Helsings' hands and been passed down from generation to generation. It was a who's who of monsterkind and the go-to resource whenever Max was in a creature conundrum.

He flicked through the pages to the chapter on ghouls, which outlined five different variations of the beast. It was there in inked script: they were all strictly carrion feeders. Max double-checked the appendix for any recorded attacks upon humans, finding only a single entry from three centuries ago, and in that instance the ghoul had attacked in self-defense. That one had chosen Max for a meal was an aberration for their kind, and a worrying one at that. And the ghoul wasn't the only creature that had tried to take a bite out of him that morning.

"I wonder," he muttered, thumbing through the book, the pages illuminated by the fluttering flames of the furnace. "Good-bye *G*, hello *H* . . ."

The rain continued to patter on the basement windowpane as it creaked and groaned in its broken bracket, but Max's attention was focused on the bestiary. Many of the illustrated pages were embellished with a host of horrible stains—blood put in plenty of appearances, as did mysterious blotches of black and green and the odd cloud of dried-up ectoplasmic residue. Max flipped past the hag, the half elf, and the hantu demon, followed by harpies, haunts, and the Headless Horseman. With a grin, Max slapped his hand down, holding the book open.

"Now then, Eightball," he said, tracing his finger over the entry for *hellhound*. "Let's see what got you howling and growling . . ."

But before Max could read about the feeding habits of a Level I juvenile hound, the fire in the furnace spluttered out, plunging the boiler room into darkness. He clapped the bestiary shut instantly. The hairs on his neck rose, his exposed flesh shuddering with goose bumps. It had gotten cold very quickly in the boiler room, unnaturally so. His breath steamed before him. A ghost, perhaps? The only light source came from the busted window at street level overhead.

"Aw, c'mon," said the monster hunter, standing and searching the shadows for a sign of the intruder. "That's a rotten trick, putting out the fire. Do you *see* what I'm wearing?" He edged closer to the furnace, peering past his swinging sneakers through the grille. The oven interior was pitch black, no sign of light or heat. "I'm down to my unmentionables. A guy could catch his death of cold!"

"Not . . . cold . . ." came a quiet voice from within the iron oven.

"Not what now?" asked Max, turning his ear and taking another step closer.

The reply was a whisper.

"Fire."

It started with the tiniest spark in the deepest recess of the furnace, before bursting into life like a newborn star. Max was already reeling back as an enormous ball of boiling flame erupted from within the huge industrial oven. The grate was blown off its hinges, narrowly missing Max as it rocketed past and embedded itself into the wall below the leaking window. His sneakers, singed and smoking, were still attached, bouncing against the wet brickwork like novelty baubles. Max scrambled clear as the fire spilled out of the fractured furnace, licking the floor all around him. His hair was smoking, as was the *Monstrosi Bestiarum*. He went straight for the book, smothering it with his chest and protecting it from further damage. Max backed up against the wall, beneath the grille and Chucks, shocked to see a figure taking shape within the inferno.

When the fire found the ground, coal-dark feet coalesced, rising as they transformed into legs. Torso, arms, and head swiftly followed, appearing as if fashioned from soot, and shot through with veins of shimmering white heat. The specter's charred head cracked apart, mouth and eyes splitting the black skull wide open, three fires guttering from its face. Max recognized the creature from the bestiary, but this was the first time he'd ever faced one: a fire phantasm. Born out of a human's terrible, fiery death, these could be good or evil. Max hoped this one was the former, but that seemed highly unlikely. The figure extended a flaming finger toward Max, the youth wincing beneath the intense blaze.

"You are Mark," hissed the fire phantasm.

"Nope, I'm Max," said the boy. "Close, but no cigar—guess you got the wrong furnace. What's this Mark's last name? Maybe I can—"

"Silence!" cried the apparition, its grating voice cracking.

"Not a conversationalist, then," muttered Max, eyes flitting about for a way out of his fix. Once again, his messenger bag was out of reach, on the floor across the basement, smoke curling from the canvas. "Can we start again? Hi, I'm Max. You must be Flaming-Hellspawn-Ghostly-Guy. Pleased to meet ya!"

"You must die, Mark!"

"Max, actually, but whatever," he said with a shrug. "Seriously, though, what is *happening* today? Is it open season on me or what?"

FIRE PHANTASM

ORIGIN: Universal

STRENGTHS: Fire form makes conventional weapons useless against it; choking smoke can asphyxiate opponents.

WEAKNESS: Water, unsurprisingly.

HABITAT: These phantasms are ghosts, doomed to haunt the site of their demise. The circumstances of their death are inevitably horrific and connected to fire in some way.

Although born from a frightful fate, a fire phantasm isn't necessarily evil. There ARE instances of benign phantasms who seek to protect and warn the living of the dangers of fire. That said, there are plenty who are the cursed spirits of wicked men and women, connected to the scene of their crime forever after. And even being in the presence of a "good" fire spirit can bring about immolation or serious harm, their smoke capable of crippling even the hardiest constitutions.

—Erik Van Helsing, November 5th, 1851

FIELD ACCOUNT—
THE ST. LOUIS CINDER SPECTER

On the banks of the Mississippi, where it joins the Missouri, we found the wrecked remains of _The White Lady_, a half-sunk, burned-out paddle steamer. Lore told of a ghastly apparition who stalked the decks at night, aflame. In the scorched cabin, by the light of the moon, I found the blazing spirit of the boat's skipper. Bankrupt and drowned by despair, he had set light to his own boat, hoping to claim its insurance. The fire took boat, crew, and captain. With the help of a local priest, we exorcised the tortured phantasm and finally put him to rest.

—Esme Van Helsing, August 8th, 1869

ODIOUS CRUMB reckons there's a FIRE PHANTASM at Gallows Hill Middle School! Maybe I need to improve my attendance and get down there more often. If there were monsters in school that'd make things a LOT more fun!! :)

MAX HELSING
Sep 22nd, 2015

"*Marked!* You are Marked!" cried the flaming phantom, staggering ever closer. Max could smell his hair burning now, the stink assailing his nose and throat. It was now or never. "You must die! The fire take you!"

The fire phantasm drew itself up, raising its flaming fists over its head, the blaze brightening around it. As its limbs flew down, Max leaped up, bounding vertically up the wall, his feet landing on the furnace grille protruding from the crumbling bricks. Fire roared where the specter punched the floor, cracking the flagstone and sending shrapnel flying. The iron grate Max perched on groaned, threatening to tear loose beneath his weight. The monster looked up at the boy, Max's whole body almost collapsing as the relentless heat rolled up the wall around him.

"Face the fire, Marked One!"

The fire phantasm's mouth yawned open, belching fire like a Balrog's kid brother. Max made one more desperate leap—again, straight up. His left forearm swung over the window ledge while his right hand ripped the glass panel off its splintered hinges. Below, the fire built in intensity. Max could feel the flesh on his back and legs searing, the air burning in his lungs.

"You cannot run from the fire!"

"Who's running?"

Max threw both of his arms out into the street, seizing hold of the swinging drainpipe and yanking with all his might. The curved end grated across the sidewalk as Max twisted it about, suddenly finding the rainwater surging straight at him, hard in the face. With his fingers and toes gripping the brickwork, he danced to one side before the torrent blasted him from the wall. The fire phantasm's glowing eyes blinked once in surprise as the waterfall crashed down, dousing its flames and consuming it in a giant, hissing roar of rage. With a woeful wail and thrashing of thinning limbs, the specter crumbled to nothing, blasted to oblivion by Max's improvised hose.

The entire basement was transformed into a steam room as Max slid from the wall and landed in a puddle, the rain still rushing in over his head. Of the fire phantasm there was no sign.

"Marked?" said Max, checking himself up and down for a telltale sign. He was clean, except for a pair of soaking, soot-covered boxer shorts. He hopped through the growing puddles toward the furnace, where his clothes remained draped over the pommel horse. They were scorched dry after the encounter, which was a small blessing considering how thoroughly soaked his sneakers were now. He scooped them up in his arms just as the door to the boiler room swung open with a clang. The school janitor stood to one side as Whedon's furious face peered into the basement.

"Helsing!" the principal roared. The boy winced and raised his hands.

"I can explain," Max lied.

TEN

SHORTCUT

Max slouched in the bike seat, the Chopper's wheels cutting a wake through stagnant puddles. His spirits were bruised enough, but the rain was now battering them into submission. His previously dried and now soaking-once-again clothes clung to his clammy flesh. As mornings went, he'd had better ones.

Since when did monsters attack him—and in daylight, too? What happened to them skulking in shadows and lurking in abandoned mills, hidden from human sight? It went against all that Jed had taught him, especially the ghoul. They might be undead, but as the mortally challenged went, ghouls were harmless enough . . . ordinarily.

Max checked his wristwatch. It had only just turned ten. Halfway through the morning and he'd already been in two scrapes, three counting Eightball. Principal Whedon had instantly suspended Max after the boiler room fiasco, and no doubt Jed would have received the news by now. How would he react to his ward being sent home in disgrace on his thirteenth birthday? Max shook his head, rain flicking from the tip of his nose. Ordinarily, he could expect the mother of all scoldings from the old man, but the morning's events had been *so* extraordinary that there had to be more to it. It wasn't just bad luck that had resulted in those attacks. What had the fire phantasm said? He was *marked*? This had the whiff of monstrous mischief to Max, no doubt about it.

He shivered as he cycled, and not just on account of the weather. Max felt as though every pair of eyes was upon him, every passerby a potential threat. Was the mailman across the street simply on his daily rounds or following him? Max pedaled harder. The crossing guard watched him approach, beckoning him toward her junction. Why was she smiling? She may have just been cheery, but Max didn't wait to find out, giving her a wide berth and riding on. An old lady stared out of a thrift shop window, her wizened features transforming into those of a hag in Max's mind as he raced by, toward the next intersection.

A mighty roar came out of nowhere, exploding from a side street and nearly bowling Max off his Chopper. He slammed on his brakes as an eighteen-wheeler thundered through, its massive wheels churning up every puddle and sending a wave of filthy water over the hapless boy. Max hunched over his handlebars, clutching his chest, checking that his heart still beat. At this rate a panic attack would kill him before a monster got him.

He turned down the side street and cycled on, crossing over once he caught sight of the woodland. It wasn't a path he would have taken at night—the old forest was home to vagrants and gangs—but on a wet and miserable day like this it would be the quietest and quickest route home. He hopped the curb and left the sidewalk, dropping onto the trail through Hemlock Woods.

Soon the noise of the street was muffled as boy and bike were swallowed by the foliage. It wasn't the largest green space in Gallows Hill, but it was probably the wildest. Trails that had once been well kept had been reclaimed by nature, roots and branches making certain paths impassable. Max found himself bunny-hopping each obstacle, ducking beneath each blocking bough, as the Chopper weaved deeper into the woods.

The path wound down through an old gulch toward an ancient-looking bridge, the logs lashed together by rotten rope and rusting nails. It spanned a rocky ravine, a stream surging below, the waters foaming thanks to the downpour. Max stood on his pedals, freewheeling between the rocks as he descended the gulch. The forest flanked the ravine, rain rattling on branches as it fell. The boards clattered as Max rode onto the bridge.

He was halfway across when he pulled hard on the brakes. Dead ahead on the opposite bank, standing in his path, was a coyote. Its gray-brown pelt glistened with rain-drops, and it sent them flying with a lively shake. Max half expected the beast to lurch toward him, canines bared and eyes wild. Instead it simply stood appraising him. Right on cue, the sun broke through the rain clouds, throwing its rays onto the animal. Even the rushing water quieted at that moment, the stream's spray sparkling like diamonds in the daylight. It was the most perfect, beautiful thing Max had ever witnessed, and it was gone in a heartbeat.

The sun vanished, gloom settling again. The rain fell heavier, and the coyote flinched. Max heard it whimper. He raised a hand, hoping to show he meant it no harm. It backed up, dipping its head and crying louder. Was it afraid of him?

"Hey," called Max, somewhere between a whisper and a shout, not wanting the beast to bolt. "No need to fear me."

The coyote's tail had dropped between its legs now, body language changed entirely. Max could see its coat trembling. Finally, it showed its teeth and let loose a harsh bark before turning and bounding up the trail, back into the darkness of Hemlock Woods. Max sighed, slumping as he gripped his handlebars. A chilling wind raced through the trees, their branches grating like death rattles.

Resigned to the idea that perhaps he wasn't an animal person after all, Max pushed off once again, but the Chopper remained motionless. Max looked down, searching for the obstruction. Nothing blocked the front wheel. He peered over his shoulder. The larger, rear wheel had somehow snared itself on trailing ivy. A green tendril was bound through the spokes and entwined around the chain cog.

"My day gets better," he muttered, climbing off the bike and kicking out the stand. He crouched to get a better look, aware that he was still balanced on a rickety, decrepit, rain-slicked bridge that was probably built by the founding fathers. He reached toward the emerald vine and stopped.

Max shivered, the hairs on the back of his hand standing on end. He looked back the way he had come, up the rocky incline toward the forest's edge. The rain, branches, and shifting shadows obscured his vision, hiding whatever was out there. The only things that caught his eye were the bright green vines that clung to the trees, climbing their trunks. A particularly thick one trailed out of the woods, growing over stone and root toward the stream. Max realized this was the actual vine that had bound itself around his rear wheel. It was almost as if it had slithered out of the forest and secured itself to the bike.

Carefully—slowly—he reached into the messenger bag on his hip, hoping to find a diamond dagger of dismemberment or, at the very least, his lucky penknife. Instead, his hand closed around his pencil case. He cursed inwardly. This just *had* to happen on a school day, didn't it?

Quick as a flash, the vines came. They flew out of the woods, racing through the air and across the ground toward Max. The first wrapped itself around his right ankle, knocking him onto his back. The next whipped him across the face before binding itself to his left wrist. A third darted forward like a cobra, stabbing at his other leg before coiling around his thigh. Max cried out, the grip of each vine like iron.

His right hand emerged from the satchel accompanied by a shower of pens and pencils that scattered a[cross] the bridge. Grasping a number two pencil, he stabbe[d the] vine on his left wrist, thick sap oozing as it release[d its] hold instantly. The vine on his right ankle took a ballpoint pen through its body, which sent it flopping off the bridge. The one around his thigh took a few more blows—he had to strike with the stationery compass five times before the vine finally relinquished its grip and slithered back up the bank, weeping sap all the way.

**

That left only the original vine, bound tightly around the Chopper's cog, a tremor rippling along its length. The protractor slashed down, the semicircular plastic blade scything through the vine like a guillotine. The severed tendril flailed wildly, oozing green fluid into the air with a sound not unlike a deflating whoopee cushion. Max leaped onto the Chopper, back-heeled the kickstand, and stamped hard on the pedal.

He felt rather pleased until a new vine lashed around his neck and tugged him—hard. The Chopper lurched forward, disappearing off the bridge as Max was yanked backward through the air. He landed with a thump on the rocks, fingers finding the noose, flush to his throat and tightening all the time. He turned, scrambling off his knees and slipping among the dead leaves. He looped the vine around his right arm once, twice, three times for good measure, winding it in until it went taut. Max placed a sneaker against a rock and braced himself. His eyes bulged, a snot bubble threatening to burst from his nose as the vine squeezed his windpipe.

"Don't be shy," he spat through gritted teeth.

Max pulled hard, every muscle in his body straining like never before. The noose loosened from his throat, his opponent clearly surprised by the switching focus of the fight. Through the rain Max could see movement between the trees and among the brambles, as something thrashed about, drawing closer. The young monster hunter hauled his foe in, hand over hand, gathering the vine like a length of rope. He was a fisherman, reeling in his catch: was it a guppy or a great white on the end of the line? The bushes parted.

The creature loomed above Max, teetering on two spindly, goatlike legs, cloven hooves clattering on the rocks. It shared its features with the trees around it, bark skin covered in knotholes and moss. Crooked arms ended in long, curling claws, the severed and squirming vines retracting like tentacles into puckered, pulsing palms. An overlarge head was held aloft by a withered neck. Erupting from the top of this crude, faceless skull, a collection of gnarled and twisted branches rose like antlers. The towering terror was perhaps fifteen feet tall, twenty including the wooden horns. Slowly, its face split, sharp splinters appearing where a mouth should have been.

It didn't happen often, but Max was lost for words.

The tendril around his arm tightened like a hungry python. It was the monster's turn to play tug-of-war now. The vine withdrew into the creature's limb, disappearing like an emerald tongue, dragging Max inexorably closer. It spun the boy, wrapping him up further, pinning his arms to either side of his body. An inhuman shriek tore forth from its jagged jaws as it ripped its arm back, lifting Max off his feet and up the rocks to where it stood.

The grotesque mouth creaked open further. Centipedes and woodlice scuttled from within, making room for the approaching monster hunter. As Max readied himself, three words kept ringing in his head.

Worst. Birthday. Ever.

ELEVEN

BROTHER IN ARMS

Max had come to terms with his grisly fate. As teenage warriors went, he reckoned he had enjoyed a few good innings. He had thought he'd gotten a good handle on all the spooky, scary secrets that were hidden in the world's dark places. Sadly, it seemed he'd transformed into a monster magnet.

"Get it over with, branch breath," he spluttered as the woodland spirit lifted him toward its jaws, grubs spilling from between its terrible teeth.

Even over the din of the rain and sound of the blood thundering through his asphyxiating head, Max recognized the sharp *twang* of a bow. An arrow flashed out of nowhere, tearing into the thick vine around his torso. Sticky sap sprayed his face as violently as an arterial eruption. The tendril instantly released its grip, flailing free, stuck with a black arrow. Max tumbled to the mulch, snatching lungfuls of air as more arrows whistled past. They peppered the tentacled horror, striking its bloated head and bark-skinned body. Max counted five more missiles striking home, each one hissing where it quivered in the monster's flesh, green smoke curling from each weeping wound. The creature went down in a thrashing heap, its life quickly ebbing away.

Max peered into the woods, in the direction from which the arrow attack had come. He blinked, wiping sweat and rain from his vision. Slowly, a silhouette disengaged from shadows, pacing forward. Two legs, two arms, torso, and head; that hardly narrowed things down. But there were plenty of humanoid monsters out there. The way it moved reminded Max of a big cat, a black jaguar stalking its prey. Was he next? The way the morning had gone, it wouldn't surprise him one bit if this devil wanted the kill for itself.

"Well, if it isn't Max Helsing!"

His accent was English, upper class; Max had Jed's fondness for period drama to thank for that knowledge. He'd endured enough episodes of *Downton Abbey* to recognize a posh voice when he heard one. Young, too, unless Max was mistaken.

"Where?" said Max, rising unsteadily, face masked in mud and hair full of twigs. While he let the stranger think he was punch-drunk, Max was already weighing every aspect of the surrounding terrain for potential weapons.

"Funnyman, eh?" said the young Englishman as he stepped out of the woods. "I like that. It's good to see the humorous side, especially in this line of work."

A mountain of a youth, probably in his late teens,

emerged from the trees. With shoulders as broad as an ox yoke, he wore battered bike leathers and a pair of enormous, steel-toed boots. A bow was slung across the youth's shoulder, and a quiver hung from his hip, bristling with arrow flights. He had a wild head of hair that put Max in mind of the latest invading British boy band. No doubt the girls went wild for that look. And his tanned skin and deep brown eyes. They probably really dug his dazzling white teeth, too. And the accent. Max hated him instantly. The giant held open his jacket, revealing a host of shining weapons within: knives, knuckle-dusters, and other grisly tools of the trade. He placed a glass-stoppered vial in an inside breast pocket, letting it fall back into place.

He grinned. "Concentrated sulphuric acid, Max. Always find it tremendously helpful to dip the arrowheads when there's time. Takes the blighters down that bit quicker. I take it you've never faced a forest guardian before. Nasty beggars, aren't they? It's the tentacles that get you every time. Ordinarily they attack only those who'd harm their woodland. Looks like you got his roots in a bunch!" He reached behind his shoulder and unhitched a long-handled ax from his back. Giving it a twirl, he spied Max regarding the weapon warily. "You appear scared, Max."

"Not scared," said Max, getting a good look at the wicked blade as the older youth approached. "Just intrigued."

"How so?"

"You seem to know me, yet I don't know you," said Max, glancing down the gulch toward the bridge. He could see

FOREST GUARDIAN

OTHER ALIASES: *Child of Gaia, "Green Man"*

ORIGIN: *Universal*

STRENGTHS: *Camouflage throughout nature, accelerated regeneration.*

WEAKNESS: *Fire!*

HABITAT: *Woods, hills, forests—any green spaces at all. Often work alongside druids, especially across Europe.*

Benign protectors of the woods, forest guardians can often be mistaken for trees. They can prove especially dangerous if their "flock" is harmed.

—Erik Van Helsing, Thanksgiving, 1849

PHYSICAL TRAITS

1. Antlers—When a guardian is enraged, this mass of branches is as deadly as the tines of a charging stag!

2. Vines—These whiplike tendrils can extend great distances, lashing at or securing their enemies.

—Esme Van Helsing, January 31st, 1864

The Forest Guardian is as old as the earth, hence the nickname "Child of Gaia." Not to be confused with animated trees, which are the mindless pawns of enchanters, Forest Guardians protect nature from the ills of man.

—Algernon Van Helsing, April 30th, 1938

JED reckons one lives in HEMLOCK WOODS!!
If there IS one, I'VE never seen it . . .

MAX HELSING Aug 14th, 2014

his Chopper in the streambed, and his messenger bag abandoned on the bridge. There'd be no swift getaway today. "Did you Google me? I wouldn't believe half the things you've read on my Wiki page. And I'm not dating Selena Gomez, no matter what she or Twitter says."

"You're quick with the jokes," said the stranger, smiling as he stepped ever closer, boots squelching through mud. "Father said the Van Helsings were unpredictable. I'd assumed he meant you were, what do you Americans say . . . badass? I never imagined he meant comedians."

"Just one of our many talents," said Max, his eyes settling on a fallen branch by his feet. It was better than nothing, he supposed; might prolong his life against the giant for all of two seconds. "You should see me tap-dance!"

The bigger teen ran a thumb along the edge of the ax head. "This is the Woodsman's Ax. It dates back to fourteenth-century Germany, and as well as doing a sterling job of chopping down trees, it's jolly nifty at cutting werewolves into tiny little pieces."

"You borrow it from Red Riding Hood?"

The other laughed. "Funny you should mention her. I'm told this very ax was used to slay the lycanthrope in that instance. After all, you know as well as I that the Brothers Grimm didn't peddle fairy tales. They were writing a historical document, a warning for future generations to stay out of the dark places, keep out of the woods." He waggled the ax in Max's direction. "Perhaps you should've taken their advice this morning, eh?"

If he was planning on killing Max, the giant teen was taking his merry time. Max could grab the branch, get one good swing in, and then be on the run. He just needed to keep this rich boy talking. Keep him distracted.

"What can I say?" Max shrugged, the forest guardian thrashing feebly at his back in its final death throes. "I like the wild side of life."

"Don't we all?" replied the stranger, now just ten feet from Max. "My name's Abel Archer," he went on, bowing as if he'd just walked out of a fairy tale of his own. He straightened, sending a crisp white card Max's way with a flick of the wrist. "Your father used to work with mine. His name was Archibald."

Max caught the card, reading the embossed details in fancy script: "Abel Archer, Fiend Fighter. No beast too big to butcher." *Wow*, thought Max. *Bloodthirsty* and *alliterative*.

"Archibald Archer?" said Max, pocketing the business card. "For real? Dad's never mentioned anyone by that name. And I'd have remembered, because—let's face it, Abel—it's kinda corny."

Archer smiled politely. "I'll let you have that one, as I rather agree; it's a ridiculous name. However, let's not play silly games, *Maxwell*. Your father's told you nothing. He's been dead for a decade. Murdered by a vampire, wasn't he? You're on your own, Max Helsing, barring that crippled custodian you keep in the attic."

Max winced. So it appeared Archer knew plenty about him, then.

"Now that's not nice," said Max, struggling to keep a lid on his anger while playing along with Archer's game. "Don't talk about Jed like that. If you want us to be friends, you need to work on those manners."

"I'm sorry," said Archer. "Truly I am. Because I do so want to be your friend, Max. I get frustrated seeing you held back by that old man, when you could be learning so much more by coming under my wing."

"You have wings? Cool! Let's see 'em!"

"I'd like to make you an offer, Max. I want to take you on as my apprentice."

Max didn't even try to stifle his laugh. "An apprenticeship? How old are you?"

"Eighteen."

"And you think you're qualified to teach me? This is a joke, right?"

"No joke, Max. You turned thirteen today. I've waited until now to approach you, given your old friend a bit more time. But you're a man now—"

"I'm a *teenager*!"

Archer snorted. "That's a man in our game, Max. You're a monster hunter, just like your father before you. He was taking down the big boys at your age."

"Thanks, but I think I'll stick with the mentor I already have. Better the crazy you know, so they say. Jed knows where it's at."

"Does he? When was the last time that toothless old boxer went toe-to-toe with a tentacled terror? I'm surprised he can make it up and down all those stairs without falling over, let alone swing a punch."

"Jed's just fine—thanks for your concern." He wasn't about to let this clown bad-mouth his friend. Jed was all the family he had. "Thanks for the offer, but I'm good. And not *all* monsters are bad. Maybe *I* could teach *you* a thing or two, like tolerance."

Abel Archer closed the distance in one gargantuan stride. The Englishman's huge hands squeezed the ax haft, his words angry and passionate, his cool composure gone.

"In eighteen years I've put more horrors back in the dirt than you've had hot dinners. I've seen a world of weird that you could only dream of. You think Gallows Hill's the center of the monster universe? You're not even close. They're everywhere, lurking in the shadows of every nook and cranny, hiding under every rock and floorboard across the planet. The whole damn lot of them are vermin, and we're the exterminators. There's no room for tolerance. Without people like my father and me, they'd take over!"

Max could see the veins bulging on Archer's neck, straining like cords of steel rope, his eyes wild. He scared Max more than any monster.

"I'll take your word for it," said Max with a passive smile. "Thanks, Abel, but no." He patted Archer's lapel. Even through the leather biker jacket, his chest felt like iron.

The Woodsman's Ax went up over Archer's head, quick as a whip-crack. Max ducked for the branch, but the weapon was already descending. He expected to feel it break his back apart in one savage swing. Instead, Archer released it from his grasp, sending it spinning through the air over Max. The Helsing boy looked around as the ax struck fast and hard into the forest guardian's enormous head where it had risen quietly behind him. The bulbous wooden skull tore in two, an explosion of splinters, sap, and grubs filling the air. The twisting antlers went their separate ways as the butchered tree-being collapsed into the mud.

Archer strode over to the twitching corpse. He reached down, tearing the ax out of the forest guardian's ruined face. Flicking green gore from the blade, he turned back to Max.

"You *will* join me, Max. Perhaps not today, but it'll happen. You'll be begging for my help before too long. That old cripple has taken you as far as he can. You need me to take you the rest of the way."

The Englishman snapped the ax into the holster on his back and disappeared into the dark forest, leaving a slightly stunned and very confused Max at the top of the gulch. He ran onto the bridge and grabbed his bag up from the boards before slipping down the incline and scrambling under the bridge to manhandle his Chopper back out of the stream. He shook his head all the while, questions rattling through his mind. That Archer knew so much about Max's family history was alarming enough. But knowing today was Max's thirteenth birthday—who could've told Archer about *that*?

TWELVE

xxx

THE HUNTER IN HIDING

"I bet he sounded like Hugh Grant," said Syd, pausing from her task at the woodwork bench to inspect the rival monster hunter's business card. She clasped her hands in mock breathlessness. "A real dreamboat."

"If your idea of a dreamboat is a well-bred, muscle-headed psychopath, then you'd have been in heaven." Max sighed as the girl grinned, returning her attention to the crossbow she was tinkering with. She'd already hammered the Chopper's front wheel back into shape that afternoon. "The guy was a maniac. He really went to town on the forest guardian. I'd rather have just left it in peace; Abel Archer left it in pieces."

Max had finally limped home to a quiet Helsing House. Jed had been out running errands, Wing had been studying, Syd was still at school, and Eightball had the run of the attic. In no hurry to rekindle hostilities with the hellhound, Max had let himself into the garage and found a spot to shelter from the rain. Curling up on a dusty old sofa, he'd drifted off into a troubled sleep, featuring guest appearances from his favorite night terrors. He'd finally awoken when Jed and Syd entered the garage a little after six, surprised and relieved to find Max snoring on the battered chaise longue.

"So come on, Jed," said Max, curled up on the sofa beneath a blanket. His yo-yo lay unraveled in his lap, his mood listless and dispirited. "Who's Abel Archer, and how does he know so much about me?"

Jed stood by the garage door, holding the plastic blinds apart, peering through a dirty pane of glass into the rain-swept evening. He turned to face Max, his brow furrowed, and let the blinds fall back into place.

"The boy's father, Archie, fought alongside your dad years ago. Brute of a guy, built like a brick outhouse."

Max realized Archer had the same look as the man who'd posed in that old photo with his dad and Jed wearing desert robes and turbans, and carrying scimitars. As the last of the Van Helsings had inherited his dimple from Conrad, so Abel must have inherited his gorilla arms from Archie.

Jed limped to the worktable, picking up the business card and giving it a once-over. His look was disapproving. "Like your father, Archie came from a long and distinguished line of monster hunters over in England. But he was what you'd call 'old school.'"

"Old school?" asked Syd.

"That means he killed anything with even a sniff of the monstrous about it," replied Max. "Am I right?"

Jed nodded. "You ain't the first of your profession to seek out alternatives to slaying, Max. Your father had a compassionate side, too, though not to the degree that you've shown. But Archie? He loved the kill as much as the hunt, and never spared the life of a single beast when our paths crossed. His smile chilled me. It never slipped, even when he was up to his waist in slaughter."

Max blanched. "He sounds like a big-game hunter, not a paranormal investigator."

Jed snorted. "He was a stone-cold killer. And you think this Abel's the same?"

"Seems like he's his father's son." Max's chin rested on his chest as he averted his eyes from Jed's gaze. "He said I'd seek out his apprenticeship one day."

A harsh laugh from Jed. "Worried you've missed your opportunity?"

"I'm sure I'll get another chance to turn him down again. How did you come to team up with his dad?"

"Only when we faced a greater foe. For the most part the Archers kept to their own stomping grounds."

"Where would that be?"

"England mainly, and the rest of Europe. The last time we collaborated with Archie was in the Middle East, and that would've been thirty years ago. The appearance of an Archer is never a good tiding. Trouble's usually hot on their heels."

"Europe sounds cool," said Syd, looking up from the crossbow with interest.

"You think?" said Jed. "It's home to some of the oldest necromantic family trees imaginable, Syd. The vampiric roots alone stretch back to pre-Christian clans that dominated Eastern Europe. The undead abominations we face pale compared to some of their European counterparts. *Cool* ain't the word I'd choose."

"So why has all this happened today?" asked Max. "On my thirteenth birthday?"

"What did the fire phantasm say to you again?" asked Jed, turning stiffly at the bench. "He described you as being marked?"

"Yeah, whatever that means. What are we going to do, Jed?"

Jed mumbled something to Syd, pointing at a component of the crossbow, suddenly terribly interested in her work. Max hopped off the sofa, well versed in Jed's crummy attempts at answer-dodging. The boy placed a hand on his mentor's forearm and gave it a gentle squeeze.

"Jed . . ."

The old man turned to his young charge. If he was a doctor charged with delivering bad news, the patient would've been weeping from twenty yards.

"Max, I'm at a loss. Your father never experienced anything like this, nor did your grandfather, as far as I know."

"So if you don't have the answers, who does?"

Jed scratched his chin like he might conjure an answer from his stubble.

Max suggested, "Maybe someone in the Undercity . . ."

"Are you *insane*?" shouted Jed, slamming his hand onto the workbench and causing the crossbow, tools, and Syd to jump. "You're a wanted man; that much is clear after this morning's chaos. And you propose going downstairs? Why don't you serve yourself on a silver platter with an apple in your mouth?"

"I don't see you coming up with any bright ideas, old man!"

Syd stepped quickly between them before they came to blows. "What about Odious Crumb?" she said.

"What about him?" said Jed warily.

"Yeah," agreed Max. "He might be able to help us. He's super well connected with the Undercity."

"No," said Jed. "You can't go near Crumb. It's too dangerous—"

"But it's just *Odious* we're talking about. He's harmless!"

"Ordinarily, yes. But something convinced a passive forest guardian, a harmless ghoul, and friendly little Eightball to attack you. Until we know more about what's going on, you've got to steer clear of anything remotely monstrous, Max. That includes the neighbors in Helsing House: Mr. Holloman in 2A—hell, even the Fairweathers at the front door. They're all potentially dangerous. And so is Odious. I'll go and see Crumb in the morning. If anyone visits the Undercity, it'll be me, not you. For the time being, you stay right here, in the garage."

Max looked about the dusty workshop. "You're kidding, right?"

"How many hours have you spent in here, training for situations like this?"

"I don't think anyone predicted a situation like this," muttered Syd as Jed continued.

"Any monster comes for you, we'll be ready."

"We?" said Max.

"Yes, you and me," said the old man. "You don't think I'd leave you in here alone, do you?"

Max smiled, comforted to hear that Jed wasn't making him go solo just yet. He was a monster hunter, but still had plenty to learn, and he hoped there were many more years ahead of him with the grumpy ex-boxer as his mentor.

"As long as Eightball stays out of my bedroom," grumbled Max.

"Your bedroom's off-limits to both of them."

"*Both* of them?" said Syd. "Who else is up there?"

"Wing Liu, of course."

"You left *Wing* in the apartment?" said Max. "Have you been taking crazy pills? I love the kid, but what if he's snooping around up there?"

Jed smiled reassuringly. "All the good stuff is out of reach on top of the cupboards and bookcases. Nothing incriminating has been left out. Believe me, he's just thrilled to have the puppy to play with."

"Remember me when I was his age?" said Max. "I was forever climbing on chairs to get to things I shouldn't . . ."

Jed's smile slipped. "I'm sure he's fine, but I'll go check on them." Unlocking the garage door, he turned back to the teenagers. "I'll bring some supper back down for you."

The old man reached for the door handle, but Max wasn't finished.

"Archer knew too much about me, Jed. Him and the monster attacks; it's all connected somehow. I'm sure of it."

Jed opened the door and was about to depart when a high-pitched scream cut through the night. The cry came from the mansion roof, accompanied by the sound of shattering glass.

"Wing!" cried Max, already moving. Jed staggered aside as his young charge barged past him, the blinds rattling in his wake as he sprinted through the rain toward Helsing House.

THIRTEEN

xxx

SMASH AND GRAB

The front door rebounded on its hinges as Max ran full tilt up the stairs, skidding around the second-floor landing. All around, apartment doors were opening as he dashed past the tenants of Helsing House. They shouted after him, but the youth had no time to stop and chat. Max's usual banter was in short supply as he bounded up the final flight and up toward the cramped attic landing.

His keys were out on their long chain, whipped into his palm, fingers flicking through them as he sought the one he needed. The door opened an inch before hitting an obstruction. The teenager pushed hard, putting his back into it, and the door shifted a touch farther. Bracing himself against the wall opposite, he lifted one booted foot and placed it against the door. Straining with all his might, Max cried out, straightening his leg as the door slowly opened.

A crowd was gathering on the floor below, peering up the dark staircase toward the teenager.

"What's happened?" asked Mrs. Connolly, her youngest child in her arms, one of the older ones squeezing past her mother and taking two steps up the stairs.

"Keep back!" shouted Max, his face now purple as he gave the barricaded entrance a final push. The door finally gave way, the heavy obstruction grating across the floor inside the apartment. Max slipped through the gap.

A bookcase lay behind the door, its contents spilled across the carpet and littering Max's path. He stumbled over crumpled scrolls, ancient tomes, and Jed's extensive vinyl collection.

"Wing!" he cried.

There was no sign of the boy or Eightball. The family room area had been turned upside down, the La-Z-Boy tipped over, pictures ripped from the wall. The lamp that had stood over Jed's chair now lay across it, bulb flickering and threatening to blink out. Through the disorder Max could see shards of glass and broken struts of wood peppering the ground. He looked up to the dormer skylight above the breakfast counter: the entire unit was busted in, its remains hanging from the ceiling. Rain steadily came in through the broken aperture, pattering directly onto Max's upturned face.

With a sickening dread Max found his thoughts returning to Eightball that morning, and the menacing mood the dog was in. The hellhound had meant to do serious harm to him earlier. Puppy or not, what damage could a hellhound inflict upon a helpless boy like Wing?

Syd was the next into the apartment, as the onlookers on the landing rubbernecked.

"I heard a scream, I swear!" The unmistakable Bostonian twang of Mrs. Connolly.

"It sounded like a child." Madame Rochelle, the tarot reader. "One of yours?"

"Mine are all here," replied the matriarch. "They're never out and about when it's time for supper."

Max had already clambered onto the kitchenette counter. Perhaps the hellhound had dragged the boy out to the roof? Syd stood below, watching with concern.

"No sign of either of them?"

Max shook his head as he examined the ruined window. Portions of the frame were torn from the joists, insulation exposed and hanging down into the apartment. He looked back toward the ground, seeing the wide spread of broken glass and timber, even a number of shattered slates lying among the rubble. Max removed Eightball from his list of suspects.

"It came in through the window. It came in and it grabbed them."

"It? What's *it*?"

Then they both heard the voice they'd dreaded hearing.

"Has anyone seen my boy?" Mr. Liu's words were almost lost beneath the hubbub.

Max leaped directly upward, snatching hold of the

broken window frame and hauling himself out of the opening. Tiles shifted as he dragged himself onto the treacherous roof, the slates slick with rainwater. Max fought a bout of nausea as he caught sight of treetops. He'd seen those trees from ground level plenty. They were *tall*. A noise below drew his attention back to the apartment, where Syd was preparing to climb onto a stool.

"What are you doing?"

"Coming with you," she replied as the stool wobbled precariously.

He admired her moxie. Syd's impulsiveness could often get her into trouble, but wherever possible, Max preferred to keep her out of danger.

"No way. You're staying put."

"But aren't you scared of heights?" Syd called after him.

He gritted his teeth as he blinked through the drizzle. "Yes."

"Be careful up there, then."

"I'll try not to die."

Max rose carefully beside the smashed skylight, arms out on either side like an acrobat. A distant peel of thunder rolled across the sky, reminding Max that he wasn't best placed should lightning come knocking. Glancing around the rooftop, he gathered his bearings. The dark gray tiles sloped steeply toward a rickety gutter below, beyond which was a drop of some forty-odd feet to the graveled drive. Decorative wrought-iron spikes ran along every peak, ending in finials that rose like black spears into the night. Max checked his footing again, spying moss and lichen on the slates, in addition to the fast-flowing rainwater.

"Great," he muttered. "We have lightning, vertigo, slime, rain, spikes, and an enormous drop. And whatever grabbed Wing and Eightball. It's ways-to-die Bingo."

Max hunkered low, spying a series of tracks scrawled across the grimy tiles. Paw prints and claw marks criss-crossed the slates, leading directly across the rooftop toward the front of the house. Max followed the trail, sneakers slipping, fingers gripping wherever they could find purchase. He reached a chimney stack, grabbing hold of the brickwork before clambering around it. The roof was an uneven hodgepodge of peaks and dips, turns and turrets. There were no footholds to speak of, only strips of lead flashing and flooded gutters zigzagging their way around him.

The twilight gloom had long since departed, replaced by the grim black of night. Moving hand over hand, Max followed the iron rails toward the front of Helsing House, sneakers sliding as he went.

"Wing!" he shouted, praying the kid might call back.

Max straddled the rails, careful to keep his undercarriage clear of the rusty spikes, before arriving at the roof's front elevation. Immediately, he began a slow descent, sliding down the roof over a sea of shifting grime, tiles, and rainwater. Directly ahead of him, at the base of the slope, Max could make out the distinct, dark outline of Eightball. The hellhound was alone, his back turned, facing out into the night. The pup whimpered and whined, his lament only ceasing when he heard the boy's scraping passage along the tiles toward him. The dog turned his head.

"Eightball?" whispered Max as he skidded ever closer.

The puppy's eyes glowed white. He snarled as Max approached, stubby teeth bared. Eightball's wobbling torso shuddered as the growl reverberated in his throat. Three bright red stripes were cut through the flesh of his face, running from his brow, straight over his right eye, and down into his jowl. The wounds still oozed. His stubby paws clattered the tiles, muscles trembling as his hackles rippled.

"Hey now, little guy," said Max, unable to slow his descent. "You can quit that hollerin' right away."

Eightball snarled.

"I mean it!" shouted Max, the slide bringing him inexorably closer to his puppy. "I've had the worst day ever, and if you think for one minute I'm going to let you drool, slobber, or fart me to death, or whatever it is you hellhounds are supposed to do, I am *not* in the mood."

The dog's growling quieted slightly. Did he understand him?

"You're smarter than you look, fella. So here's how it's going to be. You want a fight? Gimme your worst. But if I take a fall, you're coming with me. You may be the same shape as a basketball, but I don't reckon you bounce."

He readied himself, prepared for the puppy to pounce at any moment. Five feet, four, three and closing . . .

"So what'll it be, Eightball? Friends or enemies?"

Max slid to a halt in front of the hellhound, his feet braced against the groaning gutter on either side of his pet. Eightball's eyes narrowed, as if considering whether Max was really worth the effort. Then there was a deep rumbling from the pit of the puppy's guts, rising through the back of his throat as something hideous emerged from the depths. Max winced, ready for whatever horror was coming. A great glob of phlegm erupted. Eightball hocked it squarely into the youth's chest, spattering his face in the process. Then the hellhound turned away, gazing back into the night.

Max retched, trying to shake the hideous coating of gloop loose. Eightball stared into the storm, his growls turning to whimpers. "Wing, Eightball," said Max, spitting the foul drool from his lips. "Where's Wing?"

More whines from the dog, his stumpy tail thumping pathetically. Max wondered what the poor pup had witnessed, what manner of monster had seized their friend. He was scraping more goo from his chest when he found something hard and solid within the slobber. Max picked it up, wiping the slime away with his fingers. He raised it up in the rain, the moonlight catching its curved edge. It was around two inches long, with a broken base and a sharp, pointed tip. He ran his thumb over the broad end, testing its brittleness, the material crumbling beneath the pressure.

It was a stone claw. A stone claw that Eightball had

bitten off and swallowed. Max patted the dog, who snarled at him before returning his gaze to the night.

"Good boy," said Max, an idea slowly forming as Jed's words about Eightball rang in his head: *He's a remarkable wee beast*. Max squeezed the severed digit in his fist. "Good fetch."

FOURTEEN

xxx

THE WRONG WRETCH

The man stood upon the balcony and looked out over the skyline of Gallows Hill. The place bore little resemblance to the town he'd known and lived in. It was little more than a village back then, a settlement for those who had crossed an ocean and claimed the land as their own. Since he had first set foot on the shores of those Americas, much had changed, not least the skin he now wore. Removing the dagger from his belt, he raised and angled it, catching his reflection across its silver blade. He pinched the flesh of his face, doughy, loose, and slack. His green eyes narrowed disapprovingly, never losing their ghastly glow. No doubt there were healthier, better bodies he could have taken, but beggars couldn't be choosers, and neither could the warlock.

He glanced at the brass name badge on his breast pocket: "Cunningham." Judging by the uniform he wore, the man had been some kind of officer of the peace. A soldier, perhaps. It seemed the militia of Gallows Hill were none too fussy about the men they enlisted, if Cunningham was any example. In a pudgy hand he twirled the long knife, a deadly memento purloined from the museum. The rippling blade was about a foot in length, its crosspiece fashioned into the spread wings of a scarab beetle. The script had informed him it was ceremonial, used for animal sacrifice by the ancient Egyptians. The warlock wondered how it might fare on a human target. Judging by its wicked edge, quite well. He smiled at the possibilities. A peal of thunder coaxed his gaze back to the stormy world beyond the balcony.

Giant towers of stone rose across the horizon, a man-made mountain range pockmarked with myriad twinkling lights. He wondered what kind of people could build such edifices, what manner of god they worshipped that they should rise into the heavens, reaching for the stars. Perhaps this was a world he could get used to, once he found an adequate vessel to inhabit. Unnatural lights soared by overhead, roaring through the night. Were these their gods? Had mankind turned its back on its pathetic invisible deities at long last and embraced darkness, as the warlock had always desired?

Gallows Hill might have been unrecognizable, but the balcony he stood on wasn't. He turned his back on the city's streetlamps and disappeared into the dark tower, fingers trailing over the rain-slicked stone. The walls spoke to him, whispering of wickedness centuries old. He grinned, casting his mind back. If he closed his eyes, he could hear the screams, the baying of the mob, the cries of the children. This ancient building, perhaps the oldest in the town, had been the setting for his finest work. And it would be again. He was returned, and his greatest task was at hand.

The sound of powerful wings beating caused his smile to grow further. He turned as a hulking figure approached through the sky, its enormous bat-wings causing updrafts of rain to spatter the warlock as it alighted on the balcony. The floor trembled when the creature landed. It looked up, horns rising from either side of its heavy head, eyes hidden beneath a slab of overhanging brow. A lantern jaw jutted from its chest, its underbite revealing a row of symmetrical teeth. Muscles rippled across the monster's torso, its over-enlarged arms bound tight around its prize. Stepping forward on powerful stone legs, it deposited its trophy before its master.

"Excellent," said the warlock gleefully, slapping the flat of the dagger blade into his open palm.

It was the boy.

A burlap sack had been thrown over his head, a trailing length of rope binding his wrists behind his back. In the warlock's experience, it was better to take no chances. Underestimating his foe so close to the end would be disastrous. He looked the boy up and down where he teetered unsteadily; a little shorter than expected. The Van

Helsing he had crossed wits and swords with back in the day had been a warrior. Clearly the bloodline had been diluted down the years. Nevertheless, he wasn't about to quibble.

"Fine work, my robust friend," he said, clapping the hulking monster on a solid shoulder. "If I had known that your errand was to be so pedestrian, I might have undertaken it myself. No matter," the warlock went on, readying his grip on the sacrificial dagger as he tugged the rough bag off the child's head. "The Mark is delivered."

It wasn't the right boy.

The warlock lashed out at the monster angrily, sparks flying as the silver dagger scored its stony skin. The creature might have dwarfed the man, but it staggered back, cowering as its master shouted.

"You cumbersome cretin! I ask you to do *one thing*, one simple task, and you foul it up!"

"Not boy?" growled the gargoyle, its rumbling voice causing the warlock's ribs to rattle.

"It was a Van Helsing I sent you to retrieve! At the very least I expected you to know roughly who you were looking for, you gravel-brained imbecile. This child . . ." he said, struggling for words, wagging a pale finger at the boy who stood blinking around at the tower's interior. "He isn't even Caucasian. He's an Oriental!"

"Whoa there," said the boy. "Asian American, thank you very much." He looked back at the monster that had brought him to the warlock. "What is that, some kind of black-ops flight suit? It's Kevlar, right?"

The warlock shook his head. He pointed the dagger at him.

"Stay your wagging tongue, jabbering infant, lest I separate it from your gullet."

"Okay, so first, I have a name, not that you cared to ask; it's Wing Liu, but you can call me Wing. Second, don't point that thing at me, you nutjob. And lastly, what's with the cheesy, old-timey talk? Are you a LARPer? Did you take a wrong turn on your way to the Renaissance Fair?"

The warlock seized Wing roughly about the throat. He raised the knife before the boy's eyes. They blinked fearfully. He gave Wing a shake, cocking his ear the boy's way. "What's that? You're done blathering? Good. You and I will get along better if you speak only when spoken to. Do you think you can manage that, little whelp?"

Wing nodded. The warlock released his grip, Wing's knees sagging as he almost fell onto his face. The man slid the dagger back into his belt.

"I am showing you trust, child, trust that I hope you can reciprocate. Know this, though; should you attempt any transgression, my friend remains at my beck and call."

The boy glanced at the frightening figure behind him. Gradually the winged giant retreated into the shadows as the sorcerer began untying the rope from around Wing's wrists.

"Let us remove your bonds. So uncivilized, boy, especially as you are my guest. My name is Udo Vendemeier, and we appear to be in . . . a predicament. As you may have surmised from my tirade, there has been a case of mistaken identity. My friend has made a blunder. This is what happens when one hires a construct to do a monster's work. No matter—we make do, eh?"

The long rope fell onto the floor in a coiled heap. Vendemeier smiled, trying to diffuse the situation with a friendly wink. It didn't work: the dead flesh twitched, the lid below his right eye sagging open to reveal more of the sickly green cornea than he'd desired. He placed his palm over the socket, trying to massage the skin back into place. Wing winced.

"The boy we were looking for goes by the name of Van Helsing. You know of whom I speak?" The child remained mute and wide-eyed. "Please, young Wing, speak. You have my permission."

"I don't know him."

"Come, come, of course you do. Master Van Helsing. Close to your age, no doubt, and clearly you were in his residence at the time of your abduction; otherwise my friend would not have made such a spectacular mistake."

Wing shook his head. "Nope. Never heard of him."

Vendemeier's ugly smile slipped. The boy was lying, it was plain to see. Everything about him reeked of the warlock's nemesis. Vendemeier sighed and held a cold hand to Wing's perspiring cheek. The child flinched.

"You could have cooperated, Master Wing. That would have ensured a swift punishment for fraternizing with this odious family. As it is, you have instead guaranteed your-self a lingering, agonizing period of suffering. You have no idea who stands before you. I am Udo Vendemeier, Keeper of the Unspeakable Oath, Brother of the Endless Night, High Priest of Hastur, and most humble servant to the King in Yellow. I have condemned countless innocents to the dark-ness, sacrificing those purest souls to my Master, defying death itself, commanding—"

"Love the sound of your own voice much?" broke in the boy as his knee shot up, connecting hard and fast with the warlock's groin.

The body the warlock possessed may have been a bag of bones and slowly putrefying flesh, but some human reflexes remained. He went down in a heap as Wing turned, sprinting for the balcony. It was a four-story drop to the earth below. Perhaps Wing preferred a swift, sudden death as opposed to what the sorcerer now planned for him. Vendemeier's mon-strous servant bounded from the shadows and snatched the boy before he reached the stone banister. The giant raised Wing above its head, as if it might dash him against the rain-slicked flags of the balcony.

"Wait!" gasped Vendemeier, clutching the ceremonial knife as he struggled clumsily to his feet. "He's more valu-able alive, for now."

He brought his drooping face level with the boy's and glared at him with his emerald eyes.

"Know this, child; your friend *will* come for you. He's a

Van Helsing. Noble fools, the lot of them, when it comes to you pathetic humans. And when he does, you'll do exactly as I say or suffer the consequences. Live bait is *always* better," he said, pressing the dagger against the boy's ribs, "but I'll stick a hook through a worm if it gets the job done."

FIFTEEN

xxx

THE SCENT

Max pedaled hard through the drizzle, struggling to keep up with Syd's BMX. The Chopper had been bent out of shape mere hours earlier, in his encounter with the forest guardian. It had taken all of the girl's smarts to get it back into a roadworthy condition in such a short space of time. Every inch of the boy's battered body hummed like a hive of bad-tempered bees. Not only that, but the smaller bike was state-of-the-art, able to climb uphill with far greater ease than Max's vintage velocipede. And Syd was kind of cheating. It wasn't just her legs that propelled the BMX up the road. She had a little monstrous help.

"Seek," said the girl, urging Eightball on.

The puppy's stubby legs were a scrambling blur as he dragged Syd's bicycle up the sidewalk. The long chain leash was wrapped about the crossbar, its other end looped around the hellhound's straining throat. His already goggling eyes bulged further as he pushed on, sniffing at the air, ignoring the choking noose. The familiar railings of Gallows Hill Burying Ground flickered by. Max followed behind, catching a face full of spray in Syd's wake.

"You sure he knows where he's going?" Syd called over her shoulder.

"I've never been less sure of anything in my life," Max replied, "but something's got him agitated. I'll be ticked off if this is all for a fire hydrant, though!"

Max had a hunch this wasn't all about a place for the puppy to pee. Back at Helsing House, Eightball had been transformed from a cute bundle of blubber into something that resembled the *hellhound* moniker. The dog had fought their foe, even biting off one of its claws in the process. If a bloodhound could follow a scent, then what could a hellhound do? Chase down its quarry to the gates of hell, Max hoped.

They were reaching the top corner of the burying ground now, on the route they took to school. Max glanced through the railings, half expecting the remaining members of the slain ghoul's pack to come spilling over the spikes, snatching at him. They were like rats; find one, find a nest. But the only beasts he spied were crows, squawking at the trio as they raced past.

"Any sign of Jed?" called Syd.

Max looked back down the road in the direction of home. The streets were empty, thanks to the thunderstorm, with no sign of the beat-up station wagon.

"Negatory. We're on our own."

Perhaps Jed was still back at the house, dealing with Mrs. Liu. No doubt she was asking all the pertinent questions. What was the commotion? Had there been a robbery? Where was her boy? The more time passed by, the tougher it would be to convince Mrs. Liu that her son wasn't in danger. And Max was under no illusions: the boy was in *terrible* danger.

Suddenly, the dog came juddering to a halt beside a flaking white picket fence, the girl and her bicycle speeding straight past. Syd jammed on her brakes too late, and they squealed as the wheels were pulled from under her. Eightball barely flinched as the chain leash clanked taut, the girl flying from her saddle and splashing into the sidewalk puddles. Max's Chopper came to a halt alongside the dog, and the boy peered over his handlebars at his prone friend on the ground.

"Nice landing."

"You can take Eightball next time," said Syd, rising, soaking wet.

The puppy was panting, tongue lolling from between his stubby teeth, steam rising from his pitch-black coat as if he might combust at any moment. His eyes were fixed beyond the wooden fence.

"Why can't it ever be a pillow factory or candy store?" Max muttered, following Eightball's gaze.

One of the oldest buildings in town, All Saints Church was a reminder of New England's darker past. Gallows Hill

Burying Ground had once been the church's cemetery, until the place of worship had fallen into ruin. There had been numerous attempts by well-meaning community groups to restore the ramshackle structure to its former glory, but red tape and last-minute legislation had always scuttled those schemes. With its grim architecture and crumbling stone bell tower, it was as if the powers that be had willingly allowed it to fall into irreparable ruin.

"Fallen Saints," said Max.

"Why do you always call it that?"

That was the nickname the Van Helsings had for the building.

"It was from this church that men and women were dragged sobbing, pleading, or cursing to the gallows," said Max, pulling his phone from his pocket and punching keys. "Ever since then lots of other terrible tales have begun or ended here: dead bodies discovered, specters sighted, killers chased here by cops to a final furious shoot-out. If the walls of Fallen Saints could talk, they'd wail and run red with blood."

"You're all about the drama, huh?" said Syd, unraveling Eightball's chain from around her bike's handlebars. "Who are you texting?"

"First rule of monster hunting: let Jed know where we are and where we're going." Max pocketed the phone and tried the gate in vain: padlocked. Shifting the strap of his messenger bag, he hurdled the fence with ease. Syd struggled with Eightball, hoisting his blubbery mass over the gate. The puppy growled as Max received him, his eyes flashing white and demonic. The boy couldn't drop him quick enough, and the dog landed with a thump as Syd followed only slightly more gracefully.

"The leash!" cried Syd as Eightball set off at a mad dash toward the church, the chain zipping after him. Max dived to the ground, the leather loop flashing between his fingers. He grasped too late, puppy and leash disappearing toward the church.

"Nice," said Syd, stepping over Max to follow Eightball toward the derelict building.

The building was obscured by a choking curtain of creepers. The remains of windows were barely visible, twisted struts of lead jutting from the foliage like broken fingers, glass panes long gone. The odd patch of stonework that had avoided the ivy was daubed in graffiti, bright and garish against the sooty black bricks. The arched and open double doors were green with moss, a shadowy chasm yawning open between them.

"Eightball?" hissed Syd, hopefully. She flicked on her flashlight, aiming it directly at the gloom.

Max looked up, his eyes scouring the building's familiar exterior and the ancient bell tower. Something wasn't quite right, but what? It was bugging the heck out of him. He turned back to the doors as Syd slipped through the gap, and he swiftly followed.

Inside, the church looked more like a flophouse, pews toppled over and detritus abounding. The building had clearly been used as a shelter by countless squatters and homeless folk. Soiled sheets and blankets were bundled and strewn among the refuse, buzzing flies the only sign of life. Syd's flashlight beam drifted over the uneven terrain. The light caught an archway, illuminating wooden steps that led up to the belfry.

"Wing!" called Max. His voice echoed back through the cavernous hall.

"Eightball!" hissed Syd, trying her luck where Max had failed.

Instantly, the hellhound replied, his bark bouncing down the bell tower stairwell before cutting off with a sharp yelp. The girl was off and running, following the puppy's cry and dashing through the archway in the wall.

"Wait!" cried Max, cursing his friend's impulsiveness.

He heard her feet pounding up the ramshackle staircase, and quick as a flash, he was after her. The steps groaned beneath each footfall, threatening to splinter under Max's weight. Dust and dirt showered down over him from Syd on the flight above. It was a miracle she hadn't crashed through the rotten stairs in her urgency to reach the summit.

This was why Max tried to keep Syd away from the "pointy end" of his business. She had a tendency to charge into dangerous situations without thinking them through. Max's own battle plans could be pretty haphazard at times, but at least he attempted to form them in the first place.

Eightball had followed Wing's scent, which meant Wing was up there, in the bell tower.

Unless Eightball was tracking the monster. Which would mean . . .

"Syd!"

Max bounded up the remaining flight and burst into the bell tower.

The little dog was suspended from the rafters by his chain, the links bound tightly around a beam. His face contorted, eyes bulging as the metal cut into his jowly throat, stumpy legs kicking at thin air. Wing lay on the flagged floor in a crumpled heap beside a long coil of rope, unconscious. Syd's flashlight rolled across the flags, coming to a bumping halt beside Wing's prone form. And there stood Syd, on the bell tower balcony, beside an odd-looking man.

He was disheveled, out of shape, and, judging by his uniform, some kind of security guard. One hand gripped Syd's shoulder; the other was hidden behind her back. His eyes glowed with a sickly green hue, lighting up further at the sight of Max.

"If you're the security guard of Fallen Saints, you're doing a pretty crappy job," said Max, his eyes flitting between Syd, Wing, and Eightball.

"Sweet, joyous delight," said the guard, shaking Syd excitedly. "And I had wondered, nay, *questioned*, whether this moment might ever come to pass. The last son of the Van Helsings, come hither finally. I cannot find the words to express my sheer unmitigated delight at what your presence here means to me!"

"Really? Sounds to me like you're giving it the old college try."

"How I've missed that Van Helsing arrogance," said the man. "You dare to mock me?"

"What's with the goofy accent?" Max edged toward Eightball, making little effort to disguise his movements, and awfully aware that time was running out for the choking hellhound.

"Not another step, Van Helsing."

The man shifted, turning Syd to one side and revealing a long, wavy-bladed knife held against her back. Max looked back at Eightball in desperation. The puppy's kicks had grown weaker, and the eyes were rolling in their sockets. He hadn't exactly bonded with the little guy, but he sure as heck couldn't bear to see him die.

"Heavy metal," said Max.

"What?" asked the man, baffled by the statement. In his defense, though, anyone would have been confused. Anyone except Syd. Her head rocketed back, smashing the security guard square in the face with a sickening crunch. Cartilage crumpled, flesh tore, and dark blood erupted with the impact. He staggered backward, hit the stone parapet, and disappeared over the side.

Syd didn't wait to see or hear him land, dashing to join Max as he hoisted Eightball up. The chain went slack as

Syd's fingers unhitched the chain and strap above. It came free with a jangle, and the three of them fell to the ground in a heap. Max smiled as Syd rubbed the back of her head.

"Heavy metal," she said. "Thanks for the heads-up."

"Headbanging," said Max, patting the flabby flank of a wheezing Eightball. "Accept no substitutes." He looked past her to where Wing lay on the floor. Even by the poor light he could see the younger boy's chest rising and falling softly.

"Better see how our little buddy's doing," he said, rising from their tangle of limbs as Syd cradled the weary puppy. He couldn't help but smile.

"Why the dumb grin?"

"Wing is safe, my dog hasn't kicked it, and you dispatched the bad guy in spectacularly badass fashion. Who'd have thought you could kick butt like that?"

"Don't push it, Helsing."

"Come on, this is the first thing that's gone right for me today. Looks like I've shaken loose the curse. We could pick up a celebratory pizza on the—"

"Slow your roll," said Syd, interrupting Max. "This doesn't make sense."

"Gimme a break," sighed Max. "Let me have this one moment of triumph on what's been—let's face it—a truly lousy birthday."

"Fine, don't listen to me," she grumbled. "I'm just saying."

"Saying what?" asked Max, looking down at the

unconscious boy. His clothes were covered in a fine layer of powder. He dabbed it with his finger and lifted it for closer inspection. It appeared to be masonry dust.

"Whatever brought Wing here had wings of its own. If the maniac who just swan-dived off the balcony had wings, he was doing a great job of hiding them."

Max looked up into the recesses of the bell tower, with its great alcoves swathed in shadow. A cold dread washed over him as he reached out, fishing around for the flashlight, never taking his eyes off the black nothingness. He found it at last, picking it up and turning it upon the darkness.

"Just saying," repeated Syd at his back, "the security guy wasn't your monster."

The flashlight beam cut into the shadows just as the creature hidden within turned toward the young monster hunter. It stepped into the light, massive stone foot striking the flags mere feet from the unconscious Wing. Max scrambled back, dragging his small friend with him.

The beast seemed hewn from the walls of the bell tower, its body matching the stone around it, even mottled and discolored by the same mildew and bird droppings. Cracks were visible across its enormous, boulderlike torso, fissures running through the flesh like jagged fault lines. Gray dust billowed from these cavities, fluttering into the air with each movement. Wings rose with a creaking, cracking *snap*, their colossal span blotting out the moon and stars. Its growl was rocks in a tumble dryer, its clawed hands fistfuls of daggers. And there it was, one great talon missing, broken in its melee with the hellhound.

Eightball whimpered and Max gulped. When Syd next spoke, her words were a threadbare whisper.

"Now *that's* your monster."

SIXTEEN

xxx

THE BEAST IN THE BELFRY

Throughout his fledgling monster hunting career, Max had prided himself on quick, witty retorts in the face of fiendish foes, but with so many loved ones in danger around him, those quips had deserted him now.

"Run!" shouted Max.

He practically threw Wing to Syd to get him clear of the creature before tumbling to the ground himself. Its fist flew down to smash him where he lay. Max rolled, the flags cracking beneath him with the force of the blow. He came up into a crouch, the monster's attention fixed upon him. The teenager had managed to turn the creature, positioning himself on the balcony with the giant between him and his friends. Whatever "mark" was upon Max clearly remained firmly in place, no doubt blazing like a beacon above his head.

"Get them out of here!"

Syd dragged Wing and shoved Eightball toward the staircase that circuited the interior tower wall. Max aimed the flashlight directly into the winged giant's eyes, hoping to dazzle it and spring a surprise attack. The light passed over those granite pupils, now refocusing their attention on Max. They were lifeless, unblinking holes carved into the stone.

"Gargoyle," whispered Max.

Only now did he realize what had been amiss outside the church: that hideous face was usually staring out over Gallows Hill. The *Monstrosi Bestiarum* had numerous pages on these creatures and their various incarnations, but Max hardly had those fact files on speed dial. He knew only one thing for sure: they were animated beings, not living, breathing beasties like most of the monsters he faced. They could be brought to life by powerful, arcane magic but weren't necessarily servants of evil. There were plenty of tales from European folklore that celebrated gargoyles as guardians, warding the wicked away from churches. Sadly, it seemed this particular stone scaremonger hadn't received that memo. Furthermore, there was nothing in his messenger bag that could help save his hide in this instance. Whatever its weaknesses were, he was going to have to discover them the old-fashioned way.

"Okay," said Max as the monster dipped its broad head and snorted. "Let's see what you're made of, besides stone."

It charged like a bull, the tower shaking as it came. Max dived aside at the last moment, and the gargoyle crashed

GARGOYLE

OTHER ALIASES: babewyn, boss, chimera, gargouille, grotesque

ORIGIN: France

STRENGTHS: Stone flesh makes the gargoyle invulnerable to slashing and piercing weapons. Immune to any attacks against the nervous system, poison, paralysis, sleep, etc.

WEAKNESS: Very few physical frailties. Low intelligence can possibly be exploited.

HABITAT: Urban environments, specifically places of worship such as churches, cathedrals, and minsters.

In architecture, a gargoyle is a grotesque figure, carved from stone, with a spout to convey water away from a building. On occasion, these granite monsters are gifted with life, charged with the task of protecting their holy abode from harm or invasion. As such, they may be considered nonmalignant for the most part. There have been rare cases of sorcerers and necromancers animating them for use as lackeys, assassins, or beasts of burden.

—Erik Van Helsing, May 8th, 1850

PHYSICAL TRAITS

1. <u>Camouflage</u>—Granite flesh allows them to blend in against most manmade structures. Even when visible they are frequently dismissed as statues.

2. <u>Claws</u>—Stone talons afford a gargoyle a viselike grip that can puncture flesh and grind bones. Stay out of their grasp!

3. <u>Wings</u>—One should be doubly wary of those monsters with wings. It defies logic and reason that a stone sentinel should be able to take flight, so a silent, gliding gargoyle makes for the perfect killer.

—Esme Van Helsing, January 31st, 1864

Keep a HAMMER handy! Works well against ROCK GOBLINS so you gotta figure it'll hurt a GARGOYLE!

MAX HELSING Dec 12th, 2014

through the stone parapet and followed its master over the edge into the dark night. But Max's triumphant whoop was short-lived, as the magical construct reappeared, rising through the air on those impossible stone wings.

The teenager retreated into the tower, glancing back for a glimpse of Syd, Wing, and Eightball; no sign. Good. He had come to terms, long ago, with the inherent dangers in his profession: secretarial work could bring paper cuts, garden maintenance backache, and monster hunting swift and brutal life termination. But he couldn't bear to imagine anything happening to his friends. If they were safe, he could relax and do what he did best: taking down monsters.

Max stumbled over a coil of rope on the floor, sending him toppling backward as the gargoyle landed on the balcony. Max spun, letting loose a very un-macho shriek as he careened toward the great iron bell that hung from its beamed mooring within the tower top. His momentum ensured he wouldn't stop in time, and if he continued staggering he would plummet over the rickety wooden balcony to his doom. Clean out of options, he leaped high.

Max almost straddled the huge metal bell as he collided with its curved body, hands clutching, his life depending upon maintaining his grip. He heard the rotten timbers groaning as the bell shifted but didn't clang, splinters showering down on him. Max's knees compressed into his chest, his body recoiling like a spring as the gargoyle thundered toward him, wings folded against its back. Then Max was leaping, propelling himself over the charging stone sentinel. He landed even higher on another beam, with the grace and dexterity of the finest circus acrobat. *Okay,* figured Max, *a drunken monkey might be closer to the truth.* His long hours in the home gym had been well spent.

The gargoyle went through the spindly banister and crashed into the bell, causing it to peal loudly. Max felt every timber in the rooftop tremble, including the beam he was perched on, the bell threatening to break free. The monster's wings saved it once more, flapping out, propelling it back onto the top floor and away from the drop. It turned, heavy solid feet finding the flags as it searched the tower top for Max. The boy held his breath, wishing he could conjure up a chameleonlike power of concealment. *The Mark.* The monster turned its head up toward his beam and fixed its gaze upon him.

Max leaped, springing from the wooden strut as a stone fist smashed through it. He landed on the next beam, which suffered the same fate as the former, stone claws snatching for the boy on high. Max dropped to the floor, landing within that treacherous coil of rope as his perch disintegrated beneath the savage blow. Again, the entire tower shook. Hundreds of tiles fell through the holes that pockmarked the roof, shattering across the flags around him. He snatched up the hemp as shrapnel flew, backing into a wall in the hope of protection.

"Get out of there!"

Max heard Syd's cry. She must have gotten Wing and Eightball to safety, out of Fallen Saints. His hands were already working the rope, fashioning a noose from one end. He wondered if a jump from the balcony would be his best means of escape. No doubt the crazy security guard had painted the ground a lurid shade of red. He doubted he'd fare any better. But with the rope attached to the balcony? Maybe, just maybe . . .

Max looked back as the gargoyle covered the distance in swift strides, a fist flying toward the teenager. Max ducked, the bricks crumbling at his back where enormous knuckles hit the wall. The youth darted forward, skidding between the creature's legs and scrambling out behind it, rope trailing. Then came the lightbulb moment. He switched his plan of action to one that didn't involve vertigo. Instead, he gathered the hemp coils into his hands, slackening the noose until he could've fit a train through it. Or a giant, enchanted church ornament, at the very least.

"Yo, Rocky! Over here!"

Max ran and leaped high again, praying the bell would hold out for one more collision. He landed upon the pitted iron shell, the fingers of his free hand gripping the rusted bolts that fixed it to its bracket. Bell, boy, and beam seemed to drop. It was only perhaps an inch, but it felt like a foot to the nauseous Max. He didn't look down, instead readying the rope as the statue lunged one last time, wings flush to its back. As the granite gargoyle charged at the bell, Max leaped back the other way, high, channeling his inner capuchin once more. Only this time, he let loose the noose, dropping the rope over and around the oncoming monster's body as it thundered by beneath him. He kept hold of the other end, feeling it go tight as the creature struck the bell again with another deafening clang. It tried to beat its wings and carry itself back out of the tower's void, but found them caught fast by the rope, pinned to its torso. Instead, it continued on, careening into the open stairwell and plummeting toward the ground. Max let go of the rope, nearly deafened by the booming bell that no doubt woke every resident of Gallows Hill. He peeked down the stairwell just as the gargoyle landed far below with an apocalyptic crash and accompanying dust cloud. Max dashed down the shaking staircase after the fallen statue.

The dust was settling when he reached the bottom, the gargoyle still twitching where it lay. The rope had come loose during its descent, but too late. One wing had snapped off, and its left leg lay shattered, reduced to rubble. Half of its head was sheared away, a great portion missing, revealing speckled granite within. Spasmodic shivers sent new cracks zigzagging across its broken body. Max wondered how best to put the monstrosity out of its misery. It had been trying to kill him moments earlier, but now he felt only pity for his stone adversary.

"Are you suffering? Do you feel the pain?"

Max was still musing about how best to dispatch it when a clawed hand shot up, catching his chest. He felt the fingers dig into his flesh. The pain was instantaneous, only his bomber jacket slowing the progress of the claws toward his heart. He cried out as the hand burrowed in, coat and hoodie tearing as the talons scored his flesh. To his relief, it was at that moment the bell above finally came away from its mooring, bringing the beam down with it in the process. With a clanging descent, it reached the ground in three heartbeats, landing square on the gargoyle's chest. The torso exploded, its remaining limbs going their separate ways. Max's world went dark as the walls came tumbling down.

VENDEMEIER STOOD IN THE BUSHES OF ALL SAINTS churchyard, a broken hand gripping a bare tree trunk.

"What in my Master's unholy name happened?" he asked himself, his voice gurgling in his throat.

He glanced back the way he had crawled, to where he'd landed after his fall from the bell tower. By the light of the moon he could see the dark smear on the flags where his borrowed body had impacted with the earth. It had taken all of the warlock's powers to stir the body back into action, forcing it back to life as he slithered, stumbled, and then staggered into the undergrowth, leaving the church behind him. He inspected his form.

Everything about his body was wrong. He was broken, held together by will alone. His limbs seemed twisted, one elbow turned back at an impossible, hideous angle. His collarbone jutted out from his chest, a compound open fracture revealing a snapped white branch that poked through the material of his shirt. His right foot was turned out, the leg broken at the kneecap. Vendemeier felt no discomfort, just a dull ache, as if a surgeon had plied him with a powerful medication to numb the pain.

"Useless fat oaf," he gurgled as he glared at his bloodstained chest. Cunningham's corpse was already outliving its usefulness. As he moved forward with his plans, he would need another body to possess, a fresh puppet to manipulate. For the time being, however, this shell would have to suffice.

The sound of fighting within the church continued at his back as he weaved through the trees and shrubs toward a faded white picket fence. No doubt his gargoyle was busy with the Van Helsing boy. Good; all had not been in vain. The boy stood little chance of surviving against Vendemeier's stone-born servant. The warlock would now stand clear and wait for the beast to emerge, the boy limp in its mighty grasp.

He chuckled, a glob of gore catching in his throat. That wretched girl had assisted the boy, along with Wing. A kick to his nether region and a head butt all within the hour; who could have imagined that the children of this strange future world would all be such despicable, sneaky rapscallions? He would take great pleasure tormenting them both when the time came and their friend, the Van Helsing boy, had fallen. Vendemeier might have hung around to witness the gargoyle's victory, but Cunningham's pathetic body needed strapping and splinting back together. No point in leaving himself exposed to any further dangers after the night he'd endured.

Reaching the picket fence, he lurched over it, his clumsy body catching on the jagged edges. The warlock landed with a wet thump on the street beyond, just as one of those strange, horseless carriages came to a halt nearby. Vendemeier pulled himself upright, remaining in the shadows, as he heard the growls from within the carriage splutter to a halt.

An old black man emerged from within, limping toward the rear of the carriage. This new world baffled the warlock; this wasn't the first slave he'd seen wandering about freely. The newcomer looked in each direction, straightening his flat cap before flicking some kind of lever at the back of the carriage. Hinges creaked as a door shot up and open, quivering in the air. As with the other peculiar vehicles, it appeared to be forged from metal. How it moved, Vendemeier had no clue. The magic that the people of this modern world used was baffling to the sorcerer, like nothing he'd witnessed in his life from long ago. The warlock stepped a little closer, concealed within the shadows of the overhanging foliage. He might have dismissed the fellow and headed on his way, until he spied the clutter of articles that the man had stored within the rear of his carriage.

It concealed an arsenal. There were stakes, a great many of them, recognizable instantly as the weapon of choice for a Van Helsing. Vendemeier heard the clinking of bottles of liquid, very possibly holy water. He even caught a whiff of garlic on the air, unmistakable. The warlock chuckled; fools, to think they were dealing with a vampire. They weren't, not yet, but would be soon enough.

The old man turned suddenly as if he'd heard Vendemeier. Had he made an involuntary sound? Curse this useless corpse! The stranger slammed the door shut in the back of the carriage, looking back into the shadows to where the walking corpse was hidden. A scream from the church made both of them look that way, the cry unmistakably that of the girl.

"Get out of there!"

The old slave smiled at Vendemeier, who remained partially concealed in the darkness. His hand reached for the strange metallic lantern on his belt that he'd discovered beside the corpse in the museum. The warlock pressed a button and a beam of magical, wondrous light shot out from one end, straight into the eyes of the stranger.

"Just kids messing around, I reckon, officer," said the old man, squinting in the light as he limped out of the road and onto the flagged pavement. "They won't be the first kids to play around in this old ruin, or the last either."

He gave Vendemeier the briefest sideways look before fixing his gaze upon the wrecked church. Perhaps he expected the warlock to do the same. Instead, the corpse kept staring at him, wreathed in shadows.

"Well," smiled the old man, doffing his cap. "Guess

there's nothing to see here. High spirits is all. You have a good evening."

He turned, clearly dismissing Vendemeier as harmless; perhaps hoping the man might move on, mind his own business. His young charges were no doubt depending upon him, after all. The warlock flung the strange lantern, hitting the friend of Van Helsing savagely from behind. The old man's head snapped to one side, his legs going from under him as his body went slack. The blood that trickled from his temple began pooling in the corner of his eye as he looked up at his assailant.

Vendemeier turned his head as he regarded the battered and bewildered man with fascination, the peaked hat tumbling from the warlock's head to reveal his deeply dented skull. The old fool's horror at the sight of Vendemeir's demonic green eyes was writ large upon his transfixed face. The warlock laughed, and when he spoke, his broken jaw grated, splintered teeth catching as they struck one another clumsily.

"High spirits indeed."

SEVENTEEN

xxx

THE DUST AND THE DARKNESS

The church shook violently. Windows shattered, shards of glass flew, boards blew away. Syd gasped as an immense wave of dust billowed out from between the decayed church doors. It washed over her, Wing, and Eightball where they had collapsed on the ground. She slapped her hands over the boy's and dog's mouths, throwing her body over them as she held her breath. When the maelstrom finally died down she looked up, coughing and hacking as she gazed back at the church. The dust settled, leaving the trio blanketed in a fine powder, the gap between the doors a pitch-black ravine through a world of gray. There was no movement within.

"Max?" she said, horrified at the thought of what might have happened to him. She called out again, louder this time, struggling to her feet. By the starlight she could see that the bell tower was gone, a mushroom cloud rising out of the church roof where it had stood only minutes earlier.

The din that had accompanied the explosion had been deafening. Somewhere within that terrible noise she had heard the toll of the bell, clanging as it crashed to the earth, followed quickly by the tower itself. Her friend was in there.

"Oh, Max," she whispered, her voice cracking. Tears streaked her cheeks, cutting through the layers of dirt. "You stupid, stupid dumbass!"

"Not quite the heartfelt eulogy I'd hoped for."

Syd turned. Max stood close by, beneath the trembling boughs of a battered tree. He teetered, covered in dust, a clawed gargoyle hand still hanging from the lapel of his bomber jacket. He tore it off and tossed it into the bushes behind him, brushing himself down. She stepped up to him, shaking her head.

"Well," said Max. "I thought that went quite well, all things considered."

Syd punched him in the arm. Hard.

"What the . . . ? Where's the tearful embrace, lady?"

"I thought you were dead, numbnuts. How did you get out of there?"

He hooked a thumb and gestured over his shoulder. "Through a window. Not exactly by design. When the bell came down I was kinda thrown through the air. I was going through either a window or a wall. Turns out it was the former—yay me!"

"And the gargoyle?"

"He's kitty litter." Max crouched by Wing and checked him over.

"He's unconscious," said Syd. "They roughed him up, without a doubt."

Max moved across to Eightball, half-expecting the rotund pup to growl at him. The bulbous eyes swiveled in his fat little face, fixing on Max mournfully. Regardless of the mood the hellhound had been in earlier, Max couldn't help but reach out and stroke him. Eightball whimpered.

"Monsters," said Syd angrily.

Max shook his head. "There are plenty of monsters out there who are kind souls. Good monsters. The guy who took a dive from the tower and his gargoyle buddy—they were wicked, plain and simple. Speaking of which, what was left of him? That must have been messy."

"Nothing left of him."

"What? He was eviscerated?"

"No," said Syd, casting her hand around them. "He's simply not here. He must've gotten up and walked away."

Max smiled as he picked up Wing, the boy murmuring in his arms. "That's good news."

"*Good* news? I'd hate to see your bad."

"Monsters I get. It's humans, the norms, that pickle my brain. Now we know he's monstrous in some way, and unless he has some kind of accelerated healing ability, he's going to be a mess. We should look around. He can't have gone far."

"If he's here, I haven't seen him. I reckon he's long gone."

"We'd better get Wing home. If he was my kid I'd have called the cops by now. Not to mention that we've just played our part in demolishing one of Gallows Hill's oldest buildings. We'd better get a move on before Chief Boyle and the boys in blue turn up. I'll call Jed."

He shoved a hand into his pocket and fished out his phone, punching Jed's number on speed dial.

"Where is he, anyway?" asked Syd. "No disrespect to the old dude, but I thought he was your backup?"

"He is," said Max as they walked toward the picket fence that circuited the church grounds. "He's never let me down yet."

"Hush," said Syd, squinting into the gloom. She grinned. "I can hear his cell. He must be here already. Jed!" she called, picking up the pace.

"See," said the boy, letting it ring, the shrill tone leading them to him. "I told you he wouldn't let us down. The guy's a pro."

Max's smile slipped as they approached the spot where Jed's cell was ringing. The old man's station wagon was parked on the street, but there was no sign of him. The driver's side door was open. There was Jed's flat cap, the hat he never left home without, lying in a puddle. Inside the hat was his phone. The display glowed blue, Max's name showing up as the caller.

"The back door," said Max, his voice serious now as he directed Syd to the rear of the car. She opened it and stood aside as Max gently laid Wing out on the backseat. He quickly returned to the cap and cell. Eightball let out a low growl. Max patted the dog's head.

"I know, buddy. This is all wrong."

Max hit "end" on his phone and Jed's cell blinked off. He picked it up, tossing it into the driver's open door, then lifted the hat from the puddle. He turned on his flashlight, inspecting the cap's sodden black felt. Fishing inside with his fingers, he pulled out a fold of paper. Max winced.

"What is it?" asked Syd.

"Blood. On the inside. He had his skull cracked. How hard's impossible to tell." Max unfolded the paper, its edges blotted with blood and rain. He held up the flashlight, reading the scrawled handwriting. It was a flowing, archaic script, punctuated by spots and splatters of pooled red ink. Max grimaced as he realized it wasn't ink after all. Syd craned in as the two read the bloody script:

> If you wish to see your friend alive, Van Helsing, return to Gallows Hill Burying Ground at sunset tomorrow. Alone. UV.

"What does *UV* stand for?" asked Syd. "Ultraviolet? Has this got something to do with vampires, Max?" She shivered, glancing over her shoulder as if a sucker might appear there upon mention of its name. It was well known among monster hunters that ultraviolet light was as effective against vampires as daylight.

Max shrugged, sweat prickling across his cold, clammy flesh. "I don't know."

Those three words made Max feel sick. He hated being in the dark about anything, and always prided himself on having enough smarts and common sense to give him the edge over the enemy. At this point in time he was decidedly edgeless—blunt, in a word—and his mentor was missing. No, *missing* made it sound like he might pop up at any moment. Jed had been kidnapped.

"Eightball," he said, crouching before the puppy. "You ready for round two yet? Think you can find Jed?"

The pooch tucked his stumpy tail between his legs and lowered his head with a whimper. He'd taken a beating this night. Heck, Max doubted the poor little guy would ever track something down again, let alone charge into a fight. He gave him a comforting pat on the head.

"So, what?" asked Syd. "You're supposed to come back here tomorrow night and hand yourself over? In exchange for Jed?"

"That seems to be the gist of it."

She gulped. "And? Will you?"

Max considered. He'd never been in a fix like this before. For the first time ever, Max felt truly alone. Sure, he had Syd still, but his friend was only partially aware of the horrors that were out there. He pushed the fear into the pit of his belly, allowing the words of the ransom note to rattle back through his head. Ever so slowly, with each nervous heartbeat, his cockiness was returning.

"Oh, I intend to be here tomorrow night, for sure, but

I won't make things easy for our uniformed friend." He clapped Syd on the shoulder and smiled. "The way I see it, I have until dusk tomorrow to prepare for this. I'd hate to waste a minute of that time."

Max strolled around the car and flipped the trunk open, rummaging around within. He hefted a jelly jar of colorful glass marbles from the clutter, rattling them just once before depositing them into his satchel.

"What do you mean, you'd hate to waste a minute?" asked Syd, watching her friend as he went through the trunk's contents like a man possessed. "We've got no leads, nothing to go on."

"Nonsense," said Max, shoving more gear into his messenger bag. "We have all the information we need right here!" He waved the bloodied paper in the air.

"We do?"

"Of course. It's me he's after—his speech in the church confirmed it. And we know that Jed's still alive—so the note says."

"It could be a lie."

"You're right, it could. But for now, I'm going to trust the insane gargoyle wrangler on that one. Call me crazy."

Syd managed a lopsided smile.

"Last of all," he said, picking up Syd's BMX and placing it in the station wagon's spacious trunk, "this church and the burying ground—they're important to our enemy. They *mean* something to him."

"Like what?"

"That's your job to find out," Max replied, slamming the trunk shut.

"My job?"

"Yep. Head back to Helsing House. Get Wing back into Mrs. Liu's arms; I'm sure you'll be able to think of some cockamamie tale to explain what happened to him."

Max handed her a key from the chain on his hip.

"Get some sleep and then get into Jed's library. Find out everything you can about All Saints, Fallen Saints, whatever you want to call it. Check Wing, see if there's anything he can tell us that might help when he comes to. And keep Eightball by your side. As bouncing balls of blubber go, he kinda suits you."

He reached into the open driver's side door and flipped the sun visor, a spare ignition key dropping out into his hand. Max handed it to Syd. She looked shocked.

"Oh, please," he said, grinning. "Like you don't know how to drive this thing. Now get out of here before the cops arrive."

They both looked at the church and the dust cloud that still hung around it. Right on cue, sirens sounded in the distance. Lights had come on in the neighborhood, voices now audible as inquisitive residents came out to investigate. Syd hopped into the car and deftly slipped the key into the ignition. It fired up instantly and the girl smiled. Sure, she didn't have a license and was too young to drive, but when had that ever stopped her? She closed the door and wound down the window.

"And where are you going?" she asked Max.

Max straddled his Chopper and threw the cowl of his hoodie over his head. "Downtown, for some answers of my own."

EIGHTEEN

xxx

THE PAWNBROKER

Max hid in the shadows of the bus shelter, eyes fixed on the pawnshop across the street. The neon sign flickered above the door, the words *BUY* and *SELL* stacked on top of one another. The *B*, *U*, and *S* blinked out intermittently, leaving a garish pink *YELL* illuminating the crumbling storefront. Metal shutters had been rolled down over the windows and door, each one decorated with great swathes of graffiti. Much of it was in English, mostly scatological and anatomical in nature, but there were other words in incomprehensible script. Norms would have dismissed them as ordinary graffiti artist tags. Max, though, recognized them well enough. These symbols and ciphers didn't come from the human world.

Of course, he had no intention of entering via the storefront. That would be too obvious, and he couldn't risk getting spotted by any local "characters." This dilapidated downtown district was the wrong side of the tracks by any-one's standards. Max checked his phone's display: twelve thirty. Still deep within the witching hour. Content that the street was deserted, he stamped down on the Chopper pedal, launching the bicycle over the sidewalk. He hit the cobbled road, wheels rattling before he hopped the curb across the way, disappearing down the alley beside the shop. Parking the bicycle, he slipped up to the wooden side door.

Ignoring the doorbell, Max reached into the bottom of his messenger bag, rummaging around until he found what he needed. He withdrew a battered coin, lifting it to check he had the right one: a silver serpent. The snake's body coiled around itself, tail disappearing down its own hungry throat. This was currency from the Undercity, almost impos-sible to come by in norm society. The coins ranged from the exceedingly valuable platinum phoenix all the way down to the common copper corpse. The latter was next to worth-less downstairs, but would take the breath away from any human coin collector. Max took the serpent and turned it on its side before tapping it three times against a knothole in the door. Slowly, the silver coin disappeared into the tim-ber, drawn through the wood, before vanishing from his fingertips. Max nodded, pleased with himself. He'd only ever visited the shop after business hours with Jed, and had witnessed the old man do the exact same thing. This was a sign to the pawnbroker. It informed him he was being paid a visit by very special clientele.

Max heard noises within, approaching the door. He

looked around, eager to get off the street and out of sight. Shadows moved across the cobbles at the end of the alley as a number of figures approached. Their shadows grew longer, broader, more defined as they neared the passage's dark entrance. It could have been innocuous, revelers returning home after a night out on the town, but Max doubted it. This was basically downtown Monsterville, USA, and to be a human out on the streets at this hour was a decidedly risky—nay, crazy—business. Especially when every monster you met wanted to take a bite out of you.

"C'mon," he whispered, stepping into the doorframe until his chest was flush to the timber. Bolts shifted and locks were lifted. Max looked back up the passageway. Voices now, deep ones, muttering and guttural. Definitely not a troop of Boy Scouts. As the first figure appeared at the head of the alley, the door suddenly opened inward, sending Max sprawling into the arms of the pawnbroker.

They both landed on the floor, the boy on top of the man, nose to nose. The pawnbroker had a face even a mother would struggle to love, great warts and pockmarks scarring his skin. To anyone else it might have been an intimidating, scary visage, but not to Max. This was Odious Crumb, an occasional friend of the family. An occasional friend of the family who now threw his rough hands around Max's throat and began throttling him. The teenager managed to get one hand up, hooking a thumb into the gap before Crumb's fingers could reach each other. Then he kicked the door shut behind him. Whoever those strangers were outside, he didn't need them walking in on the ruckus. One fight at a time.

"Crumb!" he gurgled. "It's me! Max Helsing!"

The man's wild, bulging eyes were focused on Max's forehead. Foam frothed on his leathery lips, his jaundiced skin rippling as he strained his stubby, strangling digits. There was no recognition, no acknowledgment from Crumb that he'd ever met Max before. Max pulled his hand free and wedged his own fingers around the man's neck.

As necks went, Crumb's was almost nonexistent, but there was enough loose flesh for Max to seize hold of. He gripped hard as his own airway closed. The monster hunter lifted Crumb's head before sending him back to the ground, giving him a short, sharp crack on the back of his skull against the concrete. The man's hands slackened instantly. The teenager scrambled off the dazed pawnbroker, snatching up the first potential weapon that came to hand. It was an umbrella that hung from a coatrack, but that didn't bother Max. It wouldn't be the first time he'd used a bumbershoot to save his skin. He struck a fencing pose and readied himself.

"Well?" said Max. "Are we going again, or do you quit? Please tell me we don't have a problem, Mr. Crumb . . ."

The man blinked and wiped his eyes, rubbing the back of his head.

"Are we good?" asked Max, his voice low so as not to draw the attention of anyone outside.

"Blimey, Maxwell Helsing, as I live and breathe," said

Crumb at last, his cockney accent thick but comprehensible. "What kinda devil's gotten into you there, going for a defenseless geezer like that?"

"Me going for you?" Max relaxed a little. "It was *you* who went for me! Do you strangle all your customers?"

"Give over! I got the bruise on the back of me noggin to show for your scrapping."

Max yanked the hood of his sweatshirt aside, revealing his throat. "The finger marks on my flesh tell a different tale."

"Hell's bells," said Crumb, struggling to his feet to examine the red welts. He looked at his palms as if they belonged to a stranger. "I swear, little fella, I dunno what came over me. I thought it were you that took a pop at me! That were self-defense, weren't it?"

Max shook his head, hung the umbrella back up on the wall, and slid the dead bolts and safety bar back across the door. "Sorry about the concussion, Mr. Crumb," he said. "It was either that or die, and after the day I've had I'm determined to go down fighting."

The man gestured for Max to move further into the shop, his eyes on the door and the shuttered windows. "This way, little fella. Let's go where we can talk. Walls have ears 'round here."

Max smiled as he followed Crumb. "Little fella" was hardly appropriate any longer—he was already a couple of inches taller than this oddball of a man. The pawnbroker reminded Max of Mr. Toad from *The Wind in the Willows*, with his hunched back, stump neck, greenish pallor, and bulging eyes. If he'd flicked his tongue out and caught a bluebottle, it wouldn't have surprised Max one bit.

As a pawnbroker, Odious Crumb bought and sold anything, as far as Max could tell. The shop was an Aladdin's cave of oddities, every corner, wall, and rafter loaded with clutter. If it was worth something to someone, it was worth something to Crumb. The man thrived on others' misfortunes, picking out valuables and heirlooms when people were at their lowest points before selling them back at inflated prices. The man might appear to be down on his luck, but he'd made a fortune off the luckless of Gallows Hill, both human *and* monster. The rumor that he was a fence for stolen goods had never gone away either. Ultimately, Crumb always looked out for number one. He may have been a friend of the family, but Jed didn't trust the man as far as he could throw him.

"Wasn't expecting a visitor at this time o' night, certainly not a Van Helsing, young Maxwell. Where's that old reprobate, Jed? Coming to my humble establishment on your lonesome, and at this hour, too? Streets are a dangerous place for any soul after dark."

Max collapsed behind the jewelry counter. "It's been a helluva day. Where to start?"

Crumb filled a kettle and popped it onto the stove, firing the burner to life. "How's about at the beginning?"

As Crumb prepared a pot of tea, Max went over the day's events, starting with battling Eightball in his bath towel. If it weren't for the fact he'd lived through it, he'd have called shenanigans on the whole sorry story. When he was done, he finally got around to drinking his mug of tea, which steamed reassuringly in his cupped hands.

"So you came here looking for what?" asked Crumb.

"Answers. I figured you could help. Jed always says you're a man who knows a lot of people. Says you're 'well connected.' Is that true?"

Crumb sipped at his own drink, his leathery upper lip lingering along the rim of his mug like an enormous slug. "Will he be okay, the little Chinese lad? Your friend's able to look after him?"

"Wing will be fine," replied Max, noticing Crumb had dodged his question. "So can you help me?"

Crumb placed his mug on his countertop.

"When you entered my store, some kind of . . . rage took hold of me. Ain't never happened before. I pride myself on keeping the beast in check, understand?"

"The beast? I didn't think you were a monster; thought you only dealt with them."

Crumb's lips went thin as he smiled, his crooked teeth poking out like a row of broken stalactites.

"Oh, I've got a bit o' monster in me, little fella. My dear old mother was goblin, you see. Met the old man when he was digging Tube tunnels below London. Love at first sight, they both used to tell me, bless their dear departed souls."

The thought of a human falling for a goblin didn't conjure a pretty picture to Max's way of thinking, but then again, beauty was in the eye of the beholder. "So I triggered something in you? What did it feel like?"

Crumb shrugged. "Felt like I was drunk on home brew, didn't it? Wasn't meself until you clobbered me. And then"—he clicked his fingers—"it lifted. Just like that."

"Can't you remember what you saw? Something must've set you off."

Crumb shook his head. "I couldn't tell you. But it was like a red rag to a minotaur. Good job I got me some human blood in here as well, or you might've been brown bread."

"Brown bread?"

Crumb drew a dirty finger across his own throat, sticking his tongue out in a grisly manner. "Dead."

Max smiled. After the smorgasbord of monsters he had gone head-to-head with that day, one crotchety pawnbroker hardly put the chills in him. Still, it was best to humor the fellow while he was a guest.

"I don't mean to sound like a broken record, but can you help, Mr. Crumb? I've got nowhere else to turn."

The pawnbroker scratched his jaw as he considered the boy's plea. There was a twinkle in the man's eye that made Max feel uneasy. He let his hand drift over the flap of his messenger bag, within easy reach of its contents.

"You know, your predecessors have often proved a thorn in the side of monsterkind."

"Have I ever wronged you?"

"Not personally, boy, no. But Van Helsings have made the lives of many a misery. Who's to say you're not gonna take my head to mount on your wall one of these days? I bet there's no shortage of goblin skins in the family trophy cabinet, eh?"

"If there are, I've never seen them. Don't judge me on my forefathers, Mr. Crumb. The Van Helsings might be monster hunters, but I like to think of myself as a new branch of the family tree."

A noise outside made them both start—the clattering of a garbage can lid.

"Seems if I kicked you out of this shop right now, you wouldn't last too long. Some might say I'd be doing my fellow fiends a favor, letting the last of your lot snuff it."

Max managed to smile, even though his stomach was in knots. *Play it cool, Max*; that's what Jed would have said. He gingerly placed his mug on the glass counter. Out came the yo-yo, the boy spinning it nonchalantly as if he didn't have a care in the world. Jed had warned him about Crumb, said he couldn't be trusted. Had Max judged this terribly? Could he have gotten things so wrong?

"Some might say that helping me out tonight could put you forever in the Van Helsing good books. Might even earn you a Get Out of Jail Free card or two, insurance for any future misdemeanors." Max watched to see whether Crumb would take the bait.

Crumb smiled, eyes wide with interest. "Go on."

The yo-yo rose and fell from Max's open palm. "Know this. If you *don't* help me tonight, it won't bode well for you." Crumb's smile slipped. "Turn your back on me, set me out on the streets alone, and you're as good as killing me yourself."

The pawnbroker's face darkened now, his skin mottling around the eyes. "What's that supposed to mean?"

"You think I came here without telling anyone where I was?"

Max hadn't stopped for a moment to tell Syd or anyone else where he'd been headed, of course—this was a mega-bluff—but what other choice did he have? Jed's warnings now rang in his ears; it was that kind of impulsive hot-headedness that could get a monster hunter killed. Max crashed on.

"Jed may be missing, but my friends know I'm here. They'll be expecting to hear from me."

"Are you . . . threatening me, boy?"

Max snatched the yo-yo back into his hand, his gaze suddenly fixed upon the pawnbroker. "I could ask you the same thing, man."

Crumb's face was set, hard, and humorless, his goggle-eyes narrowed as he gauged the young visitor. Then the smile reappeared, and any menace dissipated. "What are we like, eh? A pair of silly sods, that's what," said Crumb, the jovial tone returning to his voice. "Come on, sup up. Have your brew, little fella."

Max ignored the mug on the jewelry counter. "Help me, Mr. Crumb. What's happening to me?"

"I don't know, young Maxwell, may my dear old mother rest in her pit. I'm as stumped as you."

"Then who *might* be able to help? Who's the wisest soul you know?"

Crumb considered the question for a moment. "Clay."

"Who's Clay?"

"There ain't nothing that happens above, or below, that he don't know about. He's as wise as the hills and as old as the earth itself."

Max felt hope soar in his heart, almost punching its way out of his chest. "Then you'll take me to this Clay?"

"One tiny problem with that, my lad. He lives in the Undercity."

"Ah," said Max. "Your definition of tiny is different from mine."

"You walk through the gates to the Undercity, you may as well ring a dinner bell and paint a target on your chest. No, young sir. You won't be going downstairs."

"Which leaves me where?"

"Heading home without any answers," said Crumb, making his way to the back door. "I can't help you, Master Maxwell. You're on your own, I'm afraid. And that includes facing whatever nasties come after you."

"You *have* to get me into the Undercity, Mr. Crumb. It's not just my life that hangs in the balance, nor Jed's."

"What are you saying?"

Max looked deep into the man's eyes. "Both worlds, upstairs and downstairs, are full of monsters who are fighting the urge to do monstrous things. Monsters who want to get along with folks. Monsters who are, at heart, good and honest souls. Like you, Mr. Crumb."

Crumb's face gave nothing away as Max's impassioned speech continued.

"If I'm gone, who will stand up against creatures that *aren't* fighting those urges? Who'll keep the real monsters in check? If hell on earth is what you're after, then that's how it begins . . ." Max stopped. If that didn't convince Crumb to help, he didn't know what else to say.

The pawnbroker ran a pasty hand over the alley door. He rapped his fingers against the timber and smiled. "Have you brought your Wellington boots in your purse?"

"Pardon me?" asked Max, patting his messenger bag.

Crumb's laugh was an unsavory gurgle as he patted the thick wood. "There are always alternatives to the front door, little fella."

NINETEEN

xxx

HEADING DOWNSTAIRS

Not for the first time that night, Max hurled. This one was a dry upchuck, since the remaining contents of his stomach had been evacuated three heaves ago. His eyes strained, leaking tears, as he leaned against the sewer wall. When his innards stopped contracting, he placed his forearm over his mouth, sucking at his bomber jacket sleeve as he tried to block out the stench.

Odious Crumb turned in the effluence ahead, looking back at the trailing boy. He kept his voice low, aware that the sound might carry through the labyrinth. "What's the matter, Master Maxwell? Ain't never crawled through a tunnel o' turds before?"

Max retched. "You have?"

Crumb kicked a boot through the foul river of feculence as merrily as a child skipping through puddles. "Used to play hide-and-seek in the sewers as a nipper. What harm did a bit of dookie ever do anyone?"

"Besides cholera and typhoid, nothing at all. Lead on, poopmeister."

Max fell in behind his half goblin guide, flashlight trained ahead, the pawnbroker cutting through the swamp in purposeful strides. Max followed in his wake, keeping his eyes fixed on Crumb's back instead of the filth he waded through. The man had kindly sold the boy a pair of second-hand fishing waders back in his shop; Crumb was helping Max out, no doubt about it, but clearly saw no harm in making a little profit along the way.

"You're sure you know where you're going?" Max asked, his voice muffled by his jacket sleeve. "We must have traveled miles!"

"Don't worry, lad. I'll get you to Clay."

Max felt more than a little anxious placing all his trust in the pawnbroker, but he was out of alternatives. Crumb was leading him down into a world where few Van Helsings had stepped, one that no doubt teemed with creatures hungry for Max's flesh. But every monster, big and small, vicious or harmless, was after him, and until he'd solved the mystery, no place—not even home—was safe.

Crumb turned off down a tributary, narrower than the main tunnel they'd been following. His fingers traced the uneven stones of the wall, picking at the lichen-covered brickwork. Occasionally, he would place a leathery ear to the uneven surface, even stopping to sniff at the air at intervals.

What he expected to smell over the stench, Max could only imagine.

"Please tell me your nose is broken," said Max, stifling a repeated urge to barf.

Crumb chuckled. "This nose works perfectly well, my lad. I've got my goblin genes to thank for my super schnoz."

"What is it you think you can smell? Reckon it's a crap-load of crap, with a hint of crap thrown in for good measure."

"Hard as it may be for you to believe, Master Maxwell, it's fresh air I'm sniffin'."

"Now I *know* you're kidding. We're going around in circles, and I'm running out of time, Mr. Crumb. You said you could lead me into the Undercity. No offense, but this looks like an ordinary sewer. Just like the last tunnel did. And the tunnel before that."

The half goblin placed a warty hand against a dark, grimy brick, one that looked just like any other. "O ye of little faith . . ."

Crumb pushed, and with a *hiss* and *clunk* the stone recessed into the wall. No sooner had the brick vanished than the whole tunnel shuddered. Beneath the foul water the ground trembled, almost dumping Max backward into the muck. He shone the flashlight on Crumb's grinning face.

"Hold on to your Wellingtons," said the pawnbroker.

The words had hardly left Crumb's lips before the tunnel floor opened up beneath them. Max let out a shriek as he, the half goblin, and five hundred gallons of sewage were deposited into a dark chute. Almost immediately the opening snapped shut above them with a clang. The teen-ager aimed his flashlight dead ahead as the drop became a slide, the pawnbroker a body's length ahead of him as they shot down the sloping tunnel. Within moments they were both crouching, riding the slurry-slick passage like demented snowboarders.

Hideous though the elements were, Max couldn't deny it was thrilling, rocketing headlong through the darkness, surfing a wave of poop. Crumb glanced back occasionally, the flashlight beam catching the fellow across his lumpy face. His flesh appeared a shade greener now, his eyes a bit bigger and more bulbous, his teeth a touch sharper. The deeper they went, the more his spine rose to form a knuckled ridge down his back. Crumb grinned. Max gulped.

"This is the Undercity?" cried Max. They had gradually left the tide of filth behind, but the pair still sped along. His feet slipped suddenly, his footwear losing traction along the tunnel floor, sending him into a slithery skid on his bottom. He accelerated past the pawnbroker, his flashlight arcing wildly over the tunnel walls.

Crumb chuckled. "This is a tunnel," he said, seizing Max by the strap of his messenger bag, the clawed fingers of his other hand gripping the passage wall and halting their descent. The satchel caught tight around the young monster hunter's chest, riding up and across his throat as he was jerked to a sudden, violent halt. The flashlight flew out of his hand, spinning through the air before him like a pinwheel firework. Instead of clattering off the tunnel floor or walls, it continued its trajectory out into the darkness, Max's eyes following its flight until it disappeared.

"That, my lad," said Crumb, "is the Undercity."

Max's vision slowly adjusted as an alien world blossomed into life. In the depths of a gargantuan cavern, myriad twinkling lights bloomed in the dark. Surrounded by a starless gloom, high in the vaults of the incredible abyss, it was hard to judge distance, but the cityscape must have been thousands of feet below. Great spires and towers rose all around, crowding each other as they aimed for the black heavens. Each was riddled with windows, lanterns, bonfires, and braziers, turrets and steeples jostling for dominance. Bridges spanned every empty space, crisscrossing over one another as they connected the suburban sprawl, the void beneath bottomless and impregnable. The sounds of the city were carried up toward Max on gusts of warm, pleasant air, a riotous cacophony of chaos, a maelstrom of music, merriment, and mayhem. He caught sight of the toes of his filthy rubber boots now, peeking over the edge of the sheer and deadly drop that Crumb had saved him from.

"But . . . it's *huge!*" said Max.

"What were you expecting? A shantytown? Three tents and a donkey?"

"I don't know, but not . . . this!"

"That's not just a city down there, Master Maxwell," said Crumb proudly, hauling the youth back from the brink and dusting him down. "That's a civilization."

Max looked along the edge of the ledge that they were

perched on, the path skirting the cavern's crooked wall like a crude gallery within a cathedral dome. His vertigo suddenly hit him like a bomb dropping. He was ground zero in an explosion of nausea that sent him to his knees.

"No, no," said Crumb, hauling him up. "You need to keep moving. You get spotted, you'll be in for it, remember?"

"But the city's down there," said Max. "There's nobody up here. Is there?"

Crumb extended a knob-knuckled finger, directing Max's gaze over the cliffs that surrounded them. The occasional pair of glowing eyes shone in the darkness.

"The Undercity may be below, but that don't mean there ain't life up here, in the Roof."

Max's eyes picked out silhouettes moving around the cavern, clinging to the sheer, jagged stone. "The Roof?"

"Aye. Not every monster can afford to live with their brethren downstairs. The Undercity's just like Gallows Hill. Up there, the filthy rich look down on us from their penthouse apartments. Well, it's the reverse here. The deeper you go, the pricier the rent. The Roof's home to the have-nots."

More eyes could be seen now, bioluminescent orbs like those one might find in the ocean depths. Max couldn't be sure, but it seemed their gazes were leveled at him. Hisses echoed around the Roof.

Crumb squeezed Max's arm. "We need to move. Now."

The path dropped and rose, cutting in and out as it weaved haphazardly around the cavern's walls. Max would have gladly crawled along that walkway, clutching on for

dear life, but Crumb would have none of it. The half goblin was running, his leathery hand keeping a firm hold of
the trailing teen. Above and below, Max heard grunts and
growls in the dark. He was aware of movements, shadowy
forms pursuing them around the walls, clinging to the Roof
like bats.

Suddenly they were out of the dizzying cavern, slipping
through a fissure in the rock face. A broad flight of uneven
steps had been carved out of the stone, sweeping up in a
curving flight. Were they being followed? The only thing he
was sure of was that they were directly above that nightmarish, never-ending cavern, the jagged stone roof directly
beneath their feet. Crumb kept a grip on Max as he scuttled
up the staircase.

"Um, shouldn't we be heading down into the Undercity?"
asked Max.

"No, lad," Crumb whispered back. "You're lucky Clay
lives up here. He's one of the Roof's oldest residents. There
are few who know more about the world of monsterkind,
and the comings and goings of the Undercity's residents. He
sees everything, Master Maxwell. He *feels* everything. If it
weren't for Clay, there'd be no Undercity."

"He's a founder of the Undercity? You said all the big-
wigs lived at the bottom of the abyss. How come he doesn't
live down there?"

"You'll see why, soon enough."

The pair ran out of the stairwell into a large, circular
chamber where tiny torches sputtered from sconces in the

damp, dripping walls. It appeared to be some kind of cross-roads in the tunnel networks, all routes intersecting around a broad central column of compacted earth and rock. The entire height of this enormous earthen stanchion was covered in phosphorescent fungi of all shapes and sizes. Max pulled free from Crumb's grip, causing the pawnbroker to spin about.

"Hang on one monstrous moment," said Max, a terrible thought dawning on him. "Every creature I've encountered since I turned thirteen has tried to take a piece of me. Why should this Clay be any different? Won't he try and eat me, too?"

"Unlikely," said Crumb, looking back over Max's shoulder down the dark stairs they'd exited. "He's likely to have his hands full."

"He can't drop what he's doing to smite the last of the Van Helsings? What kind of self-respecting monster does he think he is?"

The rumbling voice that sounded in the chamber was so deep it made Max's teeth rattle. "The kind who has outlived countless generations of your fragile ancestors!"

Max turned sharply to face the owner of the voice, expecting the newcomer to stride out of a tunnel mouth, but nobody appeared. Only shadows danced around the guttering torches.

"Who said that?" Max asked, splashing through puddles as he backed up to the chamber's mushroom-and-mildew-mottled central column.

The pawnbroker turned Max around, directing him toward the source of the voice. "That would be Clay."

Max looked up at the pillar of packed earth. At its narrowest point it had the girth of a giant redwood, before broadening as it rose to meet the ceiling. Great branches of earth rippled outward, spanning the entire chamber roof, each "limb" loaded with mud and rocks. These arms snaked through and around the column, finding their way to the ground before spreading out along the chamber floor. The pillar juddered, a ripple running through its body and sending tiny flakes of damp earth tumbling down its trunk. Starting at the column's heart, the strange fungi burst into color like tiny flowers, a vibrant red wave rippling toward its extremities. A dozen feet above Max's head, a ragged, craggy mouth appeared in the shuddering mass of mud, more moist soil falling as huge eyes broke open. Max faltered back a step, making out more humanoid features within the support now. It may have once had legs, but they seemed to be now entirely fused with the stone underfoot. However, those branches were clearly powerful, prodigious arms, holding the ceiling across its shoulders.

Max had never encountered one before, but he recognized the being from the *Monstrosi Bestiarum*: an earth elemental, as old as the world itself, should the legends be believed. They were guardians of the land, neither good nor evil, utterly neutral to the worlds that warred around them. There were other kinds of elementals, of course—those of

EARTH ELEMENTAL

ORIGIN:
Universal

STRENGTHS: Tremendous physical power, immune to energy assault and all nervous system attacks. Older earth elementals also known to have spellcasting ability.

WEAKNESS: Engaging an earth elemental in melee is strongly discouraged. One's only hope would be fire, which is extremely harmful to the entity.

HABITAT: Belowground, subterranean environments, surrounded by and sometimes buried beneath the earth.

All four principle classes of elemental—earth, fire, air, and water—predate humanity's existence and that of much of monsterkind. Their alignment is as varied as their appearance, although many remain neutral to mortal and monstrous struggles. Young earth elementals have the ability to pass through the earth, taking form through whatever mineral is at hand. It is only as they grow older that they assume a fixed form of choice.

—Erik Van Helsing, October 3rd, 1853

PHYSICAL TRAITS

1. _Size_—Earth Elementals are enormous creatures, constructed of earth, soil, sand, and rock. Their scale should be enough to scare off even the most adventurous—and foolhardy—monster hunter.

2. _Limbs_—Arms and legs can be innumerate, although many assume the form of man.

3. _Armor_—Solid packed earth makes them near indestructible. If one is set upon a fight, don't come to the dance with a sword or bow . . .

—Esme Van Helsing, April 1st, 1867

There is a gargantuan horror beneath Gallows Hill which holds thrall over the inhabitants of the Undercity. Hidden in the darkness within the bowels of the earth, it pulls the strings of its monstrous minions, directing them into the daylight where they cause murder and mayhem. This Earth Elemental is evil, I can feel it in my bones . . .

—Algernon Van Helsing, Feb 12th, 1937

You've been WRONG before now, GRANDPA!! Let's not be hasty . . .

MAX HELSING   June 19th, 2015

air, fire, and water—each charged with protecting its own sphere of power.

There were no notes in the monster manual that dealt with how to dispatch such an entity. Max prayed he wouldn't have to find out. The monstrous column snorted, nostrils flaring as plumes of dust billowed over Max and his guide, making them cough fitfully.

"Speak fast, little human," said the column of earth. "Your enemies approach in swift and terrible number."

Max glanced back, half expecting a monstrous mob to appear at any moment. He looked up at the giant of soil and stone. "My friend said you could help me, Mr. Clay. Can you?"

"Friend?" The earth elemental chuckled. "You have friends now, Odious? It would appear those upstairs are more accepting of your . . . improprieties than your brethren in the Undercity."

Max wasn't sure what the creature meant by this, but he caught the pawnbroker's shamefaced glare. It seemed the half goblin's checkered past might have chased him into the human world at some point in time.

"Odious Crumb has helped me," said Max, drawing the monolith's attention. "For that, I judge him a friend. Whatever he's done in the past can remain there."

The earth elemental hummed, the noise reverberating through Max's rib cage. "You're confident, Van Helsing. Then again, your kind always were."

"You *know* me?"

"The Mark is something of a giveaway, child."

Max did a double take. "You can *see* this . . . this *Mark*? But you're not attacking me. What gives?"

The ancient giant's eyes rolled up toward the ceiling. "As Odious mentioned when you arrived here moments ago, I'm somewhat preoccupied. Even if I weren't, I would not attack you, little hunter."

"Then you're the first monster that hasn't since I turned thirteen."

"I am compelled to do nothing, child. I act of my own free will. Some magic is older and more potent than that which burns upon you."

"Burns upon me? You're speaking in riddles, Mr. Clay."

The earth elemental smiled. "Clay will suffice, Van Helsing. Now let me explain." The sentinel's mouth puckered up, crumbling lips pursing as if it might blow Max a kiss. Instead, a sparkling cloud of superfine dust erupted, showering the boy. The strange soil found its way into his airways, through his mouth, up his nose, and down his throat. Tiny particles of earth, stone, and silver swirled around the teenage monster hunter, whirling about him until the darkness turned into a blurred, blinding light.

TWENTY

xxx

THE WITCHES OF GALLOWS HILL

Max was lost. The world was insubstantial, ethereal; he couldn't tell up from down. He held his hands before him, tried to focus on them, but there was nothing. Trying to clasp them together was no easier—his invisible limbs passed through one another, unable to connect. He had no body, no ground to connect with. He was mist caught in a cloud. The last thing he remembered was the earth elemental and the bizarro breath bomb it had launched in his face. Panic rose within him.

Before he lost his mind entirely, ghostly shapes began forming in the white expanse of nothingness. Indistinct lines shimmered into life, transforming gradually into huge lengths of timber. These dark wooden struts connected with one another, forming the boards, beams, and eaves of a vast roof. The building grew around him, walls of stone taking shape as they materialized out of thin air. A bell tolled, dim and distant.

Church. All Saints. Fallen Saints . . .

Pews beneath him, rows of benches with people sitting upon them, a sea of bowed heads. Black dresses and coats, white aprons and bonnets. Puritans. A man stood within a pulpit before his congregation, flailing fists, gnashing teeth, castigating his flock. Fear and accusation. Fire and brimstone.

Clay's voice, in Max's ear.

"Gallows Hill, 1692. All Saints Church. The Reverend Udo Vendemeier, a holy man of Dutch descent, assumes stewardship of this tiny parish."

The preacher's name instantly set Max's nerves jangling, Helsey sense tingling.

"You see the congregation, Van Helsing? These are good people. Honest people. Hardworking and God-fearing people. They listen to the reverend. To his words. To his claims. To his commands."

Max heard the screams now as one woman rose from the pews below, men seizing her and dragging her toward the church doors. The reverend pointed all the while, the good book shaking in his other hand, held high over his head.

"What are they doing?" Max asked, but the elemental ignored him as the scene changed below.

"She was the first. Many others followed. Vendemeier's words are not questioned."

More figures vanished from the congregation below, as the voice of the boy's companion rumbled through him. Still the preacher ranted and raved, his bony finger picking out women among the thinning crowd. No sooner would that crooked digit fix upon a soul than the damned one would burst into a swirl of black smoke, dissipating where she sat.

"Awful words," said the elemental. "Words of damnation. Words of death."

"He accused them all of being witches?"

"Twenty-seven women were hanged during Vendemeier's tenure at All Saints Church, their bodies tossed into the Witch River marshes."

Twenty-seven? Max knew of Massachusetts's grisly past, the witch trials having spread across the state. Salem had most famously captured the imagination of schoolchildren and tourists down the ages, reveling in its terrible history. Twenty had been executed there. But twenty-seven, here in Gallows Hill? He'd never heard that number before. And now those horrors were being played out before him in some nightmarish vision.

"I don't understand," he continued. "Why didn't somebody stand up to him?"

"One did, eventually. A stranger came to Gallows Hill, following Udo Vendemeier here from the old country. This traveler exposed him for what he was, a charlatan and killer. Vendemeier was a holy man, but no man of any god a good soul would ever worship. The women, and the anguish and sorrow that shrouded their wrongful deaths, were like nectar to the warlock. They were offerings. Vendemeier was a high priest of Hastur, the King in Yellow, an ancient deity spawned during mankind's birth."

Max felt the elemental's voice in his head, could taste soil in his mouth as if he were buried alive.

"The God of Vampires, Van Helsing."

Max shivered. That familiar old word, so often associated with his family through the ages, ran an icy dagger down his spine.

"Who was the man who took him out? This stranger?"

A chuckle. "Not a man. Her name was Liesbeth."

"Liesbeth Van Helsing," said Max.

He knew the name well enough. She was the first Van Helsing to come to the New World, a trailblazer in every way. Liesbeth took the fight to the very heart of evil. A vampire killer of great renown, her personal crusade was against those who wronged women, a life's mission that often took her away from the world of the supernatural and into the seedy heart of humanity.

Below, the scene changed, a cloaked figure standing among the congregation, pointing a staff at the preacher. Men seized the ranting reverend from his pulpit, dragging him screaming, cursing, down the pathway between the pews. Max could have sworn Vendemeier was looking up at him as the mob half carried him out. The church vanished, replaced by tombstones and trees, bare branches speeding by beneath him, the wicked reverend still yelling obscenities up into the heavens. At Max.

"He was taken to the place of his own handiwork," said Clay.

Suddenly, Vendemeier was hauled upright, kicking and struggling, lashing out at his captors as a rope was thrown over the buckled bough of an enormous, crooked tree. The stranger stood before him, her arms crossed over her chest as the mob went to work beneath a full moon. The *preacher's mouth worked feverish and fast as the noose was looped around his neck, the language unrecognizable to all but the stranger.*

"Liesbeth Van Helsing caught every word of that ancient language, heard every foul promise in the warlock's curse. Vendemeier made a promise that night, child. One that would not be fulfilled until the sun set on your thirteenth year."

The mob hauled on the rope as Vendemeier rose into the air. Fire enveloped Max, blinding him, swallowing the gallows, the mob, the warlock, and the moon itself. Max was devoured by the bright light once more.

MAX CHOKED WHERE HE STOOD BEFORE COLLAPSING into Crumb's arms. The pawnbroker shoved his filthy fingers into the boy's mouth, scooping out soil. Max hacked and spluttered as the half goblin clapped the youth's back. Out came the clumps of earth, caught there during the elemental's arcane ceremony. Suddenly, Max could breathe once more, Crumb brushing the sparkling soil off the boy's face and clothes.

"What is it?" whispered Crumb. "What did you see?"

Max pulled free of the half goblin's embrace, turning to face the earth elemental. "Vendemeier's curse. I heard him make it to Liesbeth's face. What did it mean?"

"Look into the pool before me, child," said Clay, his eyes lowered toward the chamber's largest, murkiest puddle. Max shuffled forward, stopping at the pool's edge. He leaned forward, craning his neck to look down. His reflection peered back, shimmering as the ripples played across the puddle.

"This is what *we* see," rumbled Clay.

Max gasped. A halo of fire suddenly sprang to life upon his head, a crown of flames that snapped and crackled. Max turned his head, the fire following each movement. He reached his hand up, fingers gingerly touching the blazing circlet, but he felt no heat or pain.

"What does it mean?" asked Max, pulling his eyes away from the watery mirror and back to the earth elemental.

"The curse translates as 'Bane of Monsters' in your tongue," said Clay. "The Mark is invisible to the human eye, but every being you encounter outside the world of man shall see you for what you are: a monster hunter. Not only will you be exposed in such a fashion, but upon seeing the Mark for the first time, each monster you encounter will return to its most primal, base instinct: to kill. Even those you might consider your friends or allies."

Max turned to Crumb, who shrugged apologetically as Clay continued.

"You're Marked for death, Van Helsing."

"Tell me something I didn't know," muttered the teenager.

"Very well," replied Clay. Earth elementals didn't do sarcasm, it appeared. "Vendemeier's curse was answered by his god, Hastur."

"How?"

"On the thirteenth birthday of Liesbeth's thirteenth descendent, Udo Vendemeier would return. The child would receive the Mark, leading to his or her swift and bloody death by Vendemeier's hand. This death would trigger the Age of Unlight."

"The what now?" asked Max, trying to keep up with the tale of his twisted family tree.

"Age of Unlight," whispered Crumb, dropping to his knees as if winded. His green face was drained of color, as if it was his turn to hurl. Screeches suddenly sounded from the stairwell at their backs.

"There is a balance in both worlds at present, child. The scales tip back and forth in favor of good or evil, be it human or monstrous. But somehow, the scales are always righted. The Van Helsings have played their part in keeping this balance in order. On occasion, your forefathers have strayed down dark and bloody paths, their zealous crusades getting the better of them, but they've always returned from the brink. And now you—more than any of your kin—have tried to police that gray space between the worlds, the veil where monsters and humans mingle. You are admired by many, child."

"Good to know. So does that help me out here?"

"No."

"Bummer."

"Upon your death, that troubled history of humans versus monsters will become quite irrelevant. The Age of Unlight will see the sun choked from the sky and the emergence of the foulest fiends any world has known. They will not be content feeding upon the flesh of humankind. Monsters shall face the same fate. Every living being above and below will provide sustenance for this greatest, most ancient evil. Hastur himself shall rise again, to sit upon his throne of blood. The vampires will hold dominion over all."

"If I die, Hastur rises?"

The giant rumbled. "The King in Yellow may be risen already. He has been hidden for centuries, all of Vendemeier's work supposedly leading toward Hastur's summoning. Come the Age of Unlight, his vampires will be able to flood the earth, unhindered by the light of day. Your death would bring about an endless night."

"Okay," said Max, clicking his fingers. "So we need to keep me breathing, yeah?"

"In an ideal world, yes," said the earth elemental, "but that may prove difficult. Your Mark—"

"My Mark, yeah, I get that," said Max. "So how do I get rid of it? I'm assuming if I lose the hot hat, then the whole of monsterkind might stop trying to kill me."

"There's only one way of removing the Bane of Monsters," said Clay. "You must destroy Vendemeier."

Max slapped a hand over his face and dragged it down. "But he's *already dead*. How do I destroy a guy who was hanged over three centuries ago?"

"The preacher was a warlock, remember?"

188 × CURTIS JOBLING

"A male witch," added Crumb. "Unlike those poor women, he was the real deal!"

Clay rumbled before continuing. "His powers are staggering, well beyond those of his peers. His physical form may have been destroyed that night by Liesbeth Van Helsing and the people of Gallows Hill, but his spirit lived on. The man you encountered in the ruined church—"

"Of course! The security guard! The note he left when he snatched Jed. Udo Vendemeier would be the *UV*, right?"

"Correct. The guard is dead. His body is a shell that Vendemeier occupies."

"Okay, so the guard has to die. Again."

Even as he said it, Max could hear how ridiculous it sounded. More cries sounded from the tunnels behind them, causing Max to begin rummaging in his messenger bag.

"For the world's sake, I wish it were so simple, Van Helsing." Another tremor passed through Clay's body, causing clumps of damp earth to fall from the elemental's torso and mighty limbs. The fungi glowed once more, the red lights fluttering within their pale flesh. "Vendemeier's power comes from his own rotten heart, not the dead one that rests within the corpse he commands. You can break him, burn him, chop bits off him. But you won't kill him. And if that body fails him, he will find another. The preacher's heart is the key. Effectively, he is immortal so long as it remains intact. You destroy that, you destroy the curse. The heart's destruction will also make him vulnerable to harm, even in spirit form. You just need to catch him before he finds another host."

"So where will his corpse be?" asked Max. "The original one that was strung up from the Hanging Tree?"

"Perhaps you can consider its whereabouts as you run," said Clay.

"But Clay, there are still so many questions I want to ask you!"

"Regardless, you should be running."

"Running?"

"Run!" boomed the earth elemental as the first wave of monsters spilled forth from the dark and twisting tunnels. They came in a rolling, roaring, snapping mass, tooth and claw tearing at the air as they charged at the boy with the crown of flames.

Max ran.

TWENTY-ONE

xxx

THE TIDE OF TERROR

If the horde that erupted into Clay's cave had expected an all-you-can-eat Van Helsing buffet, they were in for a sorry shock. The first thing they caught was a pair of flash bangs launched into their midst. The smoke grenades, part of a bulk buy from an army surplus store, were billowing gray clouds before they even landed, swallowing the mob in a heartbeat. The second thing they caught was a shattering glass jar, as a hundred marbles bounced across the floor beneath their feet. It was old school for sure, but Max had always been a sucker for *Home Alone.* And besides, the marbles worked. The beasties went down in a screeching heap of thrashing limbs. The third and final thing they caught— those who'd evaded the smoke bombs and the marbles— was the sight of Max's skinny butt sprinting for a tunnel, away from the trailing terrors.

He paused to glance back, catching sight of Odious

Crumb tackling a group of the creatures to the ground. Short though he was, they were half his size, their skin a dark scaly green: kobolds. In folklore, they were known as mischievous sprites that could be helpful or hindering. In truth, they were a world away from that playful picture. Consummate carnivores and occasional cannibals, they were never happier than when chomping on raw meat. Max suspected they'd have no problem if that meat came from a certain young monster hunter. In fact, judging by their current state of frenzy, he was at the top of their menu.

"Get gone!" shouted Crumb as he went down beneath a scrum of the monsters, buying the boy a few more moments, hopefully not with his life. One of the kobolds looked up from atop the pile, its disklike yellow eyes widening as it saw Max. It snarled, leaping off the pawnbroker, followed by more of its kin.

"Run!" boomed Clay once more, the whole chamber shaking as a large pack of monsters bounded forward toward Max. Earth and stone fell from the cave's ceiling as the elemental bellowed, showering down on the charging line of kobolds and quickly burying them. But even with Crumb's sacrifice and Clay's clever avalanche, more of the lizard-skinned beasts kept coming, bounding over their fallen comrades as they leaped toward the teenager.

Sprinting, Max took the tunnel with a trickling stream that found its way into the earth elemental's cavern. He hoped if he followed a passage that ascended, it must lead back aboveground eventually. Of course, this was the

KOBOLD

OTHER ALIASES: Galgenmännlein, Heinzelmännchen, Klabautermann

ORIGIN: Germany

STRENGTHS: Infravision, strength in numbers means they swarm when they attack.

WEAKNESS: Bright light can harm them, while their penchant for gold and gems can also make them lose all reason.

HABITAT: Subterranean tunnels, mines, and caves.

PHYSICAL TRAITS

1. _Hands_—Although kobolds are adept at using tools, their shovel-like hands can break up the toughest rock-faces. Remember to wear armor if engaging these foul creatures in combat.

2. _Teeth_—The piranha of the monster kingdom, a hungry kobold can strip flesh from the bone within seconds.

3. _Vision_—Bulging, pale orbs allow the kobold to see in total darkness, invaluable considering the time they spend in the grimmest, bleakest corners of the Undercity.

—Esme Van Helsing, July 12th, 1865

There are varied descriptions of kobolds throughout history, some depicting them as helpful or playful house spirits that carry out domestic tasks for their human masters. These are anomalies, if true. Kobolds are cruel, self-serving creatures. Like gnomes, they crave gems and ores, and within monster society there are few better miners. They are known to abduct lone humans via cunning contraptions. Another feature rarely depicted in folk tales is the kobold's incredible appetite for flesh. We have fellow hunters the Brothers Grimm to thank for extensive cataloguing of kobold activity across Europe.

—Erik Van Helsing, July 3rd, 1858

Should the hunt draw you into those depths of the Undercity, beware the kobold. A greedier goblin I've yet to encounter, with a terrible craving for man-flesh. Many sewer workers have been abducted by these monsters during tunnelling work around Boston. I was hired to find the nest—the nest is no more. Dynamite is a most effective pest control.

—Algernon Van Helsing, Oct 2nd, 1940

OLD SCHOOL, GRANDPA!!
Nuke it from ORBIT: it's
the ONLY way to be sure!

MAX HELSING
Jan 7th, 2015

Undercity, a land rich with magic, and the same rules from back home might not apply, but the young monster hunter pushed aside his worries. Climb. That's all he had to do.

The kobolds might have been the size of second graders, but they were fast, easily keeping pace with Max. The torches that had lit up Clay's cave were behind him now, leaving the youth charging blindly into darkness. He cursed himself for having lost his flashlight while overlooking the Undercity. As he ran, he fished a hand into his satchel, at last finding what he needed. Out it came, and with a snap, the high-intensity glow stick cast its white light around him. He held it out as he ran, dizzying shadows dancing off the tunnel walls. The mob was hot on his heels, snarling and snapping as they gave chase.

Max regretted wearing the massive rubber waders. Effective as they might have been for stopping Gallows Hill's effluence from clogging his toes, they did nothing for his running style. His gait had changed from agile scamper to flat-footed galumphing, throwing his limbs out with each clumsy step. The tunnel abruptly split ahead, leaving Max with a millisecond to make up his mind. Pink eyes the size of dinner plates flashed in the right-hand tunnel, and the choice suddenly became easy. Taking the left fork, he didn't wait to see the owner of the giant eyes, but he heard its growls as it joined the pack of kobolds.

The distant rumbles from Clay's cavern were far behind, as were the cries of Crumb. He hoped the half goblin was okay. Whatever Jed and Clay had thought of the pawnbroker, perhaps they'd been wrong. If he survived the swarm of kobolds, Max owed him a favor. That was if the world didn't end, of course.

The tunnel was rougher underfoot now. Max stumbled, slowing down to avoid a broken ankle, leg, or neck, possibly a combo of all three. His heart was galloping, his muscles burning as he powered into a second wind. By all rights, he should have collapsed by now, after the day and night he'd endured, but somehow he found those energy reserves that set him and his forefathers apart from the norms. Not for the first time, Max thought of the phrase "touched by magic," so often used to describe the Van Helsings; after lifetimes spent within the supernatural world, had some of that unearthly essence actually found its way into their bloodline?

The incline was steep, and Max occasionally had to scrabble for purchase with his hands. Ahead he could see a narrow, jagged slit of illumination cutting the darkness in two. As he neared he saw a crack in the rock, the walls closing in on either side of him. Beyond the narrow opening was a light source. He tossed the glow stick back down the sloping tunnel he'd ascended, spying exactly what was on his heels.

The luminous bar bounced off the floor and into the air, casting white light over a dozen angry kobolds. It struck one on the head before ricocheting off the back of another. The former reached out, snatching it from the air triumphantly as if it were a trophy. His victory was short-lived, the larger beast from the other tunnel emerging from the kobolds' midst, huge jaws snapping down over the kobold's arm, enveloping the glow stick. The light was snuffed out instantly, accompanied by the smaller monster's screams.

Max hit the gap, brushing against the rough walls as they drew in around him. He kept his eyes fixed ahead, ignoring the kobolds, so close now. He turned sideways, wincing as one jagged stone scored him across the chest, his right hand reaching forward to seize *something* and pull himself through. As if the width of the fissure wasn't enough of a challenge, now the ceiling started closing in, causing him to catch his head on an overhanging spur of rock. Max fell forward, momentarily stunned as he bumped off the walls before hitting the floor.

The snarls were almost on top of him now, the higher-pitched cries of the kobolds joined by those of the larger beast. Max tried to move but found himself snagged by his satchel, the strap bound around something. He reached back, fumbling in the darkness, finding the bag's opening. He stuck his hand in, grabbing another glow stick. Max whacked it against the rock wall, the chemicals within reacting instantly and casting a white aura over the thin ravine.

"You have *got* to be kidding!"

The bag was caught on a stalagmite, leaving Max no option but to retreat back down the passageway to free himself. The glow stick also lit up the bigger beast in all its glory: a giant rat the size of a grizzly. Its enormous jaws slavered open, a long black tongue flickering as it crammed its head into the tunnel. Dark blood swilled around inside its maw, the remains of the hapless kobold's severed arm caught between its teeth. Those incisors were already closing down on Max's foot, cutting like daggers as they ripped into his wader. He half-expected to feel them shear the appendage off, but instead they held fast, buried within the rubber boot. The beast yanked him back a foot, effectively releasing him from the stalagmite. Max might have cheered, if it weren't for the fact that it was hauling him back toward the kobold-filled tunnel, where he was destined to be torn to pieces. It shook its head like a dog with a bone, big pink eyes focused on Max all the while.

"Sucks to be you," said Max as he lunged toward the giant rodent with the glow stick, striking at the monster's immense head. The end of the stick connected with the rat's massive pink eyeball, embedding itself deep into the socket. Max let go of his grip on the stick as the enormous rodent released its jaws from his leg. The hideous sewer dweller thrashed and wailed, backing away from the boy as it retreated half-blind to the main tunnel. Max slithered free, continuing on through the narrow passage, unexpectedly thanking his lucky stars for the waders.

Max wriggled the remaining distance through the cramped ravine, until he emerged into a larger, more spacious tunnel. He tumbled forward, rolling over rails that ran in either direction. Cables and control boxes covered the curving walls. He'd somehow stumbled upon the T subway system, but whereabouts he had no idea. Was the Undercity truly so big that it stretched from Gallows Hill to Boston? Still, this had to be a good thing; it was bringing him that much nearer to the surface world. Glancing in one direction, he spied a solitary light a few hundred feet away, its bulb glowing dimly within its protective fixture. He set off jogging toward it.

Judging by the garbage that littered the tracks, the tunnel was clearly out of use. Indeed, as he approached the dim light, he could see it came from an abandoned subway station, the platform's edge looming into view at head height. Cries behind told Max all he needed to know about his chasing fan club of fang and claw. He spied a tiny iron ladder, hidden below the concrete platform lip about halfway along its length. He loped toward it, the awkward boots slapping noisily against the concrete sleepers between the rails. Crashing into the metal rungs, he clambered up onto the platform, glancing back all the while. The darkness was filled with the chattering of beasties.

Turning full circle, Max looked around the dimly lit station. It was out of use like the tunnel, but at its far end he spied the faint outline of a grilled security door. Another light shone beyond it, illuminating a flight of stairs. Max could almost smell the fresh air, so close was he to freedom. He staggered along, noticing that the tracks on the opposite side of the platform were in fine condition, the other line clearly still in use. Hitting the grille with a clang, Max yanked at it, trying to pull it open. The mechanism groaned, refusing to shift. The end of a long wooden plank had some- how pinned itself against the base of the rusted steel gate, the other end wedged into a step. Max reached through, unable to knock the timber loose. More guttural cries behind only served to make him let loose a cuss that would've made a sailor blush. On the steps, he saw a pile of rubbish suddenly move. There was someone there, resting among the junk; a homeless person. The stranger turned the hood of a filthy parka Max's way.

"Hey!" cried Max. "You can't imagine how happy I am to see someone down here. Do a kid a massive solid and pull that plank loose, would ya?"

He gestured to the length of timber, and the homeless person appeared to understand, shambling down the steps toward Max. The young monster hunter felt his heart soar— saved by the kindness of a stranger! The figure bounced into the grille upon reaching the bottom, causing the whole thing to rattle noisily. Max's smile of relief turned to a gri- mace as a handful of pale, suckered tentacles, each a good foot long, whipped out from within the hood, straining through the iron bars to lash out at the teenager.

"What are the odds?" Max muttered wearily, as the crea- ture in the stairwell dragged the plank clear, keen to open the gate for altogether more selfish reasons.

There was nowhere left to turn; the only unexplored route was the line on the opposite platform. Max scurried across, boots making such resounding thwacks upon the concrete, they could have pinpointed his position to a deaf

LURKER

AKA: squidhead, schattenjäger
ORIGIN: Germany

STRENGTHS: Silent, stealthy, blessed with exceptional vision.

WEAKNESS: Aversion to bright light. ③

HABITAT: On the edges of human civilization, in the dark places and below ground.

④

PHYSICAL TRAITS

1. _Hands_—Webbing between fingers is flexible, often used to smother and suffocate the mouths of their victims.

2. _Feet_—Broad and frog-like, they allow lurkers to tread near-silently, helping them to move without detection and strike without sound.

3. _Vision_—Four eyes is the norm for lurkers, although older beasts have been known to grow additional sets. This allows them near 360 degree vision, making it awfully hard to stalk them.

4. _Tentacles_—Fleshy tendrils coated with suckers. Tiny circular teeth line these limpet-like rings, able to cut the flesh and drain the blood of its victims.

—Esme Van Helsing, June 22nd, 1862

① ②

The lurker found its way to the New World along with many other monsters from Europe, hidden in the hulls of those first settler ships. While many creatures could pose as humans, the squid-headed "schattenjäger" (shadow-hunter) had no such disguise. Unable to integrate with humanity, the lurkers found allies in the Undercity, serving the fey folk as watchers in the darkness. Distant cousins of the deep ones, sea-dwelling creatures that inhabit the waters off the east coast of the United States, lurkers worship many of the Old Gods, pagan deities from other dimensions. Used by denizens of the Undercity as guards, spies, sentinels, and hired killers.

—Erik Van Helsing, May 23rd, 1856

If they're anything like DEEP ONES I'm gonna give them a wide berth! FISH PEOPLE and TENTACLED GODS ain't for me!!

MAX HELSING Sep 30th, 2014

dreikelwyrm in Düsseldorf. Seeing no sign of a subway train, he slipped over the edge. Fishing in his backpack, he found the last of his glow sticks, wishing to high heaven he'd brought more of them instead of garlic bulbs and holy water. With a snap, the rails were illuminated. All three of them: two for the train to ride along, a third to carry a death-dealing charge of electricity. Max never let that third rail out of sight as he jogged down the tunnel, keeping a respectful distance while looking out for any oncoming trains.

"Living the dream," Max whispered, as he ran headlong through his nightmare.

He heard the kobolds spilling over the platform and down onto the tracks. Max had hoped to see the whole pack of them electrocuted by the live rail, skeletons lit up like they'd stepped straight out of *Tom and Jerry*, but no such luck. They had clearly encountered the subway tunnels before. Max fished his phone out of his pocket, its display lighting up to reveal the time as two a.m. A blessing that it was so late, as trains would be running on a limited service, if at all. Still no signal, though, since he was too far below-ground. It wasn't like he could call 911 for help. *What's my emergency? I'm being chased by a swarm of flesh-hungry monsters down a subway track. Sure, we'll be right with you . . .*

Max was so lost in his misery that he almost missed the maintenance chute. He tripped, narrowly avoiding that dreaded third rail, as he hoisted the glow stick over his head. Fifteen feet above the tracks, there was a square opening in the tunnel ceiling where filthy rungs protruded from crumbling red bricks. No doubt it had once served as an access route for engineers and rail workers, back in a less safety-conscious era. Max didn't have a prayer of jumping for it from below, but there were a number of rickety-looking, rusted rungs that still remained secured to the walls.

He climbed the first few as fast as he could, getting ten feet off the ground before he got into a fix. At one time, a safety cage had surrounded this ladder, providing anyone traversing it peace of mind as they climbed. But this had been removed long ago when the tunnels were modernized. Instead, Max now faced four feet of monkey bars before he could haul himself up into the maintenance chute proper.

"No time like the present."

Max tucked the glow stick into his butt pocket before flinging an arm out and trusting his agility. He tried to ignore the sound of the approaching kobolds, concentrating on the task at hand. His fingers reached out once more, just as the first monster appeared below. It leaped up, fortunately out of reach, but it was enough to throw Max off his game. He missed the bar, which sent him swinging back toward the first rail. Max grunted, both hands closing around the rung he was on. With a twist of his hips, he got his body going once more, kicking back off the wall behind him as more creatures gathered below. He caught the next bar, stifling a squeal of joy, carrying himself forward to the final bar beneath the access chute. Some of the kobolds were scurrying up the wall behind him, following the path he'd taken, only to find that when they reached the monkey bar portion their limbs were woefully short. They leaped out, hoping to catch the rungs, before catching only air and bouncing onto the tracks and their fellows below.

"Ha!" yelled Max triumphantly. "How d'ya like them apples, you midget maniacs?"

He instantly regretted gloating. Old Tentacle-Face from the station staircase had joined the melee, standing beneath the chute like a makeshift climbing frame as the kobolds crawled and clambered over him. The first kobold leaped up from the swaying tower, his claws barely missing the rubber sole of Max's wading boots. The boy raised his feet in the air, straining with his left hand to reach the first rung up in the chute. His fingers closed around it, affording him the chance to reach for the next one with his right. His left knee came up, followed by his right, and soon he was squirming up the square chute, hands and feet finding the flaking iron rails. His head banged into what appeared to be a manhole cover.

"Shenanigans!" he screamed, convinced the world conspired against him.

He looked below, the light from his rear pants pocket shining down upon the pile of tooth and talon. The kobolds were almost upon him now, the first ones clawing at his feet. He kicked down, catching one in the jaw and sending it tumbling, only for it to be replaced by two more. Again, his heel went down, but another seized hold, biting down on the boot's toe cap. Max hammered at the heavy metal cover above, shouting for help, while shaking his foot vigorously to loosen the kobold. It wasn't happening. Instead, a second monster clamped onto his other foot.

With all the commotion, the glow stick popped free from the pocket of his jeans, bouncing off the head of the first attached kobold before tumbling past. Max watched its descent, skittering off half a dozen of the foul-tempered fiends, and lighting them up as it fell to the tracks. When it finally landed on the sleepers, it rocked to a halt, throwing its unnatural light over the baying troop of kobolds. Somewhere within the throng was Old Tentacle-Face, playing his part in the hunt for a Van Helsing. Strangely, the glow from the fluorescent stick was far greater than Max would have expected, and seemed to be growing in intensity.

That was when he heard it, above the frantic, fevered cries of the mob. The mass of bodies was suddenly blinded by light as the approaching train raced toward them down the subway tunnel. Max watched as the tower of monsters was skittled by the front carriage, smashed into bloody smithereens, five of the kobolds left hanging from his legs as the train hurtled by below. The remaining cave dwellers were now clinging to the youth for their lives. Max could feel his grip slipping above, their weight too much for him.

He kicked his heels, wriggling his way out of the clumsy rain boots. Seeing what he was doing, the creatures tried to climb over one another to seize hold of his jeans, his belt, anything that wasn't going to come loose from his person. Their plight was in vain. One after the other, the pair of battered, stinky, ripped-up rubber waders slid from Max's feet, depositing the wailing killers down on the speeding train cars below, which carried them swiftly away into the darkness. The train was still rattling past when Max felt hands seize hold of him, lifting him up and out of the maintenance chute and depositing him back onto solid ground.

Max found himself in the middle of a cobbled road in downtown Boston. The avenue was empty but for the confused-looking street cleaner who stood over him, scratching his head and gawping at the boy. The man's vehicle idled beside the open subway shaft, its little orange light twirling merrily atop its cab, the driver oblivious to the chaos that had occurred belowground. Max stared at his socked feet, twiddling the toes to check they were all there. Not even a scratch. Rubber wading boots were definitely a *good* thing.

The service worker glanced down the maintenance shaft as the train finished passing by below. Max saw the manhole cover, and gave it a quick, firm shove with both hands to slide it across the cobbles and back over the hatch. It dropped into place with a *clang*, as an exhausted, foul-smelling, feculence-coated Max looked up at his bewildered rescuer.

"Any chance I could get a ride home?" he asked, flicking a glob of grossness from the back of his hand. "It's way past my bedtime."

TWENTY-TWO

xxx

THE MENTOR AND THE MONSTER

Udo Vendemeier stood over the sarcophagus and rubbed his hands together. It was a clumsy action, twisted and broken fingers catching against one another, but he was in a giddy, delighted mood. A great slab of crumbling brickwork straddled the ornate coffin's lid, torn from the wall of the tiny room. Beside it a wrought-iron candelabra stood, its candles dripping hot wax onto the ancient wood. A leather wallet lay open beneath it, its contents spilled out across its surface. There were paper notes and shiny coins that bore the faces of a host of noblemen, so-called presidents of these United States of America. Dead and gone, just like the warlock's mortal form. There were the strangest portraits of the Van Helsing boy on tiny rectangles of starched paper. It was as if his face had been captured in painted form, so real one could imagine his soul was trapped within them. And there was a hard yet pliable card with another portrait upon it, this of the old man, surrounded by barely intelligible text that suggested it was some kind of license. Jed Coolidge was the fellow's name, and he was Vendemeier's to toy with. He rapped his knuckles on the sarcophagus lid.

"Are you awake in there, Mr. Coolidge? You sleep like the dead. Wake up!"

He struck the Egyptian coffin with a fist, causing the occupant within to clatter about in a startled panic. Vendemeier couldn't help but laugh. It was good to have company, even if his guest happened to be an ally of his sworn enemies. The warlock wasn't alone in his lair, of course. He had another in his service, just like the gargoyle before the Van Helsing boy had reduced it to dust. However, conversations were understandably in short supply, considering his new henchman's unusual condition. In Coolidge, he now had an intelligent mind to spar with, to explore, to torment.

"I'm going to remove your lid, old man. Are you prepared to play nice?"

Coolidge didn't reply.

"I'll take that as a yes," said Vendemeier.

The warlock gingerly lifted the candelabra and placed it on the ground beside his feet. Then he put his weight behind the huge piece of broken masonry and shoved, sending it off the sarcophagus and crashing to the floor. Brushing the wallet and its contents to one side, he placed the palms of his cold hands against the lid's edge. He shoved hard, sliding it to one side, where it followed the rubble to the ground with an almighty clatter. No sooner was it open than Coolidge was springing bolt upright, heading straight for his captor. In his hand he held a wooden stake, torn from the inside of the sarcophagus lid, which he plunged deep into the warlock's chest, hitting the sweet spot for any vampire hunter. He drove it home with all the might a beat-up, aged monstrologist could muster.

Did Coolidge truly believe he could defeat a warlock so ancient and powerful with a wedge of wood? Vendemeier was schooled in the dark arts, a necromancer without equal, Keeper of the Unspeakable Oath and Brother of the Endless Night. What mortal could stop him? Perhaps the old man had expected him to burst into flames or a cloud of smoking ash; did he think him a vampire? *Too droll*, mused Vendemeier. The warlock stood there, looking at the butt end of the stake where it protruded from his breast pocket, Cunningham's brass name badge now spattered in dark blood. Coolidge flopped out of the coffin, weary and disoriented, landing in an ungainly heap at Vendemeier's feet.

The warlock clapped. "I have to say, if it were possible to kill with irony, you might have just slain me, Mr. Coolidge. Leaping *out* of a coffin? *With a stake?*"

The old man wiped the blood from his eye, looking up at the stake. Vendemeier could see the questions flitting across his confused face.

"You're quiet, Mr. Coolidge. Come, talk to me. I am sure we have much in common." More sickly chuckles as he took an unsteady, heavy step closer to the man on the floor. "Our fields of work have many parallels, albeit from different perspectives, one would imagine."

Coolidge gritted his teeth as he tried to straighten his gimpy leg, shuffling backward until he hit a brick wall. He picked up the candelabra, holding it out so he could better see the musty room they were in. The light played over dust-sheet-covered objects of all shapes and sizes. He looked up at the walking, talking corpse of the security guard.

"What are you?"

"Surely you mean *who*, Mr. Coolidge?" The warlock tapped the bloody name badge. "I'm Cunningham. See? It says so right here."

Vendemeier could see a rising panic play across Coolidge's face, a surging tide of fear.

"*What* are you?" he repeated more urgently.

Vendemeier removed his peaked hat, running a hand through his hair as if it might in some way improve his appearance. It didn't. His fingers moved unevenly over his concave skull, just as they had outside the church, where the back of his head had been crushed by a mighty blow. His entire body was now bandaged and bound together with all manner of material, the warlock doing his best to preserve the guard's corpse since his untimely fall from All Saints church tower.

"My name is . . . Udo Vendemeier."

He stood there, triumphant, waiting for a response from his prisoner.

"This the part where you expect me to crap my pants or something?"

"The name means nothing to you?"

"Should it?"

Vendemeier scoffed. "I was the greatest warlock humanity has ever seen. When I came to the New World centuries ago, I brought with me a darkness that has since taken root in your Americas. I came ahead of my Master, to spread His word, His glory, prepare your people for His coming."

"So you 'was' the greatest warlock in the world," said Coolidge. "How did that whole mission work out for you? Not so well, I reckon, considering the mess you're in and the fact that this country is still ruled by free-thinking people. At least, last time I checked."

"Don't fool yourself, Mr. Coolidge," said Vendemeier, tapping at his splintered collarbone where it protruded through his torn shirt. "You suggest that your world is under mankind's stewardship? In the brief time since my return, I have glimpsed this world of yours, and it is a broken, sorry place. War, pestilence, death, and famine; the Four Horsemen have been awfully busy. It seems in my absence that humans have been doing my job for me; I couldn't have wished for a simpler finale to the overture. My Master will be well pleased."

"And who would your Master be?"

"Does the name Hastur mean anything to you?"

Coolidge didn't nod, but his face went slack. Vendemeier's laughter was gleeful.

"Good, good. It seems my Master still casts a long and terrible shadow. I was, and remain, His High Priest. My work shall be done when the King in Yellow returns."

"And when will that be?"

Vendemeier wagged a broken finger. "Very good, Mr. Coolidge. I am not so foolish as to regale you with my Master's plans."

"It was worth a shot," grumbled the man, spitting on the floor.

"All in good time. Such a shame you won't be around to see His return. If there's some way by which I may keep you alive, ensure that weary old heart of yours continues ticking so you may bear witness to His coming, then I shall find it. It would be a shame for your life's work to come to an end without . . . recognition. I am certain my Master would be well pleased to acquaint Himself with you."

"You seem awfully pleased with yourself, considering you're—correct me if I'm wrong—undead. Tell me, what killed you?"

The warlock's sagging flesh twitched. "A Van Helsing."

Coolidge smiled. "Great at what they do, huh? Who was it that pegged you, then?"

"Her name was Liesbeth. She followed me here from Europe, tracked me down to Gallows Hill." Vendemeier shrugged. "My mortal flesh was only ever temporary. I shall be gifted with a new vessel when He returns."

"Of course you will, pal. I bet he promises that to all his thralls."

Vendemeier stooped, seizing Coolidge by the throat. The stench of decay was overwhelming, a heady cocktail of rot and ruin, sweet and sickly all at once. The guard's body might have been broken, but his strength was superhuman. The old man brought the candelabra around to strike him, but the warlock snatched him by the wrist. The fact that Vendemeier's arm was broken at the elbow didn't hinder him one jot.

"You ought to mind your tongue, *boy*, or I'll cut it out."

Coolidge had no response, though it would've been hard to speak with a choked airway. The warlock smiled. His use of the word *boy* had unsettled the old man. Vendemeier glared deep into his eyes, his own burning like verdant gems in a furnace, until the old man looked away.

"Now, I've been quite forgiving of you, all things considered. You have, after all, plunged a stake into my heart. That's terribly poor form, in any social situation. It seems you colonials have no manners or decorum. You rush headlong into trouble, not waiting for a moment to consider the consequences to your actions. Perhaps we might have gotten along in other circumstances. I would teach you some lessons, but I really don't have the time or inclination."

Vendemeier released his grip on Coolidge's throat and wrist and rose to his full height, letting the old man catch his breath once more. The warlock reached behind his back, withdrawing the long, wavy-bladed knife from his belt.

"You've got an awful lot to say, Vendemeier," the aged hunter managed, massaging his throat.

"Come dusk tomorrow, you will accompany me to Gallows Hill Burying Ground, whereupon you shall be exchanged for the Van Helsing boy. At that point, he shall gladly offer his life to me. A quick cut with the dagger and it shall be done. Your world's end may then begin."

"If you think I'll help you capture Max, you're crazier than you look. I'll do no such thing."

"You may be fortunate; it may not come to that. Considering the Mark he has upon him, he is unlikely to survive until tomorrow's twilight."

"This Mark," said Coolidge. "What does it mean?"

Could it be possible that the monster hunters were unaware of the spell he had placed upon the family at the moment of his own demise? His life's work had led to that glorious sacrifice, all to pave the way for the arrival of Hastur. Vendemeier smiled. Coolidge was clueless. What hope did the last of the Van Helsings have, if the only teacher he had was this ignorant, crippled old man?

"Your protégé is Marked for death, the Bane of Monsters writ large upon him. Every supernatural entity he encounters—and I believe Gallows Hill is blessed with more than its fair share of such beings—shall be driven into a kill frenzy by the sight of the Mark."

"You sick son of a—"

"Steady, Mr. Coolidge!"

"You wait till Max gets a crack at you. My boy will make your head spin clean off your rotten, stinking zombie shoulders."

Vendemeier nodded, impressed at how the old man's anger bubbled to the surface. He was old, far older than the fat idiot Cunningham whose body he had seized, but he had ten times the fight in him. Perhaps when this was all done, Coolidge's corpse would be a good battle-hardened vessel for the warlock, even with a bad leg.

"You have a high opinion of the boy."

"You don't know him like I do." Coolidge kept his eyes fixed upon Vendemeier. "If you were *that* powerful a warlock, why didn't you just cast a spell on Max and draw him to you?"

"If it were only so simple," said Vendemeier, genuinely irritated. "This boy has some . . . resistance to magic. He seems impervious to suggestion spells."

Coolidge grinned. "Too tough a nut for you to crack? Your powers ain't so great after all, then, are they?"

"Do not underestimate my powers, Mr. Coolidge. The Mark was my doing, and it shall end the Van Helsing line. And you will be the bait for my trap."

Coolidge glared at Vendemeier defiantly.

"You're not hearing me, you crazy sack of busted bones. I ain't helping you, and I've heard enough of your slack-jawed jibber-jabber. I've trained Max well. He's not some wide-eyed kid who's discovered some freaky powers like in a comic book. He's a Van Helsing. He's a monster hunter. He's known this since he was in diapers. Max may be just a boy, but he's got more heart than any other Van Helsing that came before him."

Vendemeier flinched, nose curling disdainfully at Coolidge's tirade. The man's blood was up, and his spirit wasn't quite so entertaining anymore.

"You may be dead, Vendemeier, but Max will show you what true pain is. And as for me? I'd sooner die than take part in your sick, sorry-ass scheme."

Vendemeier smiled. "Death *is* always an option, but I see more poetic justice in having a Van Helsing's *living* guardian as my accomplice in his downfall."

The warlock's lips suddenly moved fast, the words in a language long dead but not forgotten. Vendemeier could feel the spell taking hold of the man, tiny barbed claws latching on to his flesh and soul, drawing him into the High Priest of Hastur's grand plan. The old man fought it with all his might, but Vendemeier's words of magic washed over him, soaking through his mind, meat, and bones. With each passing second and heartbeat, more of Coolidge slipped away, to be replaced by Vendemeier's will. Soon the faithful old friend of a teenage monster hunter was a dim and distant memory to the old warrior, every fiber of his being devoted to the warlock's cause. Vendemeier stifled a sickly giggle as he watched the faded fighter fall under his spell. It was all too splendid for words. The end of everything was fast approaching, as was his Master.

TWENTY-THREE

xxx

THE DEVIL IN THE DETAILS

"You should be in bed!" exclaimed Max.

He couldn't quite believe what he was seeing. After shambling home in the early hours, Max had fallen into bed at four a.m. When he had finally awoken the next day, the last person he'd expected to find in his apartment was Wing Liu. Syd sat at the breakfast bar with her tool kit out, while the kid was sitting in Jed's La-Z-Boy, covered in and surrounded by the old man's monster manuals.

Wing barely looked up from the topmost book on his lap. "You're the one who needs his sleep."

Max scratched his head. "What time is it?" he asked Syd.

"Just after three in the afternoon, Sleeping Beauty."

"You let me sleep that long?" shouted Max.

"Chill out," said Syd, glowering at her friend from the countertop. "You were sleeping like the dead, if you'll pardon the expression."

"Yeah, and keep it down, Max!" admonished Wing. "You'll disturb Mom. She thinks I'm in my bedroom resting."

"Disturb your mom?" exclaimed Max. "*That's* what you're worried about right now? Wing, I don't think you realize how close you came to dying last night."

"Pfft," said Wing, reaching over the arm of the chair to pick up his open laptop, the backlit display lighting his face up blue. "You worry too much. I can take care of myself."

Max turned to Syd, who appeared equally immersed in her work. Max caught the distinct whiff of hot clam chowder on the stove. His stomach rumbled. When was the last time he'd eaten? Syd had laid a bunch of newspaper sheets and a greasy tarp over the breakfast counter, cluttering it with ratchets, wrenches, blades, hammers. It looked like she'd emptied the contents of her toolbox and armory in one fell swoop. Eightball lay on the linoleum beneath, his stubby tail thumping feebly at Max's return, their bad blood almost forgotten.

"You're letting him do this?"

"The kid climbed up the fire escape from his bedroom window and plopped in here at daybreak. Apart from sneaking back to his apartment for a bowl of Mrs. Liu's noodles for lunch, he's been here ever since."

Max looked back at the homeschooled wunderkind. He was wearing a plaid bathrobe and had a bandage tightly bound around his head. Wing's attention was fixed on his laptop, left hand tapping away on the keys, his right hand scribbling away in a notepad on the chair arm.

Shaking his head, Max slipped past Syd, grabbing a thermos from the shelf and making straight for the reheated pot of clam chowder. He filled the flask, a small mushroom cloud of steam displaced by the hot soup.

"That was a full pot," Syd said pointedly. She watched him grind a heap of salt and pepper into the flask before spinning the lid shut.

"Man's gotta eat, even if it's inedible," Max said with a grimace.

"Where are you taking that?" she asked.

"Back out."

"But you're still exhausted!"

"I know, but there's too much to do. And besides, looks like you and Wing are all over the research side of things. I feel like I'm gate-crashing a book club here." Max sidled close to Syd, his eyes on the boy who was lost in the computer. "Just how much does he know?"

"About what?" she whispered.

"Well . . . everything. What I do. Y'know . . ." Max made a goofy fanged monster face, hands above his head as he threw claw shapes.

"I'm right here," said Wing. "I might have taken a blow to the head, but I'm not deaf."

He finished the line he was writing on the notepad before sliding the pencil behind his ear and closing the laptop with a snap. He pushed his glasses up the bridge of his nose and smiled at the two of them.

"So listen, guys. We've known each other for a couple

of years now, right? I'd like to think we've become friends. Also, though, throughout that time, I'm sure you've noticed I've got an interest in the paranormal, the unexplained. For argument's sake, let's call it an obsession."

Max started to speak, but Wing cut him off.

"Hear me out, guys. We agree, I'm kinda all over spooky goings-on, not just around this zip code but wherever they occur. It's no coincidence that my desktop is a picture of Nessie."

"Nessie?" asked Syd.

"The Loch Ness Monster," said Max.

Syd nodded. Wing continued.

"Every time I've mentioned something weird happening, a freaky sighting or something like that, you've always been so quick to pooh-pooh it. Which is the right thing to do, don't get me wrong. Heck, if I was encouraging a younger kid to believe that monsters were real, were out there, and could bite your head off, I'd get into some serious trouble, you know what I'm saying?"

Both Max and Syd nodded, feeling very much like they were being lectured to. Which they were.

"So, when it turns out that monsters *are* real, that I *haven't* just been living a deluded fantasy for the last two years, you can probably imagine I'm all kinds of blown away. And bummed out, too. Guys, you lied to me. You made me think I was living in Cloud Cuckoo Land."

Max shrugged. "We—Jed, Syd, and I—figured we had to keep it from you."

"Why?"

"I was trying to be responsible. Your folks rent that apartment from us, and if they got wind of me filling your head with all kinds of supernatural mumbo jumbo, there'd be hell to pay."

"I could have kept it a secret," said the boy sulkily.

"You weren't ready for that kind of knowledge, Wing. Heck, I'm not even sure you are now. But you've found out."

Wing was about to interrupt, but now it was Max's turn to stop him. "I'm sure you have a million and one things you want to ask us, and you can, but not now, not today. Right now, we're in a fight, and we're trying to get Jed back. We're trying to stop a big, bad monster."

The ten-year-old shrugged, seemingly satisfied with that explanation for now. "On the subject of stopping the Big Bad, Syd and I have turned up a few things."

Max turned to Syd. "You have?"

"*He* has," said the girl as she returned to her work on the counter. "He's a maniac with that computer."

"What can I say?" said Wing. "The Internet's your friend."

Max hopped across to the boy, who now opened his laptop once more and flicked through the pages of his notepad. Wing was smiling; it was hard to believe Vendemeier and his gargoyle had almost killed him last night.

"Resilient little twerp, aren't you?" said Max.

"I'm epic," said the kid with a grin. "The sooner you learn that, the better all around. I've got our enemy's name."

"Udo Vendemeier," replied Max, putting a damper on the boy's moment of glory.

"You found that out yourself?"

"Yeah," said Max, wincing as he recalled the previous night's exploits. "I went and asked a few questions of my own. I'd better tell you about it now, in case I don't live past sunset." He filled Wing and Syd in on everything the earth elemental had told him. Syd was listening intently where she sat, while her fingers feverishly worked on the gear laid out before her. As Max wrapped up, Eightball whimpered beneath the counter, a half growl just to remind everyone he was still present.

"I have to find Vendemeier's remains, Wing. Destroy the heart of the guy who gave me the Mark, and I get to live. Fail to do that and I'm just monster bait until something inevitably takes a big old bite outta me. What did *you* discover?"

Wing straightened his glasses once more, flipping his notepad to the first page as if he were a detective going over a crime scene.

"Well, a lot of this, you already know," said Wing. "Minister of All Saints Church in Gallows Hill, yada yada yada . . . busted in 1697 . . . hanged from the same tree as his victims . . . buried with his bible . . . exact number of victims unknown . . ."

"Twenty-seven," said Max.

Wing gasped. Eightball whimpered. Syd almost skewered a screwdriver through her palm.

"Twenty-seven?" whispered Wing. "There could only have been twenty or so families living in Gallows Hill at the time."

"Then every one of them got drawn into Vendemeier's scheme," said Max, his hatred for the warlock growing all the time. "Go on."

"The strange thing was, from the moment Vendemeier was hanged and dead, those members of his flock who had participated in the accusations and witch hunt all claimed to have taken leave of their senses."

"What a surprise," said Syd, shaking her head. "Lynch mob claims insanity. They still get away with that these days."

"Yeah, but there are accounts from Vendemeier's trial and the autopsy," said Wing, excited now. "Every man, woman, and child who had gone against their loved ones claimed that a fog over their collective minds was lifted, right at the moment the reverend's neck broke." He made a yanking motion with his hand in the air, turning his neck to the side, ear to shoulder and his tongue sticking out. "Some claimed to have been in a stupor for years; one dude who had worked as a church sexton *for Vendemeier* couldn't even remember the guy turning up in the parish. We're talking about an entire village brainwashed, guys!"

"If Vendemeier is a warlock, that kind of powerful magic would make sense. In fact, sounds to me like it's not that different from the glamour a vampire might cast upon its thrall."

"Vampires are *real*?" exclaimed Wing, his eyeballs nearly rebounding off his spectacle lenses.

Max raised his hand in defense. "Another time, buddy. Let's solve this mystery first, eh? What about Vendemeier's body—you find out where he was buried?"

Wing sighed. "I looked, but there's nothing online that pinpoints the exact whereabouts. Maybe there's something in the hall of records at the central library in town, but I'd need a good day trawling through their reference section."

Max shook his head. "No time for that."

"There is one area of the burying ground that was reserved for the remains of criminals, though."

"Where's that?"

Wing brought up an old drawing of the burying ground from the municipal archives. He spun the laptop around for Max to look at, jabbing at a point on the map with a finger. "Down by Witch River, in the earth around the Hanging Tree. According to the births, deaths, and marriages website, that portion of the cemetery held the bodies of those individuals who had perpetrated the most wicked crimes in life over a span of two hundred years. The tree itself is unconsecrated, as is the ground around it."

"Great," said Max, sucking his teeth.

"I know. Like searching for a needle in a haystack."

"Well," said the teenage monster hunter, "at least we have a haystack, and that's a start."

"What are you going to do?"

"Search for a needle," replied Max, clapping the kid's back. "And a bible, apparently. Good work, Wing."

Max paused at the breakfast bar to rifle through the gear on the counter and throw a handful of goodies into his satchel. He pulled a folding shovel out of the closet and squeezed it into his straining bag. He holstered the flask of chowder inside his bomber jacket, ensuring it was a snug fit. Syd grabbed him by the elbow.

"You're really going right now? Rest. Eat. Grab forty winks. But don't head straight back out there, back to—"

"My death?" Max smiled as he donned the jacket and readjusted his messenger bag strap. "Jed needs me, Syd. That old fart's always been there for me. Now the roles are reversed, and we're the only hope Jed's got. Vendemeier's remains are out there, Syd. I have to find them. I destroy them, I destroy the curse."

"You can't go alone."

"I absolutely can. There's no point in you putting yourself in further danger. I was born into this role—"

"And I *chose* mine, Max. Let me help you find that grave."

Max shook his head. "I couldn't live with myself if you were harmed."

"We'll all be harmed if you die, Max; if the curse and Vendemeier's plans come to fruition."

"Then I won't die." Max smiled, charming, disarming, and wildly optimistic. "You need to look after Wing, Syd. And for goodness' sake, make sure he gets back in his own bed before his mother comes knocking."

He turned to leave, but Syd kept hold of his elbow. "One more thing," she said, "before you go."

"You're not going to kiss me, are you?"

"In your dreams," she said, pulling back the tarp and dirty newspaper at the far end of the breakfast counter, revealing what she'd been working on. Max caught his breath.

"Is that . . . ?"

"Yep. It fastens here and here; this strap can tighten it. The cartridge slots in there, like so, and watch out for the spring-load. Be careful. I haven't been able to field-test it yet, so the firing mechanism might be a bit temperamental."

"And does it . . . ?"

"Yes, it does."

"And if I . . . ?"

"It'll take your finger off if you do that. Do you want to do that?"

Max shook his head, fishing in his backpack. "I won't need this anymore, then." He tossed his old homemade catapult Wing's way, the younger boy fumbling as he tried to catch it.

"Okay," said Syd, wrapping the device in an oily rag and handing it to Max. "What time is dusk?"

"Six p.m."

"Enough lollygagging, then."

Syd placed a hand on Max's shoulder as he opened the door, giving it an affectionate squeeze.

"Be careful."

"When am I not?" he said as he bounded down the stairs, trying to act positive even though his legs felt leaden.

"Every moment of every livelong day," she called after him, closing the door with a fearful sigh.

TWENTY-FOUR

xxx

THE BOX

Syd sighed. Max was gone, but there was still plenty of work to do. "Okay, brainiac. What have you got?"

Wing briefed her on everything he'd dug up in the past five minutes about Hastur, the King in Yellow—a surprising amount. "There are all kinds of references to him from ancient civilizations, like the Sumerians. He was a god of darkness, worshipped by a sect known as the Cult of the Endless Night."

"Vendemeier must be one of those crazies," said Syd.

"But there's more," said Wing excitedly. "According to medieval Germanic records, Hastur's also the father of all vampires. The Knights Templar had a big hoo-ha back in the day. He was apparently a warrior prince of Carpathia who drank the blood of his enemies, gorged on their flesh, and fought only at night. Gotta be the same guy as the Sumerian god, right?"

"Could it just be the same name popping up, but a different fiend?"

"If you believe in coincidences."

"It sounds to me like whichever version of Hastur Vendemeier's aligned to, it can't be a good thing."

"Cunningham!" shouted Wing suddenly, causing Syd to leap back, fists raised and ready to fight.

"Say what?"

"Cunningham," repeated Wing excitedly as his fingers blurred across the keyboard. "The security guard; he had a name tag doohickey!"

"Badge?"

"Bingo." The boy grinned as he entered the name, followed by the words *security guard*, into a search engine.

"Anything?"

"Jackpot!" Wing clapped his hands. "From yesterday's newspaper: there was a break-in at the Museum of Anthropology downtown. At the time the article was written, there was one item reported stolen, a sacrificial Egyptian dagger."

"The curvy blade he had last night," said Syd, her own hopes rising.

"In addition to the dagger going missing, police are also searching for a Mr. Wilbur Cunningham, the night watchman who was on security detail that night, whose whereabouts are currently unknown."

"Is that all?"

"Gimme a second," said Wing, fingers clicking the keys. "Just checking police records."

"You can *do* that?" exclaimed Syd.

"What? You think I sit at home all day with my head in a book? Get with the program, lady . . ." Syd stifled a laugh. "No priors on Cunningham. There's an arrest warrant out for him now, in light of the missing weapon. They're recommending to approach with extreme caution. No sightings at all, though. Seems like he's vanished."

Syd stepped away as Wing continued searching. There was something at the edge of her mind—what had she heard about the museum? It was something Jed had said. No, had he read something? Or had Syd read something of his? She approached the kitchenette counter where her tools were spread out.

The two-day-old copy of the *Examiner* was now covered in oil and grime, but the information was there in black and white. She cleared her gear aside, straightening the page until the article was legible once more. It covered an opening-night event at the Museum of Anthropology. The theme of the new exhibition was "The Early Settlers of New England," and above the article was a photograph of the lead curator, posing beside a few choice pieces from the collection. She leaned against a wooden pedestal, with a gibbet, gravestone, and bible-bashing preacher mannequin arranged menacingly around her. Syd squinted, before retrieving a magnifying glass from her tool kit. She held it over the picture, her breath catching in her throat.

A box sat atop the pedestal, a metal plaque beneath it with a faint inscription: VENDEMEYER'S BOX.

She called over her shoulder, "Search for Vendemeyer, spelled with a *y*. Throw the word *box* in for good measure!"

Wing typed feverishly. "It's listed as an artifact of the 'Early Settlers' exhibition, but what it contains isn't clear. But it must be connected to him, right?"

"You'd think so," said Syd, snatching her raincoat off the door peg and tugging it on over her black sweater. She tried calling Max on her cell, but there was no answer. She pocketed the phone as Eightball rose from beneath the counter and joined her by the door. She gave him a friendly pat.

"You're coming then, pup?"

He gave a hearty *woof*, his stubby tail smacking his butt cheeks like he might explode at any moment. She slipped his leash on.

"I'm coming, too," said Wing, scrambling out of the La-Z-Boy.

"You are *staying*," she replied, placing a hand on his chest and easing him back into the recliner. "You're a wizard, Wing. No, not a Hufflepuff. I mean with the Internet." She patted the phone in her pocket. "Stay in touch, okay? I'll let you know what I discover at the museum."

"Okay," said Wing sulkily, shifting in the chair. "But I could've helped you out there. Max needs all the muscle he can muster."

Syd smiled. "You're helping us *here*, Wing. Truly." She leaned forward and gave him a gentle peck on the forehead. The kid blushed instantly as he returned his attention to the laptop.

"I'll stay on it," he said, shoving his glasses back up his nose.

"And Wing," said Syd, slipping out of the door with Eightball, "stay epic!"

He grinned as she thundered down the stairs. Once again he fidgeted in the La-Z-Boy, twisting to reach behind him. Something was jabbing at the small of his back, irritating him no end. He felt around, finally catching a piece of stiff paper and pulling it out of a fold in the leather. It was a business card. He stared at it intently, completely forgetting the task at hand and the computer on his lap.

TWENTY-FIVE

xxx

THE GRAVEYARD SHIFT

Max plunged his shovel into the pile of earth, slowly straightening his back in the process. He felt muscles and tendons pop and twang like broken guitar springs. He whimpered, which was fine, because nobody was watching. Max shuddered to imagine how he'd cope with life if he had to do a real job for a living. Aim him at the pointy teeth, wind him up, and watch him go; but give him a spade and ask him to dig? Watch him transform into a feeble-limbed norm. Still, it had been a busy afternoon in the dark heart of the burying ground, beneath the boughs of the Hanging Tree.

Max looked up at the twisted branches that towered over him. Its enormous limbs arched away from the trunk like arms that had been repeatedly broken and healed, knots marking their length. Those people who had been guilty of the vilest and most heinous crimes had not been afforded the luxury of headstones. Pits had been dug around the base of the leafless tree, the corpses of Gallows Hill's worst criminals tipped into them—no coffins, or prayers, for that matter. Max had unearthed a dozen of these graves so far, searching for the remains of the warlock who had cursed him. Thus far his quest had been fruitless. No bible; no warlock. All he'd discovered was twelve terrible corpses, and a fervent dislike of manual labor.

"Sorry, guys," said Max, standing above the open graves as he unscrewed the lid of his flask. By good chance, the location of the burying ground, specifically the Hanging Tree, meant that the earth here was predominantly peat. A tributary of the Charles River, known locally as Witch River, wound its way through Gallows Hill, skirting the edge of the cemetery. The closer you got to the river, the marshier the ground became. This peaty earth ensured that the bodies buried within it had remained in a petrified state instead of decomposing. It was grim to look at, but it had helped Max's search for the evil preacher immensely. He took a swig from his flask, forgetting for a moment that it was full of scalding clam chowder. He spluttered it back out, wiping his mouth.

"Smart, Max; bring a boiling flask of cream along for thirsty work."

He screwed the lid back on and dropped it onto his bomber jacket on the ground. A flutter of wings made Max turn suddenly as a crow landed in the Hanging Tree's branches. It cocked its head, glaring down with a single blink of the eye.

"How you doing, pal? Come to watch a man at work?"

The crow didn't reply, unsurprisingly, but Max could never discount the unusual happening. It came with the territory. Looking up at the sky, he tried to guess how much time was left before sunset. Having as much wilderness survival knowledge as a caged canary, he quickly abandoned that plan of action, retrieving his cell from his back pocket. He punched it on and waited for the glow of the display. He got nothing. He flicked it with a grubby finger, but still the screen was a no-show.

"You're kidding me," he muttered, as he stuck the phone back in his pocket. He smiled at the crow, which had been joined by a second. "Perfect timing for a dead battery, eh? Don't suppose you guys have the time?"

He'd crashed so late last night, he hadn't thought of charging the cell. Max looked back over the other graves and the bodies within. They appeared mummified, their skin turned the color of old leather. He looked back at the crows as more arrived. They stared at the corpses.

"So you haven't joined me for my sparkling conversation. You've turned up for the criminal smorgasbord?"

He shook his shovel, causing a number of them to take flight to higher branches. Reluctantly, Max turned to the open graves and set back to work filling them in before the birds could start pecking at their contents. It was slow going. The ground was loose underfoot, and more than once, Max found himself sliding down into the peat alongside the bodies. His eyes lingered over each of them as he piled the earth back on, their distended necks reminding him of their fate. By the time he'd filled the twelfth grave and the light had begun to fade, over twenty crows sat in the tree, watching with interest. Max wiped his brow with the back of his arm, his hoodie sleeve coming away filthy. He leaned back against the tree and stared up, watching the shadows flit from branch to branch.

"If you hang around long enough, you'll have ringside seats for my demise."

Max eased himself up onto aching legs again and looked around at his handiwork. If there was another unmarked grave somewhere in the cemetery, what hope did he have of finding it? He punched the Hanging Tree's trunk, immediately regretting it as shock waves resonated through his fist. As he nursed his knuckles, he heard a *tap-tap-tapping* sound from the other side of the tree. He stepped around the black-barked trunk, constantly aware of the movements of the birds above him. Two dozen pairs of beady eyes stared down at him, heads twitching as they followed his path.

"I've seen that movie, y'know," he told them—Jed was a big Hitchcock fan. "You don't freak me out," he lied.

Circumnavigating the tree, he found one of the crows on the ground, tapping at the earth between two raised roots of the Hanging Tree. The bird hopped to and fro, beak striking the ground, pecking and pulling at the mulch. It caught hold of something, yanking back and dragging it out of the soil: a worm, wriggling all the way. Max half expected the bird to swallow it whole, but instead the crow threw it to one side and carried on digging. Curiosity getting the better of him, Max snatched up the folding shovel and moved to join the crow. The bird hopped aside onto a wizened root, making way for the young man. The broad-bladed tool cut into the earth and came away loaded, Max tossing it back over his shoulder.

"What do we have here?" said Max, dropping to his knees. The shovel went in and out, dragging the peat and wet earth clear, taking him ever deeper. That familiar feeling that he was closing in on something monstrous began to rise around him, like a specter materializing. He trembled as he worked, the building dread making his heart beat faster, wilder. A couple of the crows fluttered down from above, flanking him alongside their brother, lining the upturned roots like a ceremonial guard. Great peaty clumps came away from the ground now, and Max grunted as he put his back into the task. The muddy clods made a sucking sound as they tore free, landing with resounding splats away from the Hanging Tree.

Max stopped digging when the shovel struck something leathery. The birds flapped clear as Max placed the tool against a root before sliding down into the shallow pit. He straddled the exposed brown leather, grimacing as his fingers set to work brushing the peat and soil away. It wasn't flesh. It was a book. Max pulled it out of the ground and opened it delicately. It was awfully old, its pages rotten and stuck together. However, the few pages that did open revealed disquieting symbols and words in an alien language, inked on the pages with a graffiti-like scrawl. The warlock's bible? Or was it a spell book? He tucked it into the back of his waistband and continued digging, his hands slowly revealing a black-robed body beneath the dirt.

"The first plot would've been *far* too easy," he grumbled at the crows. "Oh no, let's wait until he's dug up a dozen and broken his back. Then we'll come along and show him where he *should* have been digging. I can see why they call you a murder of crows now . . ."

A few more sweeps of his hands and there was Vendemeier's body, frozen in the earth for posterity. The dark burlap of the preacher's robes clung like a death shroud, following every contour of the corpse beneath. Every inch of exposed brown flesh clung to the bones of his skeletal hands and his narrow skull. The dead man's mouth was open in a silent scream, choked off by packed soil squirming with worms.

"Now for the grisly business. You may want to look away, birdies."

Max stood up, dragging his messenger bag toward him through the soil. He flipped the latch, reaching in to withdraw one of the greatest weapons the Van Helsings owned. He gave it a twirl, admiring the craftsmanship. The stake was as old as Gallows Hill Burying Ground, brought to America by Liesbeth, the one family heirloom that had survived centuries of monster hunting. Max affectionately referred to the silver-tipped mahogany blade as Splinter; every good weapon deserved a cool name.

"You may not be a vampire, but far as I know, Splinter will kill any known monster." He dropped to his knees and straddled the corpse. Gloom had descended over Gallows Hill, but the visibility told Max that the sun was still out there, somewhere, so perhaps he wasn't too late. He began his incantation, the words of magic rolling off his lips smooth, instinctive, and automatic; taught to him by Jed and practiced to perfection. This was the first step in banishing an evil spirit, vampiric or otherwise. The second step involved Max driving Splinter through the corpse's heart. If that didn't do the trick, nothing would. He held the stake in his left hand over Vendemeier's torso and raised the shovel over his head. When Max uttered the last word, he afforded himself a smile of relief. The spade fell.

The stake passed straight through the corpse's chest with no resistance, and Max's hand disappeared into the rib cage, fist still wrapped around Splinter. The crows began a chorus of caws around him, some taking flight, squawking and circling the Hanging Tree as Max ripped the robes apart. There was an open cavity in Vendemeier's breast, and it wasn't caused by Max's attempted staking.

"What the—"

The teenager clawed the soil aside with frantic fingers, finding other organs within the torso that had shriveled but remained in place, intact. But the organ that had pumped blood around Vendemeier's corrupted body—of that, there was no sign. The crows continued their baleful chorus, their cries becoming a frenzy of panic that matched the horror that bloomed in Max's fearful soul.

TWENTY-SIX

xxx

A NIGHT AT THE MUSEUM

"He's a guide dog, mister. In training."

"For real?" said the guard in the lobby of the Gallows Hill Museum of Anthropology. "Don't they usually look a little more guide-doggy than that? What happened to Labradors?"

Syd bent, patting Eightball's head as he sat at attention beside her. She was careful to avoid the three angry cuts that ran down the right-hand side of the poor hound's face, dealt out by the gargoyle. She looked up at the guard.

"If a dog's smart enough, he's good enough."

She made a silent prayer that the puppy would remain on his best behavior and resist all temptation to drag his butt across the museum's polished marble entrance hall.

"He's super well behaved, I promise. And he's got to learn how to guide around places like museums. Can I *please* bring him in?"

The man scratched the back of his head, tipping his peaked cap forward in the process. He was a heavyset, barrel-chested man, the beginnings of a gray beard stubbling his humorless, pale face. He wore the exact same uniform as Wilbur Cunningham, or Vendemeier, or whoever the heck it was that they'd encountered at All Saints Church. His name badge read DEMBINSKI, and chances were good that he'd been a friend of poor Cunningham's.

"You keep him on a short leash, young lady, you hear?"

"Thank you, sir," said Syd, hitting him with her prettiest smile. It drew a grin from the man. It rarely failed. She looked around, wrinkling her brow, the picture of innocent curiosity.

"Something else I can help you with?" asked Dembinski.

"Oh, nothing," said Syd, picking up a foldout museum map. "I just heard on the news there'd been a break-in here. I was wondering if they'd caught the robber yet."

A frown appeared on Dembinski's broad face. He leaned closer. "The police don't know what they're looking for. They seem to think it's my friend Wilbur who did the stealing, but that's crazy."

"Is he the guard they have a warrant out for?"

Dembinski flapped both of his hands in a "go away" gesture. "Wilbur's a good guy, an honest man. There's no way he'd steal anything from the museum. He loves this place. Loves his job. You make your visit a quick one, little lady. We close soon, okay?"

Syd set off into the exhibition rooms, checking her cell.

The time was just after five. What time had Max said the sun would set—six p.m.? Visiting the museum was suddenly feeling like an indulgent distraction. Perhaps she'd have been better off tooling up with weapons and following Max to the burying ground. That's where the battle would be won and lost, not in some musty old museum.

"Well, we're here now," she muttered to Eightball. "Let's take a closer look at that box and see what else we can find."

The museum was almost empty, only the odd visitor wandering noisily up and down the parquet-floored corridors. Syd avoided them all, slipping through the building and the various exhibits. She paused by the entrance to the Egyptian Room. Yellow police tape formed a cross over the archway, the fire door closed behind it, barring any access. A poster from the management was pasted onto the inside of this glass door, informing the public that the room would reopen upon conclusion of the police investigation. A law enforcement poster sat alongside it, encouraging anyone with any information to contact Gallows Hill PD at the usual number.

Syd shrugged and moved on.

The "Early Settlers" show was in the American Room. Syd remembered this room from her elementary school days, when she'd turned up with her class to rub brass and try out a butter churn. It had never been the most inspiring room in the museum. That had changed recently, though. Now it resembled a haunted house, with waxwork reenactments of the witch trials dominating half of the exhibition.

Grisly depictions of the perils the early settlers had faced were re-created around her, including diseases, ships sinking, and entire villages starving to death. Placards told stories of encounters with America's wild animals, a homestead sacked by a pack of hungry wolves, while other accounts covered the awkward and sometimes disastrous encounters between colonials and the Massachusett tribe, not least the smallpox the Europeans introduced in 1616, almost wiping the Native Americans out. Syd shook her head.

Remembering the photo in the *Examiner*, Syd went deeper into the witch trials portion of the exhibition. Life-size models of three pointy-nosed, wart-faced crones were gathered around a cauldron, as though they were auditioning for *Macbeth*. The notice on a stand beside them explained that this was the "archetypal witch," as caricatured down the years by popular culture. Behind them stood the preacher waxwork, all fury and righteous fervor before the trio of hags. The ministers in those early days were the most powerful, influential individuals in society. One would think these men could have done more on behalf of the poor people who were hanged or burned. Sadly, they were often behind the witch hunts, driving their parishioners into a furor as they sought out the wicked and guilty.

And then there was Vendemeier.

Syd shivered as she came to a placard that recounted the activity of the reverend of All Saints Church. The twenty-seven hangings for which he was responsible didn't appear in his biography—here, it suggested somewhere between five and eight. Syd snorted. The write-up described his flock lynching him at the Hanging Tree, but there was no mention of his monstrous connections, or the instrumental role of Liesbeth Van Helsing. There were some things the norms just weren't ready to face.

"You're really helpful, pooch," said Syd, looking down at Eightball, who was trying to catch his tail in his wobbling jaws. She watched him walk in tight, concentric circles, bewitched by his own butt. "Hellhound, huh? Sure you are."

Then she spotted the pedestal, positioned exactly where it had been in the newspaper photograph: a tall, polished, dark wooden plinth with a brass plaque bearing the words VENDEMEYER'S BOX. Only the box wasn't there. The top of the stand was empty, a perfect square left in the dust where the artifact had once sat. Syd stepped closer, running her finger through the dust as if it might make the cube magically reappear. She crouched, peering at the other exhibits at floor level, even lifting the skirts from around the crooked witches' ankles. The box was nowhere to be found.

Should she go back to Mr. Dembinski, the affable security guard, and ask him the whereabouts of the box? Perhaps Dembinski was in cahoots with Vendemeier. The news had all been about the Egyptian sacrificial dagger going missing— no mention of a misplaced item from the American Room. Her thoughts were interrupted by an announcement over the PA system asking visitors to make their way to the exit, as the museum would close in ten minutes. Her hands fell to her sides in exasperation. The thing she had come for was gone, and she had no idea who'd taken it. She looked at the thin windows that circuited the walls where they met the ceiling, a faded blue light visible outside. Sun was setting. Time was running out.

Eightball growled, a low gurgle that made her jump. He'd stopped stalking his rear and had returned to her side, where he now crouched. His hackles were raised; his eyes narrowed as his nostrils flared.

"What's the matter?"

She hunkered down to comfort him. Eightball let her left hand stroke him, but the right he chose to snarl at. She brought her hand away, fearful that the hound might try and take a bite.

"You don't like this hand? But the other's fine?"

He continued growling, sniffing at the air, lips slowly peeling back to reveal that row of stubby teeth. Syd looked at her hand, wondering what had gotten the puppy riled up. It was clean but for the dust smear that marked her fingertip. Dust from the top of the plinth.

"Of *course*! Your sense of smell! It took us to All Saints, following that creature that caught Wing. Where can it lead you in here, Eightball?" She held her finger out, the snarling grunts catching in the dog's throat as he sniffed at it.

"You can do this," she said, moving her right hand away and lifting his jaw in her left hand gently. "Find me the box, Eightball. Seek it."

She stood up and removed his leash. Eightball went to work, nose to the ground, snuffling. He was in and among the waxwork exhibits, bumping into the occasional one, threatening to knock a crone into a cauldron and a farmer into a fisherman. He stopped before the pedestal that had held the box, growling briefly, before continuing on his way. Syd stepped back into the main corridor that ran through the museum. She could see and hear the last remaining visitors heading for the exit. If she didn't show up soon, the guard would come looking for her. That would be the end of her museum adventure for sure. She returned to the American Room.

There was no sign of the puppy.

"Eightball! Where are you?" she hissed, rattling his chain leash to draw him out. She called again, dropping to all fours as she tried to lure him back. She could hear heavy, booted footsteps in the corridor now, drawing ever closer. Dembinski, no doubt.

There! Beyond the fake gallows at the back of the room, a velvet curtain hung from the ceiling to the floor, and before it, Syd could see the puppy's paws dancing about excitedly. She scampered between the exhibits, rushing to his side. Eightball's stubby claws were catching at the red material, almost bringing it down as he tried to tug it aside. Syd lifted the curtain's hem, the hellhound ducking beneath, and came face-to-face with a door. The girl looked it up and down, unable to find a handle. There was, however, a keyhole. She let the curtain fall behind her and fished her pick from her pocket, slipping it into the mortise lock.

Dembinski's footsteps were behind her now, close to

entering the room. Syd glanced down at Eightball, who, thank goodness, remained totally silent, his big eyes fixed on her. She could feel the lock straining to give. She pulled her wire hair clip out of her ponytail, adding it to the pick in the lock and giving it a final jimmy. The tumblers clicked and the door swung open, inward. She ushered Eightball forward into the gloom, just as Dembinski's boots found the polished floor of the American Room. By the time the guard had reached the cauldron of witches, the chamber was empty, the door was closed, and Syd and Eightball were descending a darkened staircase into the basement of the museum.

TWENTY-SEVEN

xxx

A COLD DATE

Max sat in the boughs of the Hanging Tree, watching the sun set in the west. He wondered if this was the last time he'd witness the spectacle. He was, after all, effectively gift-wrapping himself for sacrifice. Was this how life had been for his forefathers? Had their teenage years been dogged by apocalyptic curses, or did they get to date, play hooky from school, and hang out at the mall? But there was no point in dreaming about what life might have been, like if he'd been a norm. He smiled as the sky darkened to the color of an angry bruise. He was a Van Helsing, and it rocked.

"So good of you to keep our appointment!"

Max started at the voice, looking back between the branches, east through Gallows Hill Burying Ground. The entire cemetery was built on a slope, descending down to Witch River and the hideous Hanging Tree. Two figures emerged through the gloom, walking side by side between the avenues of headstones, marsh mists separating as they came. Vendemeier's gait was shambling, stiff-legged— Cunningham's corpse had taken quite a beating. Beside him came Jed, shuffling along, his hands bound before him and his head bowed. He looked like a beaten man. Max hated to imagine what the warlock had put his old friend through, and it took all his self-control to resist throwing himself at the preacher.

"You couldn't have *kept* me away, Udo. Can I call you Udo? I'm gonna call you Udo. I feel we have a . . . rapport; that's the word, right?"

The warlock's hips made a sickening, grating sound with each step as he came closer. He stopped short of the boughs of the tree.

"You almost sound pleased to be here, child."

"Not often I get asked out on a hot date." He shivered. "Maybe *hot* isn't the right word. But why the mash note? You could've asked me to come in person, Udo. Whodathunk you were so shy?"

Max could see that the guard's clothing was stained dark, a bib of blood covering his throat and chest where he'd collected an impressive collection of injuries. Chief among these was a broken neck, a compound fracture of the collar-bone, and one of Jed's stakes buried in his breast. His aged mentor remained by the warlock's side, head still down-turned. Max could see bloodstains on the old-timer's vest.

He could feel his fists clenching, knuckles popping. *Play it cool, kid; play it cool.* Apart from the three of them, the graveyard appeared empty, but Max was taking no chances. His attention was fixed upon Vendemeier, but his gaze flickered around the burying ground.

"You came alone, Van Helsing."

"Well, kind of. Just me and the birds," he said, gesturing into the surrounding branches at the mob of crows who roosted within them. Vendemeier made a gurgling, disapproving noise, causing a couple of his avian friends to flap nervously. "Don't tell me you hate birds, too, Udo. Is there anything you actually like?"

"Like?" said the warlock, rolling the word around his mouth as if it were an exotic morsel of food. "That's such a weak word, I find. A pathetic waste of speech and thought. To *like* something, one may as well have no feelings at all. *Like* is nothing. There is only love and hate. I love my Master, the King in Yellow. His time approaches."

"Gee, Udo, you do *love* the sound of your own voice, don't you? Did you always speak in riddles? Y'know, before my dear old granny got the better of you?"

Vendemeier shook Jed by the shoulder. The old boxer was still in fine shape, his muscles bulging where the warlock's rotten hands clutched his flesh, but he was like a rag doll in Vendemeier's grip.

"That witch may have turned up unexpectedly, but she only hastened the inevitable. My sacrifice was always part of my plan. I had to fall long ago so that He could rise today. I made that vow when I chose to serve Him. I took the Unspeakable Oath."

"There's a question that's baffled me, Udo," said Max. "Why couldn't you bring forth your end of days back then, when Liesbeth dispatched you? Three hundred years is a heck of a long wait for a punch line!"

"Hastur's great sleep is no trifling, mortal nap. He . . . changes. He becomes. While He sleeps, His brood multiplies. You must feel very proud of your work, Van Helsing. You think your family has rid the earth of Hastur's children? You believe them dead?" Vendemeier laughed. "An army slumbers, to rise alongside the King in Yellow."

"You're losing me again, Udo. I ask you a normal question and you vomit gibberish everywhere. It's messy, dude. Makes a conversation *such hard work*."

Vendemeier smiled, the right-hand side of his face hanging loose. He reminded Max of a stroke victim, albeit one who'd gotten a bit mangled. "Are you coming down out of the tree, child?"

"I kinda like it up here. Great view. You'd know all about that, though, wouldn't you, Udo?"

Max slapped the main bough of the Hanging Tree, the bark still smooth from the ropes that had once hung there. Vendemeier pulled the wavy dagger from his belt and placed it beneath Jed's ribs. That caught Max's attention.

"Down you come, boy."

"You release Jed first," said Max.

He shifted on the branch, ensuring his messenger bag was flush against his right hip. Vendemeier brought the knife to Jed's wrists and cut the rope that tied them together. He kept a hand on the old boxer's shoulder, looking back to the tree.

"Down, child."

"Jed," said Max, ignoring the talking corpse. "Walk straight forward, toward my voice. To the foot of the tree."

His mentor shambled forward, a hand from Vendemeier propelling him on his way. Jed came to a halt beneath the Hanging Tree's main bough, directly beneath Max. The birds squawked, some hopping from one foot to another or flapping their wings anxiously.

"Your end of the bargain, Van Helsing. Come. Now." The warlock beckoned with the Egyptian dagger.

"Stay put, Jed," whispered Max, loud enough for the old man to hear but not Vendemeier. The teenager looked back to the maniacal minister. "You choose this spot for any particular reason?"

The warlock chuckled. "Call me sentimental. This was the scene of my greatest work. You cannot imagine the thrill of seeing a pack of people turning on their loved ones. Brothers, sisters, fathers. Even children, screaming until their mothers were swinging from that bough." He pointed at the branch Max sat on. "You're touching history there,

Van Helsing. You should feel honored that I invited you, of all your family, here this night."

"Oh, I'm flattered, Udo, believe me. Knowing I get to finish off Granny Liesbeth's work is a real feather in my cap."

More gurgling laughter. "Your witticisms make you feel vigorous and full of bravado, no? I've seen such false courage before, in another life, foolishly fighting for a human monarch before the King in Yellow showed me His grace and favor. At the Battle of the Boyne, a battle-hardened corporal from Yorkshire, constantly making merry on the eve of war—he took a pike to the belly; opened him up from navel to chin. That quelled his quips and irritating jibes. Make light of your situation while you still can, Van Helsing, for soon enough we'll see the color of your innards."

Vendemeier looked past the Hanging Tree toward the river, its dark waters churning past.

"Witch River. So nostalgic of the local oafs to rename it as they did. We flung enough of the wretches in there, after all."

Max felt the anger take him. He threw himself from the tree, landing on all fours a few feet in front of the man. Vendemeier smiled.

"You hate me? Good, come closer, child. That rage in your blood can only please my Master when I cut your throat. Fear not, Van Helsing. I shall not spill a drop. The elixir will quench His thirst in fine fashion upon His return."

Max looked at the knife in the man's rotten hand. "Huh, I don't see any bottle or basin for you to sluice my juice into.

Looks to me like you're gonna make a bit of a mess."

"You underestimate my powers, child," said the warlock, striding toward the crouching boy. He ran his swollen purple tongue along the dagger's edge. Vendemeier whispered words of ancient, perverse magic over the tainted dagger. Emerald flames suddenly danced along the blade, following the waves in the folded metal.

"At the *exact* moment that the cut is made, these fires shall cauterize your wound. You will then be prepared for Hastur's return. When the King in Yellow arrives in the New World, He shall dine upon your carcass."

Max was on his knees before the warlock, right hand slipping into his pocket. Vendemeier's eyes were blinding now, the fire that played along the wickedly serrated knife matching their enchanted emerald light.

"As I said"—Vendemeier drew the flaming sacrificial dagger back with a sickly smile—"I shall not spill a drop."

"Seems like a lot of extra fuss," said Max, "when you could've just borrowed my flask!"

Max's hand came up fast, palm open in his best Spider-Man impression. The yo-yo flew straight and sure, whipping repeatedly around the warlock's wrist. Max yanked back hard like a fisherman striking the line, the string going taut and tugging Vendemeier's arm. The ancient blade flew from his hand, landing in the mud at their feet. The green fire spluttered out, the spell momentarily broken, and the warlock roared with anger. Max let go of his trusty toy, the loop of thread slipping off his middle finger as he scrambled clear of the raging madman.

Dashing back to the Hanging Tree, Max found Jed still standing there, swaying. He threw his arms around the old man, squeezing tight for a moment, before clapping his hands onto those muscular biceps.

"We have to go, Jed! Let's get you back to Helsing House, quick as we can!"

He gave the man a shake, the boxer's head still bent, gray stubbled chin resting upon his bloodstained vest. What had the warlock done to him?

"You have to wake up, Jed. Like *now*!"

Max heard noises now in the graveyard as a host of horrors materialized through the gloom. They crept around tombstones, slinking between trees as they drew ever nearer. Countless white eyes shone in the dusk light, pinprick pupils trained upon the young monster hunter. Jaws smacked hungrily. It seemed every ghoul from across Massachusetts had been drawn to the warlock in preparation for this night. And now Vendemeier had let them loose. Max balled a fist, punching Jed desperately in the chest, trying to shock him into action.

"You wanted your friend back, child," said the warlock, hidden in the depths of the darkness. "Have him."

Jed's head came up at last, eyes closed, jaw hanging loose and gormless. Max's heart froze as dread seeped through every bone in his body. He reached up, a trembling finger touching the man's throat. There was a pulse. Max gasped with relief. Then Jed's eyes opened.

They burned with the same green fire that shone in the sockets of Vendemeier's skull.

"Bring him to me," said the warlock.

Jed lunged, the crows squawked, and Max ran.

TWENTY-EIGHT

xxx

VENDEMEIER'S LAIR

Eightball strained against his leash, his collar cutting into the roll of flesh around his throat. The little dog's tail wagged furiously, pug nose flat to the floor as he followed the scent. Syd stumbled along behind, trying to rein him in, one hand bound in the chain leash, the other clutching her flashlight. If the exhibition halls of the Museum of Anthropology were confusing in their layout, nothing could have prepared her for the vaults. Since descending the staircase, Eightball had dragged her through a warren of corridors and storerooms, their route switching left, right, doubling back on itself. It appeared that the museum's basement had been designed for King Minos; Syd half-expected his bull-headed monster to pop out of a broom closet at any moment.

"Attaboy, Eightball," she said, giving up any attempt to haul the puppy in. "Seek it."

Dembinski hadn't given chase, clearly missing their

exit from the American Room. That had been ten minutes ago. She had to wonder just how big this place was, and how good Max's dog actually was at tracking; there was one particular fire extinguisher she was convinced she'd passed by a number of times already. Enormous shelving units rose up to the ceiling, each one loaded with museum paraphernalia. Each way they turned, Syd encountered another tower of oddities, crates and pallets stacked with who knew what. She didn't have the time or inclination to investigate. It was the box she sought, and she hoped the little hellhound could lead her to it.

The portly pooch suddenly came to a halt at a crossroads of shelves, picking one route and then the other, changing his mind repeatedly. Syd found herself entangled in his leash. Eightball growled as he threw his head back, sniffing at the air. Then his hackles rippled. If a chubby puppy could ever "point" like a hunting hound, that's what Eightball would be doing. His body quivered, muscles locking, eyes trained on a corridor that Syd didn't recognize. She turned around, stepping over and out of the tangle of chain. She crouched and stroked the dog affectionately, feeling him tremble beneath her hand.

"Good boy, Eightball," she said in a soothing voice. "If you wanna hold back, I completely understand."

The puppy shuddered as Syd advanced down the passageway, casting the flashlight beam straight ahead. At the end of a dingy, cluttered hall, the light bounced off a closed door, the sheet metal dull and dirty. She gave it the once-over as she drew nearer, noticing that there were marks in the grime around the handle. Even the dusty floor revealed telltale footprints where the door had recently opened out toward her. She tried the handle: locked. Undeterred, she pulled her pick out once more and set to work. Within a minute the barrel was turning. She grabbed the handle again and pulled. The door shifted only an inch before jarring to a halt. Something was barring it from within.

Syd looked around, sticking the flashlight's end in her mouth as she rifled through the shelves around her for something she could use to prize open the door. On one side she found a case of toilet rim blocks for the restroom, a pallet of paper towel rolls, a huge stack of brown envelopes, and boxes full of gift wrap. She turned her attention to the other side. Higher up, there was a glass box that contained some kind of African tribal mask. Below this there was an Australian didgeridoo, a great bamboolike pole that Aborigines would blow through to make music. Perhaps that could act as some kind of fulcrum, but she'd have to shatter the end first. Even then, would it work? On the lowest shelf, her eyes finally alighted on the perfect tool.

Syd searched the long glass case for a lid and found none. The museum had clearly vacuum-sealed the display, possibly to prevent any damage to the metal. She'd heard about how oxidation could ruin iron, and suspected that contact with air would do irreparable damage to the artifact. But what choice did she have? She made a quick apology to the Holy Mother before bringing her boot down and smashing the long panel on the top of the box. Glass tinkled into the display case and showered the item within. Syd deftly reached inside, grabbing the haft and pulling it free.

With force and maneuvering, she was able to wiggle the spearhead into the gap between the door and its frame, just above the handle. The shaft jutted out at a forty-five-degree angle, quivering like a giant arrow. The label on the glass cabinet had informed her that this was an Aztec spear. Syd pushed with all her might. The spear bowed, the weapon's head trembled, but the door didn't give. She moved along its length, to the spear's base. Drying her hands on her jeans, she bent her back and pushed hard once again.

Eightball looked up at her, kneading his little paws anxiously as she struggled. She cried out as the spear flexed, prompting a bark from the pup. Just when she thought her back might break before the spear, Eightball leaped in the air, hurling his body at the bending weapon shaft. He struck it hard beside her, adding the extra bit of weight that Syd was missing, before bouncing back to the ground. Girl and spear lurched forward suddenly, a *snap* sounding beyond the door as the flashlight tumbled to the floor with a *crack*.

The metal door creaked as it swung open, a cloud of dust billowing out of the darkness into the basement vaults. Syd scrambled for the flashlight, swinging it up into the open doorway. Beyond was a crowded storeroom. White dust sheets broke up the pitch black, materializing as the flashlight's beam passed by. She entered warily, slicing at the air with the ray of white light as if it might cut any terrors in two. She didn't see any other exit from the room. The beam flickered intermittently, losing its intensity. Syd gave it a shake, willing life back into it. On the floor she found a broken wooden bar, which must have barricaded the door shut. She also found a large piece of broken masonry, bricks protruding from its crumbling cement. Syd stepped over the detritus, scanning the room. One exceptionally large shape sat atop a wooden table, draped in a sheet. She grabbed its edge and pulled it free, catching her breath.

It was a sarcophagus, the faded script and gold paint all but vanished from its surface. Hieroglyphs were scored along its length, no doubt spelling out the name of the inhabitant. It was at that moment the flashlight blinked out. She shook it ineffectually. Now she was in a pitch-black basement, blind. Not for long.

"Let there be light!"

She said this to herself as much as Eightball and the shadows, sparking up the cigarette lighter that she carried everywhere with her. It's not like she smoked—Syd was no fool—but she liked to be prepared. Max had taught her that; she'd never been a Girl Scout. She held the lighter over the sarcophagus, noting that it was empty, the lid placed to one side against the wall. She whipped more sheets down, revealing more random boxes of both junk and antiquity.

Crouching, she petted Eightball, and found that the dog was snuffling at the ground again. She brought the flame to the floor, illuminating spatters of blood on the gray concrete. And something else; she ran her fingers over a series of raised blobs in the dust. Dried wax. The flame flickered. Holding the cigarette lighter out, she kept it low, waving it slowly before her. As the flame fluttered again, Syd felt the slightest breeze over her knuckles.

She shuffled to the wall, the fire now burning blue as the airflow caught it once more. The breeze was strongest beside a tall metal locker, nearly blowing out the lighter flame where the cabinet met the wall. Syd squeezed her fingers behind the locker's back and pulled.

There was a grinding squeal of metal against concrete that caused her to wince. The locker came away from the wall, revealing a man-size fissure where the bricks had been removed. The crumbling wall's edge matched the chunk of masonry she'd almost tripped over when she'd first entered the room. Syd raised the lighter, spying roughly carved steps descending.

"Woof," said Eightball.

"You're not wrong," she whispered anxiously, picking the spear up and setting off.

The tunnel was big enough to accommodate her, allowing for the comfortable passage of a six-foot-tall man, she reckoned. The flame twinkled, catching the undulating rock walls as she went. Syd could see finger marks—perhaps even claws or talons had gouged the route through rock and red, sticky earth. It was a stretch to describe it as a staircase, but uneven footholds hewn into the earth brought her deeper into the ground with each step. She stumbled, lighter held out in one hand, spear raised in the other. Eightball followed, hopping down the crumbling steps. The tunnel suddenly leveled out, her descent complete, as the ceiling rose and she found herself in a domed chamber.

Her foot caught something on the floor with a *clang*. Looking down, she found an abandoned handheld candelabra. Crouching, she passed the lighter over the six candle stubs, illuminating the chamber. She stood, raising the fancy candlestick aloft.

"Holy crapsacks," Syd hissed as Eightball growled.

This had to be Vendemeier's lair. The room stank of decay, a sweet, musty reek that made her bite back her bile. An exit tunnel headed off from the one that she'd entered through, probably leading away from the museum and providing the warlock with another means of access. The curving walls were adorned with scripture and symbols carved into the clay. They reminded Syd of the sarcophagus hieroglyphs, only cruder, less elegant in their shape. The more she stared at them, the more she felt chills emanating from the pit of her belly. Her guts were curdling, as if some ancient evil had taken root within her, crawling up through her insides, reaching for her heart . . .

Syd looked away, struggling to breathe. She cast her eyes to the floor in the center of the chamber. There it was. An unremarkable-looking cube, carved from a dark black wood, sat upon a plinth of earth that rose like a termite mound to waist height. She held the candelabra over it, glimpsing a green hue within the wood. Syd stepped around it, examining it carefully from all sides. If there was a lid, it wasn't visible, but it had been described as a box.

Sticking the spear through the belt loop on her skinny jeans, Syd picked it up.

Her first clue that she was in danger was Eightball's growl. The second was the candle flames flickering as something rushed toward her from that other passage. This was her cue to duck as a hard fist connected with the clay wall. Red earth fell away, choking dust clouding around her. The cube tumbled from her hand into the debris as she struggled to right herself. Half-blind, Syd whipped the spear back out and held the candelabra up in an attempt to see her assailant.

The mummy was no giant, not like in the movies. It was around six feet tall, and wasn't even that broad; it probably weighed less than Syd did. The ancient wraps that covered its body hung on every contour, hugging its embalmed flesh. The linen bandages were stained dark with age and from the gradual breakdown of the body within, crusted in places where they'd begun to peel away. Foul flakes of dried-up ooze broke free with each of the mummy's staggered steps, its head utterly hidden behind the centuries-old material. A museum piece it may have been, but judging by the crumbling cavity it had left in the wall, it still packed one hell of a punch. The monster twisted, its rotting arm pulling back, ready to swipe at the girl again.

Syd lunged in before it could strike, the Aztec spear

MUMMY

OTHER ALIASES: mumia, mūmiya
ORIGIN: Persia and Egypt

STRENGTHS: Great physical might, relentless constitution, disease-ridden.

WEAKNESS: HIGHLY flammable!

HABITAT: Crypts and tombs.

Mummies (the bandaged, preserved bodies of the dead) can be found in many civilizations, although the undead variety has recently risen to prominence. The European craze of archaeology that began in the 16th and 17th centuries will bring antiquarians ever closer to them, especially (I fear) in Egypt. As long as humanity interferes with these ancient burial sites, breaking seals and unleashing curses, so we shall see more of these infernal walking corpses. Graverobbers will always get their just deserts. Undead mummies carry a variety of diseases and an insatiable hatred—and hunger—for the living. Avoid them at all costs!

—Erik Van Helsing, August 13th, 1860

PHYSICAL TRAITS

1. Hands—The clawed fingers of the mummy are its deadliest weapon. "Mummy Rot" is a fast-acting disease that can cause the flesh of their foes to be swiftly eaten away.

2. Mouth—Saturated with the same hideous blight as the hands, the additional danger of the mummy's bite is its tongue. A probing, snakelike monstrosity, it can burrow into the flesh like a leech to gorge upon its victim's blood.

—Esme Van Helsing, January 5th, 1866

① NEVER enter a TOMB without a TORCH!

—Algernon Van Helsing, March 15th, 1940

Fortunately, we live in GALLOWS HILL and MUMMIES are pretty few and far between! Long may things stay that way too—they sound SUPER GROSS!!

MAX HELSING Apr 29th, 2015

hitting it on the left side of its torso, between the ribs. Unfortunately for the girl, the weapon carried straight through, emerging out of the mummy's back as her hand collided with its bandaged chest. The mummy's fist flew and Syd moved, but not quickly enough. It caught her in the shoulder, the blow sending shock waves through her right arm and leaving it numb. She hit the wall, bouncing, more hieroglyphs breaking loose in a shower of earth and clay.

Eightball bit the monster on the left calf, tugging at its leg and worrying the wraps free. They came loose, tangling around the dog, revealing puckered, necrotic flesh the color of ebony. The mummy kicked backward, catching the pup in his ample guts and propelling him across the chamber. The dog made a wide parabola and left an Eightball-shaped imprint in the wall, landing in another heap of rubble.

If the mummy didn't kill her, the collapsing cavern would. Syd was on the floor, moving away from the monster, her right arm still dead. Placing the candelabra on the ground, she frantically looked through the debris around her, desperate to retrieve the dropped box, but the creature was breathing down her neck. She felt a hand seize her ankle. She glanced back at the mummy, now stretching its other hand up toward her thigh, yellow nails poking out of the end of scabrous, bandaged fingers. She kicked with her free leg, catching it in the groin. Centuries old it may have been, but the blow still had the desired effect. The mummy staggered back, tripping over the unraveled bandage of its calf and toppling like a felled tree. It landed on the spire of earth that the box had previous sat upon, the spear of sculpted clay bursting straight through its chest.

"Eightball," cried Syd. "The box; seek it!"

The little dog pulled himself upright with a whimper, shaking dirt from his shiny coat before setting off into the rubble in search of the black cube.

With a mournful moan, the mummy tried to haul itself up the clay spire, but it slid back, still pinned in place. For now. Syd scrambled upright.

"C'mon, Eightball," she called. "We're out of here!"

The room was in danger of collapsing at any moment, and the mummy was still determined to remove her arms from their sockets. If the box couldn't be retrieved, so be it. She dashed toward the sloping passage that led back to the museum, only to witness the tunnel ceiling coming down, one enormous slab of earth after another. Keeping a healthy distance from the skewered mummy, Syd maneuvered around it toward the other exit.

"Eightball, let's go!"

The puppy whimpered, still searching for the precious box.

"Leave it!"

She clambered to the entrance of the other tunnel, glancing back in time to see the mummy break free, snapping the clay tower off midway up its height, the red earth tumbling loose from the great hole in its stomach.

The creature nearly crashed into Syd, bandaged hands grabbing her shoulders as she fell backward into the tunnel. The mummy came with her, stopping short of landing on top of her. It looked confused about what had halted its progress. But Syd could see the culprit well enough: the Aztec spear, still stuck horizontally through the dead Egyptian like a cocktail stick through an especially disgusting wiener, had caught on either side of the tunnel, halting the mummy's progress. If it just turned its torso, it would be through and onto her, but thankfully for Syd, the mummy wasn't so smart. Instead, it pulled her back down the tunnel toward it, long arms reeling her in. She was about to scream when a strange belching noise preceded an explosion of light in the collapsing chamber.

She saw the mummy illuminated, its body silhouetted by an explosive blast at its back. Those bandages, brittle and long dried, went up in flames, devoured by a fireball that engulfed the monster. Its fingers released Syd, letting her collapse to the ground as she felt the heat burn her face. The ancient wraps and the corpse within were swiftly consumed, and the remains of the mummy fell to the floor like ash. The antique spear tumbled, and the teenager snatched it as it dropped, backing up into the tunnel before she was caught by the cave-in.

Out of the flames, dust, and bone-rattling rubble came Eightball, bounding out of danger and landing on her chest, just as Vendemeier's lair fell in on itself behind them. The puppy's nostrils flared bright white, smoke trailing from them, while in his slobbering, superheated jaws he held that small black box. Syd plucked it from Eightball's lips and hugged the hellhound hard.

"Clever boy," she said, kissing his dust-dappled brow. "You *are* a remarkable wee beast, aren't you?"

TWENTY-NINE

xxx

A GRAVE PREDICAMENT

The ghouls poured through Gallows Hill Burying Ground, a wave of pale and putrid flesh. They turned on one another, clawing and snapping, eager to be first to their prey. More than three dozen of the foul fiends had fallen under Vendemeier's spell, rushing to play their part in the dawn of the Age of Unlight. All they needed to do was bring down the boy. They yearned for his raw flesh, far removed from their usual diet of worm-riddled corpses. Their master would have to be swift, though; Marked for death as the monster hunter was, it would be a battle of wills to make them resist devouring the boy whole.

That was if they could catch him, of course. Max was the last of the Van Helsings; he had spent the afternoon in the cemetery, and he had not been idle. There'd been plenty more to do than exhume graves. He was a resourceful young man.

At the moment, the boy's main focus was on the mob of grave-robbing monsters. He'd managed to evade Jed for now; though his possessed mentor was still out there, the ghouls were priority number one. He let the closest pair draw in close, snapping at the heels of his Chucks as he took a looping route that brought him back toward the Hanging Tree. He jumped over the trench in the ground, snatching up his shovel where it sat upright in the piled-up peat. The ghouls missed the leap, falling over one another as they landed in the open grave, directly onto Vendemeier's petrified corpse. Even with the Bane of Monsters blazing over Max's head, the two ghouls couldn't resist tearing into the corpse, fighting over his remains as a third leaped in to join them.

"Three down," muttered Max. "A small army to go!"

As he rounded the tree, two more awaited him. The first leaped, only to find itself struck across the head by the flat of the shovel. Max spun, bringing the tool around in a descending arc and burying it with a resounding crunch in the second one's shoulder. It wasn't a killing blow, but then again, that wasn't what Max had aimed for. Ghouls were peaceful beasts for the most part. The monster hunter wanted to incapacitate them until he could deal with Vendemeier. Not that he had a plan on that front. He'd hoped the warlock's grave might have thrown an answer up and into his lap, but it had given him nothing. He was playing for time, and the clock was broken.

He tried to wrench the shovel free from the ghoul's

shoulder blade. Black blood welled as the fiend wailed, reaching for the folding handle. Max looked behind; two more were converging on him from opposite directions. Max twisted at the last second, swinging the shovel handle—still with the wounded, flailing ghoul attached—straight into the path of the first incoming attacker. He released his grip when the two collided, leaving them tumbling in a tangle of crunching limbs. Max ducked, but the second attacker couldn't be avoided, landing directly on top of him with a victorious howl echoed by its companions throughout the cemetery.

Its palms slapped Max's face as one finger caught the edge of his right eye. The boy reached up for the monster's throat, but its reach was longer, its elbows locked. He felt the cold, clammy digit hook his eyelid, tugging at it, expecting it to slip into the socket at any moment. Max twisted his face, snapping his jaws and taking off three of the creature's fingers. He spat them out rapid-fire, ignoring the foul taste as the ghoul fell away.

Max was up and running again, eyes searching not only for the next ghoul but also for Jed and Vendemeier. Where were they? Were they leaving the hunt to the carrion feeders? Right on cue, he heard the gurgling gloats of the warlock resonating throughout the wooded graveyard around him.

"You delay the inevitable, Van Helsing. Cease running and hand yourself over. Mr. Coolidge desires a reunion."

Max ignored the taunts. Ahead he spied the family crypt, instantly recognizable even through the twilight gloom.

Another ghoul jumped out from the shadows, charging at Max, arms wide in a monstrous embrace. Max had never been good at sports in school—he saved his competitive edge for when it mattered—but in that moment he channeled his inner linebacker. He went in low, dipping his shoulder and catching the monster in the guts. The ghoul went up and over, somersaulting over Max's back as the boy continued his progress. He hurdled the crypt railings, leaping up onto the tomb's roof. He skidded to a halt as the ghouls closed in, the nearest already climbing the black railings that circuited the family burial plot. Max's hands worked fast, picking up the item he'd stowed there and strapping it into place. With regret, he remembered Syd had never field-tested it.

"What could possibly go wrong?" he muttered, standing and turning on the assembled mass of ghouls.

The bolts flew, one after another, the first couple going wide. The third struck its target, and soon they were catching the undead horde in quick succession. The ghouls screamed with each impact, the silver-headed missiles doing untold injury to each of them. Shoulders, knees, hands, even gut-shots would do the trick, taking the monsters out of the fight.

Firing a crossbow wasn't a new experience for Max; he'd been trained in every kind of weaponry by Jed. But this modified version, Syd's repeat-bow, was something special. The bow was strapped onto Max's forearm, with a lever across the palm that triggered the firing mechanism. With a clench of the fist the bow reloaded. How? Max had *no* idea, but he didn't need to. Thank goodness he had Syd, who understood these mechanical dark arts. A clip that housed a dozen bolts was mounted above the groove, depositing them into place after each shot was fired. If he ran out of ammo, he simply had to lock another cartridge in.

Seven of the monsters lay wounded around the tomb, but their brethren poured over them to get to the boy. He fired again. The bow clicked. He was out of ammo.

"Wow," he muttered, fishing in his messenger bag for the spare clip. "They went down *really* fast."

His fingers were closing around the wooden magazine when a hand seized his ankle and yanked hard. He fell backward, landing on his spine across the top of the tomb, his messenger bag swinging out over the granite edge and hanging behind him. He could feel a ghoul hauling itself up onto the crypt roof, using Max's aching legs as a ladder. Below his head, another ghoul had traversed the railings and taken hold of the satchel, which dangled now from around his throat. The ghoul tugged it, cracking Max's head into the tomb's stone gutter. The creature's hands raced up the straps toward the youth's face.

"Hold him there for me," said Vendemeier, emerging from the shadows as Max found himself pinned to the tomb. Dead, decayed hands appeared around him, scuttling up the crypt wall like a swarm of giant spiders. They snatched hold, grabbing his arms, securing his legs, twisting the satchel straps until they choked the young hero. Max watched, upside down, eyes bulging, as Vendemeier advanced, the Egyptian dagger in hand. Soon, Max was motionless; dead hands gripped his hair and locked his head in place. The warlock was only a foot away, surrounded by his frenzied horde of ghouls.

"You'll never win, Vendemeier!" shouted Max. "There'll be others like me. Good people who'll stop you."

"Cease your incessant prattling, child," said the grotesque figure, raising the flaming green knife toward Max's exposed throat. "There *are* no others, Maxwell Van Helsing. You are the last of your line. Know now, at the end, that you are entirely, absolutely, and undeniably alone."

He drew his hand back, the blade poised to strike Max's neck.

The next moment, Vendemeier's arm was pinned to the head of a ghoul by his side, an arrow impaling it in place. The warlock cried out, dropping the dagger as he toppled over onto the felled fiend. The monster holding Max's messenger bag straps turned, trying to see where the shaft had flown in from, only to discover a matching arrow suddenly quivering in its own skull. It went down in a twitching heap, releasing its hold on Max's satchel. The teenager tugged his right arm loose as panic seized the group. A quick jab to the throat of the ghoul who held his left arm, and his entire upper body was free. The one that had crawled up his legs remained astride him, suddenly realizing that it was alone. Max swung the repeat-bow around, smashing the weapon into the monster's jaw and causing it to fall flopping from his lap.

Max chanced a glance in the direction the arrows had

flown from. Stepping out from between the trees and graves came Abel Archer, bow loaded and already unloaded, yet another arrow stuck lightning-fast in the chest of one of the ghouls. A smaller figure accompanied the Brit through the mist. Wing Liu crept along behind the mountainlike Archer, the boy's newly acquired catapult launching marbles wildly into the melee.

Max didn't have time to question the arrival of his allies; he had more pressing concerns, specifically the monster mob baying for his blood as they clambered onto the crypt. His bomber jacket absorbed some of their blows, but tooth and claw still found their way to his flesh. He kicked and punched, jabbed and weaved, hurling them off the tomb and back into the throng. Archer and Wing had distracted many of the ghouls from their target, but plenty remained focused upon their initial foe. Max could imagine the Bane of Monsters, a crown of fire, blazing above his head like a beacon. A neon flashing sign with "Come and Get It" in big letters couldn't have done a better job of directing monsters his way.

With a boot to the chest of one of the ghouls, a gap opened up for him. Max took two strides and leaped, leaving the tomb behind as he launched himself into the air and over the railings. The ghouls watched him sail over their heads, turning to follow him as he landed acrobatically in a tucked roll. He ripped the clip off the repeat-bow and whipped the fresh cartridge out of his satchel. Unfortunately, the fracas atop the crypt had reduced the magazine to broken shards of wood, and his hand reemerged clutching splinters and crossbow bolts. He looked back at the ghouls piling toward him. Max launched the loose bolts like throwing darts. They found their marks, the creatures recoiling as the silver heads hissed into their flesh.

Max was up, sprinting back toward the Hanging Tree. Headstones whipped by, and overhanging branches made him duck and scramble. He looked back at the dozen or so creatures in hot pursuit. But where was Vendemeier? He brought his gaze ahead once more as the Hanging Tree appeared out of the mist.

The punch caught Max in the guts, lifting him off his feet, as his assailant stepped out from behind a tree. The boy landed in the mud, spluttering for breath, his face full of filth. He looked up, his vision blurred, his enemy stepping closer. This foe wasn't mindless like the ghouls. Max was facing a warrior, he realized, his eyes quickly refocusing upon his towering opponent.

He was facing Jed.

THIRTY

xxx

BROUGHT BEFORE THE HANGING TREE

Max's head recoiled as Jed's boot caught him clean across the jaw, lifting Max off the ground and flinging him through the air. He hit the deck, skidding through mud and dead leaves, before coming to a halt beneath the Hanging Tree. For a moment, he could see nothing, hear nothing, eyes blinded by lights and his head consumed by a high-pitched whine. Slowly, the white haze subsided, the world taking shape. The din of battle returned as the blurred figure of Jed limped closer. Max tried to speak, his mouth full of blood, as the man grabbed him by his hair. Jed hauled Max to his feet, his sneakers struggling to find the ground. His mentor brought his other hand back, slapping Max with furious venom. The boy pirouetted, collapsing into the tree and sliding down its trunk.

"You're beaten, Van Helsing," said Vendemeier, following Jed's footsteps as he approached the tree. He paused, looking down disapprovingly at the ghouls that were devouring his mortal remains in his grave. He shook his head, moving on.

"Don't be so precious about your life, child. You're just flesh and bone, another insignificant grub that doesn't know its place. This is not your world, boy. This world belongs to the King in Yellow."

"So you keep saying," spat Max, a glob of blood dribbling down his chin. "Still haven't seen the big guy yet. He shy or something?"

Jed seized Max's shoulder, shoving him back against the tree. His face was emotionless, eyes wild with that terrible green fire that raged within Vendemeier's slack-skinned skull.

"Are you in there, Jed?" Max whispered. "Give me a sign. Anything."

The only sign he received was a grim one, the old boxer drawing a fist back, ready to let fly.

"Steady, Mr. Coolidge," said Vendemeier, raising a twisted hand, the arrow still stuck through his forearm. "It will be *my* pleasure to take this one's life." He pulled the arrow through the dead flesh, the missile emerging dark and sticky through the other side before he threw it into the mud.

"Do you see me fretting over my corpse down there?" asked Vendemeier, gesturing toward the feasting ghouls in his grave as more gathered at his back. Max could see them forming a defensive cordon around him. Where was that maniac Abel Archer when you needed him?

"I couldn't help but notice you weren't . . . altogether yourself," said Max, looking at the exhumed grave.

Vendemeier giggled. "No, I suppose not. The piece of me that was sworn to my Master, bonded to Him by the Unspeakable Oath, was removed upon the night of my death by my acolyte. It was kept safe from harm. Did you really think you would find my heart here tonight, Van Helsing? Do you think me an imbecile?"

"You have to ask?" Max brought his gaze back to Jed, trying to look deeper than the hellish green glow of his eyes. "Jed, you've raised me as your own. You've been there for me through thick and thin. Please, snap out of it. Whatever this clown's done, shake it off."

Max kicked out at the old boxer, catching him on the kneecap of his bad leg. The man winced, the green flames flickering, faltering momentarily before roaring back to life.

"You don't want to do this, Jed. I love you. You're kinda fond of me, too. Don't let him win!"

"Hold him still," said the warlock, his jovial humor now vanished as he approached with the dagger. Jed grabbed Max's bangs, pushing his head back against the rough bark of the Hanging Tree. The murder of crows had gathered in the branches above, all silent now, bearing witness to the end of Max Helsing.

SYD'S BMX BURST THROUGH THE GATES OF GALLOWS Hill Burying Ground, kicking up gravel as she stood high in the seat. Her legs were a blur, stamping the pedals as she accelerated through the graveyard, down toward Witch River. Shouts and screams drew her in, leaving her with no doubts about where the battle was. Trees and tombs slipped past, silent sentinels that marked her path toward a scene of madness. Eightball was behind her somewhere, struggling to keep up, his brave work done after belching a fireball onto that miserable mummy.

The scared kid inside was telling her to turn back, head home, bury her head beneath her pillow, but the best friend roared louder. She wouldn't leave Max alone on this night. She had no idea what was in the box, but she knew one thing for sure: she had to deliver it to Max.

She could feel the box's hard edges pressing against her rib cage, zipped under her jacket. She was terrified of dropping it, of what might happen if she failed to get it to Max in one piece, let alone on time. The access tunnel from Vendemeier's lair had brought her out into a park, not far from the museum. Doubling back, she and the portly pooch had picked up the bicycle and burned rubber in their desire to reach the cemetery.

A figure lurched from the undergrowth as she neared a bend at the bottom of the hill, scrawny arms reaching, white eyes blind with rage: a ghoul, like the monster she and Max had encountered the other night. Syd couldn't hold her scream in; Max might have been able to face down any horror, but this monster hunting was all new to her. The Aztec spear was stashed across her back, but reaching for it would have caused her to crash. Indeed, she nearly lost control of the BMX, righting it only when she kicked out with her foot, hoofing the fiend in the chest. The ghoul tumbled back and the bike remained upright, taking the corner and speeding toward the Hanging Tree.

Two more undead monsters crashed toward her through the undergrowth, looking to cut her off. Her muscles burned as she powered downhill, jumping on the pedals to get them spinning.

The front wheel hit a rock. The BMX stopped instantly, and Syd was launched from the saddle like a boulder from a siege engine. Her body spun and the world turned around her. Then she was coming back to earth, screams and snarls in her ears. Her inner engineer told her what was coming: her angle of projection and descent was such that she was going to land on her head with no hope of righting herself. This would be a broken neck . . . if she were lucky.

The crunch never came. Before she could land, Syd was caught in the embrace of a stranger as safely as a kitten tumbling from a tree. The young man wore scuffed biker leathers, and he cradled Syd in one arm against his broad chest. She glanced up, catching his thick mop of blond hair and Hollywood smile, before he pulled a long-handled ax from a holster on his back. Barely breaking eye contact with her, he sheared the top of the first ghoul's head off as it closed on them. Then the stranger threw the blade at the second one, catching it square in the chest, black blood spewing down its torso as it collapsed face-first in the dirt.

Wing appeared, stepping out of the shadows to stand beside them, a loaded slingshot in his trembling grasp. Syd was lost for words.

"Do breathe, my dear," said the young man in a smooth English accent. "There's a good girl."

MAX SQUIRMED IN JED'S GRIP, UNABLE TO FREE HIMSELF from the man's iron hold on his hair. The sickening sound of the feasting ghouls rose from the Hanging Tree's exposed roots. The remaining monsters were closing ranks around their master. Were Archer and Wing dead? Max bit down a sob, imagining the poor kid's fate. The pale-skinned ghouls were silent as they watched Vendemeier, entranced by the warlock's dagger, green flames licking its length.

"I hadn't expected an audience for this tonight, but so be it," said Vendemeier. "It has been so very long since I've had a congregation to preach to, I'd almost forgotten the sound of my own voice."

"I find that hard to believe," grunted Max, as Jed twisted the hair on his scalp to silence him.

"You have served me well, my friends. When the King in Yellow returns, you shall all find favor beneath His gaze. There is a future for each and every one of you in the Age of Unlight."

Max ignored the ranting warlock, reaching into his jeans pocket. Out came his bunch of keys from Helsing House, the brass garage key caught between his thumb and finger. He lashed out, the jagged metal cutting through Jed's vest and slashing a strip across the old man's chest. Fury flashed in Jed's eyes, momentarily replacing the green fire as his clenched fist shook. The keys fell on their chain as Max kept his voice low, trained on the old boxer, as he risked everything. He reacted, Max reasoned, to pain, to emotion.

"Your name is Joseph Edward Coolidge, and you were born in Harlem in 1945. Your mother's name was Roberta, and she worked as a maid at the Hotel Edison in New York City. You never met your father, Joseph Senior, because he was killed on the beaches of Normandy during the D-Day landings. He got a medal for valor, which you keep at our home in a frame above the fireplace. It's your most treasured possession."

The green fire flickered further at the mention of Jed's parents, but his grip remained firm, the fist poised to strike. Vendemeier continued preaching to the ghouls at his back as Max went on, quiet but insistent. Tears were rising in the corners of his eyes, but he was locked in on Jed. His free hand moved inside his jacket, searching for his last lifeline.

"I know all this because you drilled it into me. You told me how important family was. 'The most powerful magic in the world.' Those were your words, Jed. You met my grandfather, Algernon, when he used to stay at the Edison. You tended bar and got to chatting. He showed an interest in your boxing career. When that ended prematurely, he offered you a gig working for him. You've worked for and with the family ever since. When Algernon died, you took his son,

Conrad, under your wing as your own. You two traveled the world side by side, fighting monsters and putting them in the dirt. And then my father died, and you were left with me. Still family. Nothing changed. You raised me right; you raised me as you would the son you never had. You're all I have, Jed. You *are* my family. I love you. And that's why this hurts me more than you can know . . ."

Max launched the contents of the thermos flask at Jed. The old warrior released his grip on the boy, his hands flying up to his face as the scalding soup hissed across his skin. The burning broth went up his nose, down his throat, into his eyes, and across his bloodied vest. The flask fell into the leaves, quickly followed by an exhausted Max as he collapsed at Jed's feet. The veteran monster hunter loomed above him, doubled over, green eyes hidden behind clenched fists as steam rose from his scorched head and torso.

Vendemeier was in his element now, speaking loud and proud, the ghouls buoyed by his arrogant speech as he moved among them, blessing their flesh with the burning blade. Their dead flesh hissed, the stench unbearable.

"Just as the boy is Marked, so now are you, as soldiers in Hastur's army. Could there be any greater gift than being the first acolytes of the King in Yellow, on the eve of His return?"

The ghouls clamored, desperate to feel the kiss of the green flames upon their rotten skin. Vendemeier sighed contentedly.

"And so begins the Age of Unlight, Van Helsing," said the

warlock, twirling the blade and turning back to Max. "Time to die."

Jed's punch caught the warlock on the bridge of the nose, his already decaying features crumpling in on themselves beneath a sledgehammer of knuckles. He went down into the dirt, face a mask of thick, gooey blood, looking up at a beaten, battered Jed, who towered over him. The aged prize-fighter swayed unsteadily, steaming lumps of overcooked clam flopping from his face and shoulders, his eyes human, hard, and full of anger. Max stood beside him, cheeks wet with tears, as the crows in the Hanging Tree screeched in unison.

Jed snorted. "You asked for it," he said, raising his fists, ready for a fight.

THIRTY-ONE

xxx

THE MURDER OF CROWS

With Jed returned to his former self, Max had a moment to gather his thoughts before the horde of ghouls charged for him. Jed stood in their way, a human barricade. With the spell broken, his rage was doubled, the old fighter letting his fists rip as jawbones, teeth, and rotten flesh flew. If a ghoul slipped by him, he'd change his angle, cutting it off before it could reach his young charge. He had Max's back, but it wouldn't stop the monsters from gradually overpowering them.

"Max!"

It was Syd's voice, from beyond the scrum of bodies. Max dodged as one of the ghouls broke past Jed, wincing as its claws raked his stomach before he shoved it headfirst into the Hanging Tree. The crows squawked as the fiend hit the trunk, but they remained there, watching the fight. A figure barged through, shoving the monsters aside and heading straight for Max, clearing the way for the girl who ran in his wake. It was Abel Archer, with Syd and Wing on his tail.

"The box!" Syd yelled, waving a black cube above her head as she caught sight of Max through the melee.

That wasn't a great idea.

Vendemeier leaped up from the mud, seizing her by the hair. She lashed out, striking with elbow and foot, trying to headbutt him, but he'd learned from his last encounter with Syd. He avoided her blows, hands working their way along her straining arm, past the elbow, to the box she clutched in her hand.

"Filthy little harpy," he hissed. "Give that back!"

"Go get it yourself!" cried Syd, tossing it into the throng.

Max saw it land at Jed's feet, where the bare toes of the ghouls kicked it around. He dived forward, onto his belly. The combatants went down with him, trying to stab him, bite him, kill him, as Vendemeier shrieked in a blind panic. He too threw himself forward, pushing his minions aside as he tried to reach the box.

Max felt teeth bite into the top of his head, and claws rake his throat, but he kept on reaching for that black wooden box. Jed tore monsters off Max's back, with Abel Archer joining the huddle, his ax ripping lumps out of the rotten bodies. Through the mass of limbs, Max saw Vendemeier's green eyes shining as he squirmed through the mud toward the box. The boy felt the weight of bodies on him, Jed and Archer unable to reach him, as the undead tried to tear flesh from his bones. He screamed but fought on. It was only a hand's breadth away. Vendemeier crawled desperately closer. The warlock mouthed the word *no* as Max got to it first, slamming his fist down, the cube splintering beneath the blow.

Within the broken box lay the blackened husk of a heart, preserved for all time as if pickled in tar. Max grabbed the withered lump of meat and tossed it, through the crowd, into Vendemeier's centuries-old grave. The trio of ghouls who had gorged on the warlock's remains stared briefly at the organ as if it were a hand grenade thrown into their midst. Then they leaped upon it, clawing at one another, hungry to taste this most delicate, delicious morsel. As their teeth tore the heart apart, it was as if a thunderclap had hit the burying ground, knocking everyone who yet stood flat into the blood-soaked mud.

Max rolled over, coming face-to-face with a ghoul. The monster was close enough to bite his nose off. Yet it didn't. Instead, it stared at him in confusion, big pale eyes blinking as if stirring from slumber. Those tiny pinprick pupils looked Max up and down, and then gazed past him, as the creatures around it rose from the sucking, squelching earth. Max stifled a relieved bark of laughter, realizing with delight that they no longer wanted to attack him. Instead, they turned their attention to the other figure that lay close by, struggling to rise from a peat-stained puddle.

"What . . . what are you doing?" said Vendemeier, slipping in the mud on his twisted, buckled legs. "He's there, right behind you. Seize him. Do as I command, you foolish fiends!"

Max clicked his fingers. "Don't you see it, Udo? They're no longer in your thrall." He made a halo sign above his own head as Syd, Wing, and Archer gathered around him. "Your Bane of Monsters is gone; the spell was broken when your heart got chowed. You're done, Vendemeier."

The ghouls closed on the warlock, reaching out, claws catching and grabbing him. They no longer saw a powerful necromancer directing them to attack the teenage monster hunter; they saw a corpse. It might have been moving, talking, struggling in their grasp, but it was still a corpse. Max smiled. He knew full well what ghouls' diets consisted of.

Vendemeier fought back as the remaining ghouls pulled him back down into the mud. He screamed, enraged by their betrayal, trying in vain to fight them off. Wilbur Cunningham's filthy, bloodstained uniform was stripped in seconds and tossed aside, exposing the dead flesh beneath. Syd and Wing looked away as the ghouls tore into the security guard's body like hungry hyenas. The warlock's cries ceased. Bones broke like branches, the awful sound echoing around the graveyard.

A swirling green gas rose from the feasting pack, coalescing before Max and his friends. Jed stepped forward, only for the boy to pull him back as a whispering voice filled the air.

"Do you think that body is the only one that I can occupy, Van Helsing? Foolish mortal. I have survived for centuries, not bound to the earthly confines of flesh and blood like you pathetic humans. Your victory is fleeting. I merely have to find another host, another vessel to—"

The green mist was cut off as a crow flew directly through it, breaking up its shape. The strange gas gathered back together.

"I shall simply find—"

Another crow flew through it, followed by a third, separating the emerald gas into disjointed clouds.

"What is this?" hissed Vendemeier's voice, shrill with panic.

Max smiled as the crows mobbed the green gaseous being, lancing through it and ripping it apart. The warlock's spirit shrieked with each blow.

"Twenty-seven," said Max, as the dark feathered birds swarmed around Vendemeier's spirit, driving it away from the Hanging Tree and over the marsh. "Twenty-seven innocents you murdered during your reign of terror. Twenty-seven poor souls who have waited centuries for their revenge."

The murder of crows pecked, swooped, and slashed at the green mist, striking home as surely as if the warlock were made of flesh. He screamed.

"Twenty-seven spirits waiting for you, Udo."

As the birds drove the vapor over the mist-shrouded reeds of the riverbank, more ghastly, pale lights joined it. They rose up from the marsh like will-o'-the-wisps, attaching themselves to the strange cloud. Still the crows crowded Vendemeier's spirit, breaking it apart.

"What are they?" whispered Syd as the warlock wailed.

"This isn't the end, Van Helsing!" screamed the spirit, growing thin and strained. "This is just the beginning!"

The crows dive-bombed the green mist, driving it down into the mire and the dark, brooding river. Each of the birds hit the surface, taking a piece of that evil, pea-soup fog with it, vanishing beneath the brackish waters with the tattered spirit in tow. The warlock's cries were gone at last.

The humans returned their attention to the Hanging Tree and the ghouls gathered around Cunningham's remains. Abel Archer hefted his ax and grinned, but Max reached out to stay his hand.

"We must let them go, Archer. They're victims here, too. See them off, scare them away, but don't harm them."

The young Englishman sneered, but joined Max as they hissed, clapped, and jeered at the monsters, seeing them on their way. Those that lingered were shown the crucifix or threatened with Archer's ax. Soon the fiends had fled, and Max and his friends stood around what was left of Wilbur Cunningham.

"I don't know who he was, but he didn't deserve this," whispered the boy. He picked up the shovel. "I need to bury him."

Jed stepped up, taking the folding spade from his young charge's grasp.

"You've done enough work today," said the old man, gently but firmly pushing Max back. He began digging around the roots of the Hanging Tree, Syd, Wing, and Archer gradually joining him as Max watched, exhausted.

THIRTY-TWO

xxx

JIGGITY JIG

Max pulled his sweatshirt hood up as he stepped out of the front door of Helsing House, feeling the chilly wind. The rain had ceased, but there was still an inclement nip to the air that suggested winter was on its way. Leaves were piled up on the steps, plastering the stone flags and crying out to be removed. That job could wait, Max figured; he was done doing chores for the immediate future. Some kind of vacation seemed in order. He would just have to work his charms on Jed, get the old man to take him away somewhere—preferably a tropical island.

Eightball bounced past him, down the steps, and onto the gravel drive, finding a suitable spot for a restroom break. It was only nine p.m., but it felt an awful lot later. Max had just popped into the Liu apartment, checking in on Wing, but the kid was fast asleep, exhausted after their exploits. There would be time to talk things through with Wing in the following days. The kid had come through for Max in a remarkable fashion. The boy wasn't alone, of course. Others had played their part in saving the day. Saving the world, more like.

"Home again, home again," said Syd, from her perch on an old bench around the side of the house.

Max smiled when he heard her, and Eightball released a very contented *woof* of his own. He skipped down the steps and followed the hellhound toward her.

"Jiggity jig! What are you doing sitting out here in the cold on your own?"

"I'm not on my own," she replied as he drew close.

To Max's surprise, Abel Archer sat beside her, his hands buried in the pockets of his leather jacket, breath steaming above his head. His weapons lay at his feet, a small arsenal that would get him into trouble the first time a beat cop saw him. How he avoided their attention, Max could only imagine.

"Abel," he said, smiling as best he could. "I thought you'd be long gone by now."

Eightball growled, barely audible, but Max didn't miss it, and neither did Archer. The young Englishman glared back at the hellhound briefly before turning to Max.

"I suppose I should be tootling off, eh? Been a long night for all, hasn't it?"

"Long couple of days actually," said Max, stretching and flexing his muscles ineffectually beneath his hoodie. "I haven't really stopped. It's been one monster after another.

Don't know if you've ever experienced anything like that."

"Can't say I have," said Archer, standing and smiling. Even hidden within the house's shadows and the night's black shroud, his grin still dazzled.

"Yep. All part of the job, I guess," said Max, Eightball's growl still rumbling at his feet.

"You're not wrong there, Maxwell," said the other, hefting his pack and buckling his equipment into place. He looked like some postapocalyptic freedom fighter, all black leather, biker boots, bows, and blades.

"Sayda," he said, bowing elegantly at Syd and sharing a sly grin with her. She giggled. Since when had Syd been a girl who giggled? "It's been a pleasure to meet you, my dear. I very much hope this isn't the last time our paths cross." The girl didn't answer, but judging by her smile Max reckoned she felt the same way. Archer stepped up to Max, towering over his rival by a good foot.

"You know, Maxwell, it can't possibly work."

"What?"

"This," said the giant Brit, pointing at Eightball. "Befriending monsters. It's going to get you killed."

Max smiled. "Worked out well this time. If my monster friends hadn't helped me as much as my human ones did, I'd probably be ghoul chow."

Archer grinned. "You're lucky your little friend Wing called me. Consider this one a freebie, old bean. The next time you're in over your head, it's going to cost you. I can't drop everything and come running every time you get in a fix, can I?"

Max's jaws clenched as he smiled at the big idiot. Archer punched him in the shoulder. He was probably the kind of clown who would try and break a hand when he shook it, thought Max.

"You have my card," said Abel Archer, turning and walking down the drive, the gravel crunching underfoot. "And remember, when you're ready, come work with me. I'll show you what it means to be a *real* monster hunter."

Then he was gone.

"That guy is such an A-hole," said Max.

"You think?" asked Syd, heading back indoors. "I think he's a hottie."

Max was lost for words as he followed her into Helsing House.

His mood lifted as he climbed the stairs, though. He had an awful lot to be thankful for. He was alive, and that was one thing. Even better, the world hadn't ended, swallowed up in the Age of Unlight by Hastur. Max feared he hadn't heard the last of that name.

Back at his own apartment, his weary legs carried him over the threshold, the ever-ready Eightball bouncing in after him. Syd picked up her toolbox from the counter and slipped it into her backpack, checking that everything was securely in place. She turned to Max.

"Welcome to teenhood, dude," she said, giving him a

rare hug. "Trust me when I tell you, it gets better."

"I'll hold you to that. Thanks for everything, Syd."

"Hey, it's what friends do. I have your back, Max. Always."

"And I have yours."

She straightened her backpack, pausing to pat Eightball, who licked her enthusiastically.

"Oh, and hey," said Max as she opened the door. "Archer called you Sayda back there. What's up with that?"

"It's my name."

"I thought it was Syd?"

"Right, because *that's* a Hispanic name."

"It's not?"

"It's short for Sayda, Maxwell," she said, putting extra emphasis on his own full name.

"I didn't know that."

"You never asked." She smiled, closing the door behind her.

Max shook his head, still irked by Archer.

"Penny for your thoughts?"

Max turned, surprised to see Jed limping out of his bedroom and into the lounge. The old boxer moved slower than ever, looking like he'd aged another decade since his abduction at Vendemeier's hands. Beneath the paisley bathrobe and old slippers, Max could see he was still wearing the clothes he'd returned home in, no doubt still spattered with blood and gore.

The boy shrugged. "Keep your change. My head's pretty

vacant at the moment. I'm exhausted, just about ready for bed. What happened to the shower you said you were taking?"

Jed poured himself a warm mug of coffee from the stove. "Are you my boss now?"

Max was tempted to say something glib right then, but for once he thought better of it. Jed was hurting, there was no doubt about it, and it wasn't just from the physical and mental mauling Vendemeier had dealt him. His pride was battered.

"I'm sorry," said his mentor, before Max could think of something else to say. He trudged back past him, settling in his reclining chair.

"For what?" asked Max, sitting down on the rug before it and leaning back against the La-Z-Boy. He'd grown up in that position, crouching at Jed's feet while the old man read.

"All that's happened in the last two days. Every damn minute of it; I'm sorry."

"You've got nothing to apologize for."

"It happened on my watch. I'm supposed to look out for you, protect you."

Max swiveled and placed a hand on Jed's knee. "You *can't* always look out for me. There are going to be times when you're not there—at school, in the street, when I'm with my friends—but that's just life. It'd be just as true if I was a regular kid and not a monster hunter, Jed. You can't always be there."

"But if I *had* been there—"

"I'd be mad as hell!" finished Max. "I need my space, dude. You cramp my style."

Jed clipped him with a rolled-up copy of the evening newspaper, provoking a chortle from Max.

"When you are there, I know you have my back, Jed. That's all that matters."

"I didn't have your back tonight. I was under that monster's spell."

"For a while, sure, but you snapped out of it when you had to."

"It wasn't me, Max. I wasn't . . . myself. I remember so little of what happened. But you brought me back . . ."

"Me and a flask of clam chowder." Max laughed, patting his leg again. "Seriously, Jed? You don't need to explain yourself. That was witchcraft. Don't sweat it. It's done."

"Done?"

"The Bane of Monsters spell is broken. The fiery crown's vanished from my head. I've got you back. I'm not dead. Vendemeier most assuredly is. And the world hasn't ended. Everything's hunky-dory, Jed. Things can return to normal now."

Max smiled. Jed didn't.

"What?" asked the boy.

"The Bane of Monsters might have been removed, Max, but this Vendemeier business is far from over. You may not be Marked for death anymore, but the prophecy remains in place. Should you die an unnatural death at the hands of a monster, it will still trigger the Age of Unlight. The world as we know it will crumble, and the vampires will seize it from mankind."

Max's throat was suddenly dry. "Hastur? The father of vampires, right?"

"Indeed."

"Vendemeier spoke of him like he was some kind of god."

"To the vampires and their thralls he *is* a god, albeit a living one. Or an un-living one." Max nodded. "Udo Vendemeier was one of his priests on earth, but there'll be others."

"Others?"

"Other humans perverted by Hastur's dark promises, those who've taken the Unspeakable Oath and are sworn to serve him throughout life . . . and death."

Max shivered. "He did mention an acolyte having taken his heart for safekeeping."

Jed nodded. "Fortunately for us, that acolyte allowed the heart to end up as a museum piece."

"But if I don't die, Hastur can't return, right?"

"Oh, I think there's *every* possibility Hastur may return. Vampires hibernate, do they not? They feed to a point where they can go into a slumber, sometimes for decades, until they gestate into something else. A metamorphosis, if you will, from Adolescent, via Mature, through to Elder. Hastur's been gone for centuries. If and when he does rise, who knows what form he will take? One thing we can be sure of; a returned King in Yellow will be like nothing the Van Helsings have ever encountered before."

Max sat silent for a moment, brooding.

"When the chance comes to strike Hastur," he said finally, "we gotta bring him down. The trick is keeping me alive in the meantime."

"Son, you put your life on the line every time you step out that door and go sniffing after monsters."

Max shrugged. "It's what I do, what I was born to do, and what I'll continue to do. And as long as I have my friends and family around me," he said, squeezing Jed's bony knee as he rose, "I'll be fine."

"That's all well and good, but with Principal Whedon breathing down your neck, it'll be a miracle if you make it to high school."

The boy laughed. Eightball fell in alongside him again as he started toward his bedroom. He paused by the door, fishing something out of the back of his jeans, beneath his hoodie.

"What you got there?" asked Jed, as Max pulled an ancient leather book out and tossed it to his guardian. He caught it in deft hands.

"Vendemeier's bible. The Egyptian dagger should be sent back to the museum, but I reckon we should hang on to this particular artifact."

"You're not wrong," said Jed, placing it carefully into the bookcase.

"So listen," Max went on, "I was thinking of taking a few days off. Recharge my batteries and all that good stuff."

"You can sleep in tomorrow until ten."

"Ten in the evening?"

Jed glowered. "Those steps need sweeping." His face quirked into a half smile. "But don't make any plans for the weekend."

Max's face lit up. "Why? You got a surprise up your sleeve?"

The old man threw the newspaper at him.

"What's this?" Max asked.

"A newspaper. We're going on a trip."

"Cool!"

Jed's bushy brow twitched. "You may want to check out page eleven. Two college kids went missing in the Pine Barrens of New Jersey. Police report reckons some kind of animal attack. A third student survived. However, he claims they were assaulted by some kind of bat-winged creature with horns, hooves, and a forked tail. His words."

"Jersey Devil?"

Jed shrugged. "Like I said, don't make any plans."

"I can live with that," said Max as he disappeared into the darkness of his bedroom, Eightball in tow. "It's the closest I'll ever get to a vacation."

EPILOGUE

BUZAU MOUNTAINS, ROMANIA

The helicopter touched down on the snow-covered meadow, deep in the shadow of the mountain. The passenger disembarked with the rotors still spinning, kicking up a blizzard as the man hurried across the crisp white field toward the forest's edge. His long, finely tailored black coat flapped as he strode, the wind racing off the mountain nearly blowing him off his feet. The foreman, a short fellow in a thick woollen jacket and a battered yellow hard hat, met him at the tree line. He guided the visitor through the woodland and up the crumbling scree of a goat track that led to the site. As they walked, the man in black looked around.

The Buzau Mountains remained relatively unknown to the outside world, little-explored even by the people of Romania. The man had spent the last week lodging in a guest house in the closest settlement, the village of Nucu, his only link to the outside world a spluttering satellite phone. There had been no road to bring him here this morning—hence the helicopter. The stunning scenery reminded him of where he grew up in France, near Chamonix, at the foot of Mont Blanc.

Breathtaking though the area was, the Buzau range was no tourist destination, not yet anyway. For the time being it remained uncharted, forgotten, a region where mystery and myth still ruled over the superstitious locals. No wonder this had been the chosen place so long ago.

The two men passed a tiny campsite as they climbed. There were three large tents, one for the work crew to sleep in, one for the quartermaster stores, and a last one that was used as their living space, to dine in and shelter from the inhospitable weather. The workmen had been brought over from Poland, cherry-picked by the visitor's man in Warsaw, chosen for their trustworthiness, reliability, hard work ethic, and, possibly even most importantly, lack of ties back home. There were six of them, including the foreman. A good number.

"We are here," said the foreman, speaking in English but with a thick Polish accent, his walruslike mustache twitching nervously. He stopped as the man in black caught up with him.

It would have been difficult to spot the cave entrance from almost any angle. From above, the overhanging cliff ensured it was masked by the mountain, while from below there were trees and bushes blanketing it from sight. What had once been a natural opening within the rock had been adapted centuries ago. The rock face had been hacked away, apertures acting as shrines around a dark, arched doorway, for pilgrims to deposit offerings in. The nubs of black candles could be spotted within these alcoves, their dark wax staining the lichen-covered rock. The visitor paused, letting his fingertips trail over the frozen trails the wax had left down the rough stone. There were other carved churches within the Buzau Mountains, dotted around the village of Nucu, but none like this. He looked to the foreman, who stood at the entrance.

"After you," said the man in black with a smile.

He followed the foreman into the church. A generator chugged away in the corner of the compact cavern, an arc light throwing its glow around the roughly carved room. A couple of tiny stone benches were placed before an altar, behind which was a mosaic. The man in black stepped closer, inspecting the picture. Knights could be seen marching into battle beneath a huge, boiling cloud of darkness, their armor black and their weapons raised. Instead of foreign enemies meeting the sword, though, the Crusaders' fallen foes in these pictures were also Europeans, recognizable by their livery as the Knights Templar. Some of these knights were crucified, hanged, or impaled upon giant stakes that lined their bloody route. The man in black smiled once more.

The foreman stepped through a fissure at the back of the cave, great blocks of rubble gathered around its base. The visitor looked at the opening in the rock, noting the place where at one time the passageway had been bricked up. He followed his companion through the gap and down a set of stone stairs. A different kind of cold gripped the man in black as he walked deeper into the mountain. This one didn't prick at his flesh like the harsh wind outside. This one gnawed at his heart and soul. So close now.

The cave chamber at the foot of the flight of stairs was roughly the same size as the church up top, another arc light illuminating the excavation site from its place suspended from a rig. The five other members of the work team sat on camping stools beneath it, crowded around an electric heater while they sipped from tin mugs. The man in black nodded to them as he passed, though none returned the greeting. One even managed to spit on the rocky floor in an open display of contempt.

"What's the matter with him?" whispered the visitor to the foreman. None of the other men spoke English. The man in black had selected them for that quality, too.

"They want away. Their work is done. You pay them now, yes? The final fee?"

"Of course," said the visitor. "Do tell them I have the money with me, in the helicopter. All of it. I'm very happy to give them their final payment . . . once the job is complete."

"But the job *is* complete," said the foreman, frowning. "Can you not *see* what we've unearthed? This is a tomb."

The man in black turned back to the walls and their grisly tableau. Skeletal bodies were exposed within the earthen walls, lining the chamber, shoulder to shoulder like members of some grotesque assembly. They appeared to have been buried upright, packed into the rock face like hideous statues. At a glance, he counted thirteen bodies.

He closed his eyes and made a silent prayer for their sacrifice: acolytes, disciples—noble souls one and all. There was only one area of the cavern where the dig remained unfinished. A tall, wooden structure was half exposed within the rock, packed into place by centuries-old mortar and soil. It was perhaps ten feet tall and rectangular, its surface scored where the tools had caught it, leaving welts crisscrossing the timber's dark stain. The visitor's breath caught in his throat.

"They'll have no more part in this work," said the foreman. "This is unholy."

The visitor turned on him quickly. "Then they don't get paid," he snapped. As the foreman flinched, the man in black controlled his temper. The smile was there once more. "I was under the impression that none of your crew were religious souls, and therefore this undertaking should have been straightforward. If they wish to not be paid . . ."

He looked past the foreman toward the men. They might have been Polish, but they clearly understood enough English to get the gist of what was said. They nodded at their boss.

"They want paying."

"Then they finish the job," said the visitor, standing aside and gesturing to the far wall as the men picked up their tools once more. "They open it."

The workmen closed on the wooden paneled construct. None of them were fools; they recognized a coffin when they saw one, and an enormous one at that. They were suspicious. For what reason would this Frenchman hire them for this peculiar, specific work? They were superstitious, too. They'd heard the legends of Romania, especially old Transylvania, but they were just stories, weren't they? Above all else, the thing that unified these men was money. Bad debts and worse decisions had driven each of them to the Buzau Mountains and this record-breaking payday. It had been too good an offer to refuse.

The men wedged axes, crowbars, and chisels into the edge of the timber panel, splintering it in places and causing it to flex. It was fully ten feet high from floor to ceiling, but it wouldn't budge. Curses were muttered among the workers as they bickered about where the best point was to prize the coffin lid open. Finally, the foreman stepped before his men, directing each of them to key points up and down the strange casket. Raising a hand, he counted down, before dropping his fist as a signal. They all pushed as one, putting their backs into a combined effort as the dark timber bowed and buckled. The men cried out as a snapping, rending sound came from the box and the wood broke out into the chamber in an explosion of splintering shards. The workers staggered clear, choking as something large toppled out of the coffin, accompanied by a cloud of foul-tasting dust.

One of the workers tripped over a stool, crashing into the lighting rig and launching it swinging from its mooring.

This sent a dizzying beam of light lurching around the room, to nauseating effect. As the lamp creaked overhead and the men spluttered, its glow passed over the strange object that had tumbled from the coffin, the details only visible in fleeting, terrifying glimpses. It looked like a giant black seedpod, perhaps nine feet long and three feet wide at its center, thinning at either end. The men edged closer, trying to see it by the careening illumination. The pod's surface appeared to be covered in thick, trunklike arteries that webbed their way around it entirely. One of the workers gave it a jab with the head of his pickax before his colleagues could stop him. A cracking noise emanated from the pod, followed by a hiss, as if a seal had been broken.

Then nothing.

The light continued to swing crazily overhead. One of the men pointed, indicating a great jagged line that had appeared on the pod's surface, leaving a gaping darkness within. The crack was only a centimeter wide, the contents invisible. The workers craned in to examine it once more. Only the foreman was wise enough to begin backing up, retreating toward the exit. One more tap from a workman's tool was all it took, as a crowbar teased the split carapace.

With a squealing animal cry, a darkness rushed out of the pod, the crack widening in the blink of an eye until the chrysalis tore apart. The men screamed as the entity whipped through them, lashing out, seizing hold, and breaking them like kindling. Oily fingers found their flesh, latching on, tooth and talon slicing the men open like rich, juicy fruit so that the monster could gorge upon their blood. The foreman had seen enough, spinning to run up the steps, leaving his five companions for dead.

He staggered to a halt, the man in black before him. He tried to speak, his lips twitching uselessly as he found no air in his lungs. Only a gurgle emerged, as he felt his insides flooded. He glanced down as the visitor withdrew a smoking, silenced handgun from against the foreman's chest. The visitor smiled, turned the man about, and gave him a gentle shove back toward the emptied coffin, where his colleagues were being quickly drunk dry. He prayed he would die before the monster in the dark took hold of him. He wasn't so lucky. A crooked, clawed hand reached out and drew him into the madness.

The man in black dropped to one knee, whispering praise to the Master, mouthing the magical, arcane words of the Unspeakable Oath. His powers of suggestion were limited, nothing like those of the fallen high priest, but he had still managed to cloud the minds of the Polish work team, convince them to remain here against their better judgment. The workers' death rattles echoed around the room, a steady gulping guzzle rising as they fell, one by one. The foreman's corpse was the last body to topple to the floor, an emaciated husk, as the specter swept before the visitor. The shadows moved around the beast, easily mistaken for a cloak, but these were great and terrible wings of darkness. The Master rose to his full height before his kneeling servant, towering ten feet tall and filling the room, the light still in motion at his back.

"Vendemeier?"

The voice was like a cold knife through the man in black's skull. It felt like his eyes might burst from their sockets, forced out by the all-consuming darkness that invaded his mind.

"High Priest Udo is gone, Master. Never to return. I am Guillaume, Keeper of the Unspeakable Oath, Brother of the Endless Night, and your most humble servant."

The entity hissed in fury, lashing out, tossing the corpses about the room until they bounced off the walls and the lighting rig crashed to the ground, plunging the chamber into darkness, only the faint glow from the church finding its way down the staircase behind the Frenchman. The Master's voice was in his ear now, the breath a whisper of ice that reeked of death and decay.

"And the offspring?"

"The last of them yet lives, Master." Before the darkness could rage again, Brother Guillaume spoke more urgently, his head bowed, unable to look upon the beast. "But Udo did not die in vain. Wheels are still in motion; the boy *was* Marked. The first part of Vendemeier's prophecy holds. Should the boy now die as you desire, the second part will be completed. The Age of Unlight *will* come to pass."

The cavern was silent, the Master considering his acolyte's words. Slowly, a low, sickening chuckle rose, causing the man in black's innards to reel and roll.

"Bring me the boy," hissed Hastur, the King in Yellow. *"Fetch me Van Helsing!"*

ACKNOWLEDGMENTS

Massive howls and hat tips to Kendra Levin, my eagle-eyed, ghoul-grappling editor at Viking. Additionally whopping thanks to my vamp-vanquishing agent, John Jarrold. Kate Renner, cheers for giving Max Helsing such a stylish, killer cover design. And high fives, fist bumps, and tentacle slaps to Jake Wyatt for his fiendishly fine jacket art.

Here's to many more monster hunting escapades together, folks!

TURN THE PAGE FOR A LOOK AT
MAX'S NEXT MONSTER HUNT ...

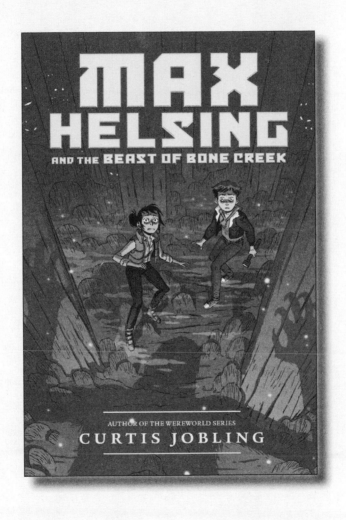

PROLOGUE

xxx

THE MERMAID OF THE MYSTIC RIVER

The fisherman sat on the end of the jetty, huddled beneath his blanket, the hulking behemoth of the Tobin Bridge straddling the night skyline at his back. With its green painted girders lit up, the cantilever crossing dominated this corner of Boston, towering over the rolling waters of the Mystic River. The blood, sweat, and toil of good and honest Massachusetts men had gone into the bridge's construction in the 1940s. If there was a greater piece of engineering, or more handsome manmade structure, Henry Fitzpatrick hadn't seen it. Fitz might have been biased, of course, as his father and uncles had helped build it.

He hunkered down in his deck chair, a rod on either side of him, both set upon their rests. The lines disappeared into the darkness, out onto the water, the fluorescent markers on the nylon quivering in the breeze. If there was a bite, the elderly angler would see it. He checked them over. The one on the left, fine. The one on the right, fine. His feet were up, resting on the cooler, a trio of empty brown beer bottles stacked neatly beside it. Beneath the deck chair, his bulldog slumbered, snoring to his heart's content.

"Fine company you are, Shamrock."

The sound of traffic passing over the Tobin Bridge was a gentle reminder to Fitz that he wasn't the only soul awake at that ungodly hour. Not so long ago, there would've been company for him, up and down the wharf, other night fishermen sharing the river. Those days were gone. Fitz was the only one who remained, the only one who hadn't been scared off.

He glanced up at the moon, full and white overhead. He'd been warned by the gang in the bar not to go, to head home to his wife, Maggie, but Fitz wouldn't hear it. Not that he was averse to spending time with Maggie, of course, but Fitz was at his happiest on the jetty, and everyone knew it, even Maggie. The lure of the river was in his blood, as it had been in his father's, and his father's before him. Fitz checked the lines. Left, fine. Right, fine.

The folk who lived around the docks, who'd worked there all their lives, were a fearful bunch. Gullible, in Fitz's opinion. Two poor saps had gone missing over the previous full moons, so naturally the superstitious said this was the mermaid's mischief at work, luring the men to a watery grave with her siren voice. The Mermaid of the Mystic River. Fitz chuckled. Utter hokum. The two men simply had one too many ales and walked off the wharf to their watery graves. They wouldn't be the first fools to get washed away down the Mystic.

Fitz reached down and opened his cooler, removing a fresh bottle of beer. He cracked the cap off, flicking it into the tide, a dozen feet below. It spun through the air, reflecting the moonlight before it plopped into the waves. He tipped the bottle back, taking a hearty swig, his eyes glancing at the rods. The one on the left, fine. The one on the right, bowing, flexing, the fluorescent marker humming on the line.

He placed the bottle down carefully, reaching across to take the rod off its stand. He stood and braced his feet on the rough timbers of the jetty, hand gripping the reel. He'd been here for three hours and this was the first nibble of the night. It was almost as if, until now, the fish had been scared away. Striped bass was what he was after, and his stomach was rumbling already as he imagined one cooked in butter and lemon. What a treat that would be for tomorrow's dinner. He wound the reel in.

The bulldog was awake now, whimpering beneath the chair.

"What's the matter, Shamrock? Get out here, ya lazy mutt."

The dog didn't come, instead knocking the deck chair over as he backed away fearfully.

"C'mere, ya dumb dog," snapped Fitz, irked by Shamrock's sudden and unexpected cowardice. The bulldog scampered down the wharf, abandoning his master. The rod suddenly yanked hard, almost shooting out of Fitz's grasp. The angler was an old hand and a canny fisherman, though, and he quickly struck back, cranking the reel.

"Big fish, are ya? That's fine by Fitz. The more bass for my plate," he snarled, grinning as he wound in the line.

"You might want to let this one go."

The voice came from the shadows at his back. Fitz half turned, not wanting to take his eyes off the bowing rod and taut nylon. A boy was walking forward, some young punk who was clearly lost and more than a bit deluded if he thought he could tell old Fitz how to fish. His drainpipe jeans had seen better days, his Chucks were so dirty they could've walked away by themselves, and if Fitz wasn't mistaken he was carrying a lady's handbag across his shoulder.

"Who the hell are you?"

"Me?" said the kid in the bomber jacket and ratty jeans. "I'm your new best friend."

MAX HELSING WATCHED AS THE OLD MAN CONTINUED to wind in his catch, struggling and straining. The fisherman wasn't listening to the boy's sage words of advice. This was nothing new. Folk of most ages seemed more than ready to disregard what the thirteen year old had to say. He was obviously kicking off the wrong vibe, one that said pimply teenager as opposed to kick-ass monster hunter. The bulldog had the right idea. The hound was probably downtown by now.

As he leaned over the wharf edge and took a peek at the

choppy waters below, the battling old man raised an eyebrow at him. The fishing line was vertical now, pointed straight down, as it cut one way and then the other through the water.

"Okay, I'm no fisherman, but I *do* know you're fishing for bass. And I also know bass are about . . . yea big." Max made the shape with his hands. "I don't think you've got a bass on the end of your line, dude."

"Like I said, who the hell are you?"

Max was rummaging around inside his messenger bag. "That's not important, but what *is* important—"

"Is that a purse you're carrying?"

"Purse? Really? I like to think of it as my manbag." Max shook his head and pulled his hand out of the messenger bag. "What I was *trying* to tell you before you so rudely interrupted was that you might wanna stick these in your ears."

He held out a pair of wax earplugs, placing them atop the cooler.

"Will it mean I don't hear your voice?" grunted the man, wincing as he cranked hard on the reel.

"Probably, but more importantly, it'll save your life."

The man's laugh was sarcastic. "Get lost, ya little jerk. A man's at work here."

Max sighed with regret and popped his own plugs into his ears. "Ditto."

He leaned back over the side just as the "catch" emerged from the briny water. Max had been following this story from a distance for three months now. Local legend had always said there was a mermaid in the Mystic River. There was some truth to the story, of course, but this was no mermaid. It was a selkie, an ancient creature that had followed the Irish immigrants across the Atlantic centuries ago. Romantic folklore told that they looked like seals beneath the waves but when they emerged from the water they transformed into enchanting humans. The truth was far more grim. This particular selkie had been putting in appearances every three decades, regular as clockwork, rising for three full moons to feed before vanishing back to the deep. If it failed to feed on each of these nights, it would starve. It seemed to Max that a selkie's life was a bit of a cursed existence. Though Max felt sympathy for it he wasn't eager for any more humans to be slaughtered. Tonight was Max's last chance to send the selkie packing.

The creature that emerged from the Mystic bucked and writhed on the end of the line as the fisherman continued to winch it in. It was never going to win a beauty pageant. Its head was bald with bumpy ridges, a pair of large pale eyes glowing like headlamps. The monster's mouth was wide and drooping, like that of a grouper, with jagged needle teeth jutting out from all angles. Max could see its throat flexing, wobbling, as a frog's might when it croaks. The beast was singing, Max realized, and he was relieved to be wearing his plugs—the song of the selkie was its principal weapon, and the way it bewitched sailors and fishermen.

SELKIE

AKA: selchie, Finwife, mermaid, siren

ORIGIN: Scotland, Ireland, Orkney, Shetland, and Faroe Isles.

STRENGTHS: Great speed and agility in water, bewitching song.

WEAKNESSES: Prolonged exposure to air, low intelligence.

HABITAT: Predominantly the coastal waters of Irish and North Sea, and east Atlantic Ocean.

The selkie of romantic legend spends its time at sea in the form of a seal, transforming into a human when on land. In fact, this carnivorous beast spends most of its life feeding upon fish and seabirds, but once every three decades, by the light of the full moon, will seek out man to feast upon. Only the flesh of humans gives the selkie its preternaturally long lifespan—failure to dine in this manner will grant it a lingering, painful death by starvation. BEWARE the Song of the Selkie, for this is its greatest weapon!
—Erik Van Helsing, February 27th, 1852

PHYSICAL TRAITS

1. <u>Extremely Large Eyes</u>—Adapted for seeing in darkness.

2. <u>Saberteeth</u>—These curved teeth prevent captured meals from escaping.

3. <u>Song of the Selkie</u>—The selkie's musical song can enchant its victims, this thrall effectively convincing prospective meals that the selkie is a beautiful object of attraction rather than a hideous aquatic killer.

—Esme Van Helsing, November 1st, 1864

"The Mermaid of the Mystic River"

Reports local to Boston, Mass., of a vengeful selkie having followed Irish families across the Atlantic. Two sets of abductions, thirty years apart, suggest there may be some truth in this. To Be Investigated.

—Algernon Van Helsing, June 22nd, 1935

RE: Mystic River
It's on the <u>TO DO LIST</u>! Take earplugs to combat the power of the selkie's song—it can't be worse than Jed's snoring!

MAX HELSING

Oct 11th, 2014

Two humanoid arms ended with webbed hands and taloned fingers, while its lower torso was that of a serpentine fish, ending in a great tail that twisted and thrashed at the water. Its flesh had the pale greenish-gray pallor of a corpse that had been found floating in the sea for days. The hook wasn't in the monster's mouth, of course; it was clenched in one of those grotesque hands, the line wrapped around its puckered forearm intentionally. It had meant to be caught. It wanted the man to haul it ashore. It needed the man's assistance if it was meant to feed.

"Okay, fishsticks," said Max, waving at the selkie from above as the fisherman reeled it in, ever higher. "Here's how it has to be. I'm afraid you're done snacking from the Boston All-You-Can-Eat Human Buffet. The restaurant is now closed. I'm giving you one chance to turn tail and disappear back to Atlantis, or wherever the heck it is you've come from."

Although the monster was warbling its hideous ballad, its eyes narrowed when it spied Max, its teeth gnashing as it rose closer to the wharf.

"Guess that's a no on the skedaddling, then?" said Max, straightening up and turning to the man. He was about to ask for help, but quickly realized it was futile. Twin rivulets of blood dribbled from the old angler's ears, while his eyes were pale and glassy, utterly entranced. Max shook him violently, trying to dislodge the rod from the fisherman's hands, but it was hopeless. The boy flipped open his messenger bag's flap, rooting inside for a knife to cut the line. Without that connection, the beast couldn't rise the twelve feet out of the river to feed. It would be doomed to go without, and would (hopefully) starve. Just as Max's hand closed around his pocket knife, he felt teeth clamp around his ankle. He cried out, looking down, expecting to find the selkie feasting on his foot. Instead, he found the little bull-dog, returned to defend his put-upon master from Max. As the fisherman continued winding the monster in, the dog snarled, worrying the boy's drainpipe jeans, which ripped and frayed. Having Eightball, Max's own dog, with him right now would have been helpful—especially since he was a hellhound—but Max was alone on this one.

He shook off the dog, who bounced away then came straight back. This time he leaped, jaws snapping around the messenger bag and dragging it down to the ground. The knife went loose inside the satchel as Max hit the deck, the strap came free, and the bulldog danced away with the bag in his mouth.

"Crapsacks!" shouted Max, as the selkie's head appeared over the side of the wharf, its webbed, clawed fingers now gripping the timbers as it let go of the hook and the line.

Max scrambled forward to the empty beer bottles. One, two, three; they whipped through the air, striking the sel-kie in the head and splitting the ghoulish flesh. The inju-ries hardly spoiled the creature's good looks. It reached out, grabbing Max's foot and biting down hard. Its needle teeth punctured the tread of his Chucks.

"What *is* it with my *feet?*" he screeched, booting the river monster in the face.

The boy's hands went into the cooler, grabbing full bottles of beer now and sending them at the selkie. The creature ignored the barrage, crawling ever closer, claws digging into the decking. The cooler lid was the next thing to hit the beast, buckling as Max smashed it over the selkie's ridged, knuckled skull. Its mouth opened wide as it wailed in agony. Max could feel one of his earplugs coming loose. He jammed the cooler lid into its open jaws and then snatched up the loose coils of fishing line. He rolled over the monster, wrapping the line about the creature's neck in quick succession, three times in all. He yanked back hard.

The selkie shrieked and gurgled, big white eyes swelling wide like they might pop. Max cried out as he pulled with all his might, feeling the strong nylon cord cut into the flesh of his hands and fingers. The selkie's great fish tail flapped and slapped, striking the timber jetty as it gasped in vain for breath. One last cry from Max as the line reached breaking point, and there was a wet ripping sound, like piano wire going through an overripe cucumber. He felt the cord give as it sliced through the monster's neck. The selkie's head rolled away, the white light ebbing in those dreadful eyes as its black blood washed across the wharf.

The fisherman came to suddenly, shaking his head,

looking down in horror at the monstrosity from the deep that lay at his feet and the boy from Gallows Hill Middle School lying across its decapitated corpse. His bulldog trotted up and began to lap at the pool of oily fish blood.

"Bass is off the menu, I'm afraid, sir," said Max, anchoring his chewed-up Chucks on the dock as he clambered to his feet.

"Have you ever tried sushi?"

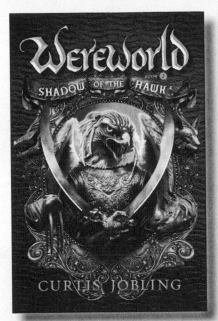

Wereworld
BOOK 3
SHADOW OF THE HAWK
CURTIS JOBLING

Wereworld
BOOK 4
NEST OF SERPENTS
CURTIS JOBLING

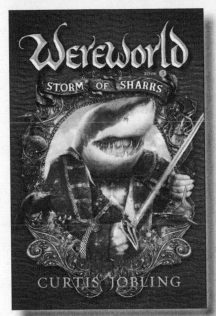

Wereworld
BOOK 5
STORM OF SHARKS
CURTIS JOBLING

Wereworld
BOOK 6
WAR OF THE WERELORDS
CURTIS JOBLING